AWAY
WEEKEND

LESLEY FERNÁNDEZ-ARMESTO read War Studies at King's College, London. She has written for *The Times*, ghosted an African president's autobiography, and adapted Shakespeare's *As You Like It* for an opera. She lives between London and Northamptonshire and is never seen without her dachshunds. Away Weekend is her first novel.

Instagram: @lesleyfernandezarmesto
Facebook: @lesley.fernandezarmesto

AWAY
WEEKEND

Lesley Fernández-Armesto

*Quadrant
Books*

Published by Quadrant Books
Suite 2, 7 Dyer Street,
Cirencester, Gloucestershire, GL7 2PF
T: 020 3290 0920
www.quadrant-books.com
info@quadrant-books.com

A catalogue record for this book is available from the British Library

ISBN 978-1-3999-5346-7

Cover Artwork by Victoria FitzRoy
Cover design by E-digital Design
Typeset by Tetragon, London
Printed and bound by TJ Books Limited

I have found out that there ain't no surer
way to find out whether you like people or
hate them than to travel with them

Tom Sawyer Abroad

Chapter One

She could not recall those few, September days in Indiana without feelings of profound panic. She had read about this: something triggers a memory, and there one might be, walking the dog in the park, or shopping for face cream, and it's as if one is back again, re-living the trauma. The breath is quickening, the heart is racing, the limbs are a-quiver. When the invitation had first been extended it had seemed like a perfectly innocent plan, a good idea; a chance to see a new place, savour a fresh experience, spend time with a charmingly suave man. Yes, he really had appeared to be charmingly suave then. Like Cary Grant in a black and white movie. How wrong one can be, she thought, turning over in her mind the horror of that long weekend, and its final humiliating moments. She shivered, relieved it was over, but half-wishing it had never happened.

When Ellis had proposed the weekend away to Geraldine, they had been friends – and she had thought that was the right designation, though it had become a little more – for about seven months. They had met at a pre-Christmas drinks party, in a part of London that is curiously defined by a mosque to the south, a synagogue to the west, and an American school in the middle. St John's Wood – now no more arboreal than any other part of the metropolis – is a cosmopolitan village, where it is easier to buy a designer handbag than a pint of milk, and pristine four wheel drive vehicles double park in the High Street, while their Louboutin-heeled drivers teeter across the pavement to pick up skinny lattes.

Mrs Mankowitz, Geraldine's hostess at that party, had been brought to St John's Wood many years before as a young bride. Her late husband had made his money churning out small electrical components in a factory that was far, far away from this pleasant place. These tiny items were essential for the workings of the great machines of industry: "Just small cogs in big wheels," Mr Mankowitz would explain to anyone enquiring about the exact nature of his widgets. His manufacturing endeavours had enabled him to purchase a yellow Rolls Royce, and knock three small mews houses into one. This ancient yellow car still sat solidly in its capacious garage, from where, one afternoon a week, Mrs Mankowitz – ferociously diminutive behind the steering wheel – would drive to an elderly friend's house for a game of bridge. It was a distance of under a quarter of a mile. She proceeded so slowly and cautiously that offers of walking in front of the Rolls with a red flag had been made, in order to alert other drivers and pedestrians to the potential hazard, but as she clung to that walnut steering wheel, so she religiously stuck to this regular jaunt. The party, too, was a piece of that same comforting ritual, an essential rhythm in her long life: she and her husband had habitually invited neighbours in for drinks in the third week of December, and that would continue, she said, till she was removed from her home, feet first.

Her guest list was always eclectic. It included tradespeople, elderly grandees of St John's Wood life, an exotic selection of those passing through – Americans, Japanese, Indians, Russians – and her immediate neighbours. Geraldine fell into the last category.

She had moved into the area a couple of years before. There had been no particular reason for her choice, other than the proximity to the park, and the discovery of an exquisite little mews house, so tiny it could hardly accommodate more than one slim woman and her small dog. It had, she thought, been the perfect choice for her.

Mrs Mankowitz had waited a week after Geraldine had moved in before asking her over to tea. The old lady had noticed the charming pieces of antique furniture being taken carefully into the little house by burly removal men, and had observed the immaculately turned out woman with delight. "We're going to like our new neighbour," she had remarked to the empty chair by the fireplace.

On the afternoon of that first invitation Geraldine had walked all of fifteen feet to the other side of the mews, wondering which of the three front doors to knock on. She settled for the one at the end, which had a more used look than the other two.

"Aha!" said Mrs Mankowitz, "You chose the right one. I always think it's a bit of a test for newcomers. The other doors are actually blocked from the inside." A long room had been created from banging through three sitting rooms and two hallways, and was elaborately arched.

"Oh," exclaimed Geraldine, "this reminds me of that Beatles film, where they each walk through the front door of a row of terraced houses, and on the other side it's all knocked through into one. Did you ever see that?"

Mrs Mankowitz clapped her hands with delight, "That's exactly where my dear late husband, Binky, got the idea. That's him there." She indicated a small round table, covered with a chintz cloth and be-topped with glass, its surface crammed with silver framed photographs. "Of course Binky wasn't his real name. He was called Bernard. But I thought of him as Binky as soon as I saw him. I named him! He was such a good-looking man." She passed the photograph carefully to Geraldine. It showed a heavy-featured, rather baggy-eyed individual, with thick, slicked back, dark hair.

"I had a stuffed rabbit called Binky when I was a child," said Geraldine, inconsequentially. "He was called after my grandmother's cat."

"There," exclaimed Mrs Mankowitz with pleasure. "I knew as soon as I saw you arrive across the road that we'd have lots in common. I shall go and make some tea, and you can talk to Gertie and Otto while I'm in the kitchen."

Two ancient, bulbous dachshunds lounged on the hearth rug, too bloated to stir from their fireside position. Geraldine bent down to stroke them, and they growled warningly.

Mrs Mankowitz apologised for their greeting. "That's just their way of saying hello. They are rather ancient now, like me. They're like an old married couple, although they are actually brother and sister. Earl Grey or Lapsang Souchong?"

"Earl Grey would be perfect, thank you."

The dachshunds glared at Geraldine while Mrs Mankowitz tottered to the kitchen, returning with a tray bearing a silver teapot and a sponge cake.

"That's Binky's chair over there," said Mrs Mankowitz, indicating the large, wing back chair with the lace antimacassar. "He's still sitting there. I can't see him, but I can feel him, and I know he's with me. I talk to him all the time."

"How very comforting," said Geraldine, taking everything in her stride.

"And isn't it funny you thought of that film when you walked in?"

"Yes," replied Geraldine. "And I was just trying to think of groups consisting of three people, instead of four, to come through the three doors."

"What an amusing idea! Well, the first trio that springs immediately to MY mind is Freeman, Hardy and Willis, but I have no idea if they were real people."

"Oh yes," replied Geraldine, "the shoe shop. My mother used to take me there when I was a child. We always had frightful arguments because she insisted on sensible footwear... Oh!" she exclaimed, "there was a pop group called the Three Degrees."

"I dare say there was, dear," replied Mrs Mankowitz, "although I don't recollect them myself. Probably after my time. I remember the Andrew Sisters, though: weren't there three of them? Of course, there's Three Degrees of Separation. Wasn't that a film?"

"I believe so, but I think there were six of those," said Geraldine, helpfully.

"Ah," Mrs Mankowitz replied vaguely, as she poured tea. "I hardly ever go to the cinema any more.

Gordon, my son, took me to see something a couple of years ago. I can't remember what it was: salmon came into it, I think, which was funny, really, as I always say I'm as deaf as a haddock. I really am! But it was terribly loud, this film, despite my dreadful deafness. I said to Gordon, half way through, 'Can't they turn the volume down?' And he said, 'It doesn't work like that, Mum'. I had to sit there with my fingers in my ears for the rest of the afternoon. I haven't been since. He's a sound engineer, Gordon – never married, can't find the right girl – so if he couldn't do anything about it, no one could. He does a lot of work at Abbey Road – you know, the recording studios. He says it's all done on computers now. Sits there all day, twiddling knobs. I can't quite understand it, myself."

Geraldine smiled sympathetically, and after a second cup of tea, took her leave. "What a sweet woman," said Mrs Mankowitz, as she settled back into her chair. "Did you like her, Binky? She'll be a very good addition to the mews. And I think I'll ask her if she can help me with the shopping… only occasionally, of course." She reached for the remote control of the television set, stuffed somewhere down the side of the sofa. "Let's watch the 6 o' clock news. See if anything has happened in the world out there."

"Nice legs," said Binky, from the other side. Mrs Mankowitz looked towards the wing back chair and shook an admonishing finger. "Naughty Binky," she said, switching the television on.

This was the beginning of a firm friendship between the two neighbours, and in months to come, Geraldine was even allowed to walk Gertie and Otto, when their usual dog walker failed to turn up. It was a painfully slow promenade, the two dachshunds shuffling and huffing their way to the park, whilst her frustrated miniature poodle pulled impatiently on his lead, but like the emergence of the Rolls Royce from its garage, it was more symbolic than just a mere outing: it was a seal of affection and trust between the two women.

Geraldine had never agonised over attending social occasions on her own. Years as an Army officer's wife had given her plenty of practice at light-hearted banter, and on entering the overheated, overstuffed room that fateful, December morning, anticipating a welcome glass of sparkling wine, she had recognised several people she knew, squashed into the corner next to the large Christmas tree, which had been exactly positioned where Binky's chair usually stood. She wondered, briefly, where the chair had been stashed, and whether he was happy with its temporary relocation. Delicately, she shoved her way through the crowds to greet her acquaintances. Each expressed pleasure at seeing the other.

"We were just saying how awful it is that Yorks is closing down after Christmas. There'll be no butchers' shops left soon. It's the fault of all those wretched vegetarians."

"But they did sell cheese," remarked Geraldine, helpfully. The two men, and the woman from the library, looked at each other. "Although," resumed Geraldine, after a pause, "I suppose that would be no good for a vegan, would it? And then again, perhaps a vegetarian wouldn't like to walk into a meaty atmosphere? I expect the very look and smell of meat must be disgusting to a vegetarian. And a vegan too, of course. But I have heard that many vegetarians lapse when they see – or I suppose smell – a bacon sandwich. Isn't that odd? I would never eat a bacon sandwich." She mused, quite randomly, out loud. Her neighbours, feeling the subject of the butcher's closure had suddenly become uninteresting and exhausted, switched to the problems of residents' parking during the cricket season. Geraldine, as the owner of a large car – although not quite as enormous as the yellow Rolls Royce – had much to add to this, too.

She was therefore fully engaged when a man sauntered over to the chatty group and said, "Hi". Perhaps because of his height, he managed to halt conversation, momentarily, while he was observed. He was considerably over six feet tall, late fifties, perhaps even early sixties, greying at the temples, his full, wavy hair cut a little short, his face tanned, his eyes blue. He was immaculate in navy trousers, striped shirt, and a V necked cashmere sweater of a lighter blue. He appearance was as a waspish American, straight out of Central Casting. The two English men, shorter and paunchier in their raspberry cords and checked shirts, bristled at his intervention. But he looked unperturbed at the resumption of chatter, as though it really didn't matter. He raised one eyebrow at Geraldine, as she clutched her empty glass, and she wondered, with some interest, who this stranger was.

"Looks like you could do with another," he said to her, smiling.

"Oh goodness," she replied, "I'm sure someone will be around in a minute to do refills."

"Ah," he said knowingly, "I guess it would be bad form." He managed to convey the phrase as if it was in inverted commas, "to help oneself."

She smiled uncertainly. "Have you just moved here?" she asked, taking him in, discreetly. He was handsome, in an old-fashioned, distinguished kind of way. Reminded her of someone – an actor, perhaps.

"Yes, I arrived just over two weeks ago. I've been based in Geneva for the last three years, and have now come here to run the London office."

She was about to enquire about the London office and its activities, when a large man in a Christmas sweater – a cheery red knitted garment with a festive reindeer depicted on the front – bore down on them, bearing bottles.

"I see you've met our new neighbour," Gordon, Mrs Mankowitz's bachelor son, said, slopping foamy liquid into their proffered glasses. His mother commandeered him every year from his flat in Marylebone for waitering duties. "Rick is from New York." He rattled this off with enormous satisfaction, pleased at remembering these essential details. He quickly moved on to the next empty glass.

"Actually, I'm Ellis, and I'm from Chicago. But I guess to you Brits we all look and sound the same." He smiled, all perfect white teeth and crinkly eyes.

"And I'm Geraldine, and I live opposite here. And no, you don't all look the same. You look nothing like the Incredible Hulk. He's American, isn't he?"

He laughed. And that was how the friendship, or whatever it was, had begun. She had left the party and gone back to her little house without much thought about him, until a few days later, she had bumped into him in the street. It was a dank, dark winter's evening, and she had dashed to the pillar box to catch the last post. He was walking towards her, his elegant grey overcoat buttoned up against the December chill. He smiled broadly at her. "Geraldine," he'd exclaimed with pleasure – how very American to remember her name – "I was hoping we'd meet again."

"Really?" she said, surprised at such candour.

"Why, sure… Hey, are you on your way somewhere, or can you come and have a drink? I could do with one after battling home on the Tube. My flat's just along here." He indicated a large Victorian villa, which had recently been re-furbished. Geraldine had watched the building works unfold – which had been prolonged, extensive and expensive – with considerable curiosity.

"I'd love a drink. How kind. Just the thing for a nasty winter's evening."

His apartment occupied the entire ground floor of the double-fronted house. Inside, every period feature had been successfully erased. The large reception room was now a dazzling white cube, minimally furnished with lumps of uncomfortable-looking upholstery, draped with faux fur throws. Ellis flicked a switch, and a gas log fire burned merrily in a chrome surrounded hole.

"Homely, isn't it," he said, wryly, opening a bottle of rather good Chablis.

"It is a little bit cheerless. My tiny mews house is very cluttered compared to this." She looked around, searching for something encouraging to say. "It must be terribly easy to keep clean."

"I wouldn't know. The agent has arranged for all that sort of thing. I think a contract firm comes in once or twice a week and moves the dust around. I'm not here much."

"And will you be in London very long?"

"Hard to say. Probably a year, maybe less. I keep putting off retirement. I slightly dread the prospect of all that free time and what I'll do with it. I'm not ready yet for travelling the world and perfecting my golf swing – that kinda stuff. So, meanwhile, I've been parachuted in to get things back on an even keel after a couple of dodgy moments in the London office."

Ah, the London office. "Which is?"

"Nathan Brothers." Yes, she remembered reading something about them in the newspaper. Insider dealing, manipulation of interest rates, excessive bonuses. Something of that sort. One of the many stories that merely confirm, to those not caught up in the world of high finance, that bankers march to a different, irregular, beat of the drum.

"And what do you do?" he asked, observing her long legs in dark indigo jeans and her cream cashmere polo neck. No wedding ring, just an expensive looking watch, pearl earrings and a gold bangle.

Geraldine took another sip of wine. "I'm afraid I don't work. Haven't for ages. I have a little dog, two grown up children, a very small garden…" She trailed off, as she struggled to think what she did do every day. She lunched with friends, went to Pilates classes twice a week, enjoyed opera, theatre, ballet. Shopped. How very different from someone who is dropped in to an alien clime to sort out global-ranking problems. "I'm afraid I'm rather boring, actually."

Did she imagine he'd challenge this, on so short an introduction? He didn't reply, but merely noted the honey-touched brown hair, the large grey eyes, the two little frown lines between them. She was a good-looking woman. Could pass for forties, but probably in her fifties.

Divorced presumably. Perhaps even widowed.

She stood up. "Thank you so much for the drink. I must dash. My dog will be wondering where I have got to." He helped her on with her black quilted coat with its little tippet of rabbit fur round the collar.

"My company has a box at the opera house in Covent Garden," he said as he opened the front door for her. "Perhaps you'd join me there one evening?"

"Super!" she said. "I adore opera." Was that one of those suggestions like 'do let's meet for lunch', she wondered – an utterance which both parties know will never happen.

From the bay window he watched her walk down the short path, and turn left at the gate. She strode a couple of hundred yards to the narrow entrance to the mews, which even taxi drivers often missed. As she turned into the enclave of six tiny houses, she could hear Bolly barking. She let herself in and faced the exuberant greetings of her apricot poodle. She picked him up – a wriggling puffball of fluff. She took him into the kitchen – white painted doors and a black granite work top. French windows at one end led into the minuscule garden, and at the other, a Georgian mahogany card table and four chairs served as the dining area. Everything was neat and tidy. Even after two years, she still took pleasure in the perfection of her surroundings. She would come downstairs each morning and just gaze at the little drawing room, overlooking the mews, with its thick silk curtains and its pretty antique furniture.

She took arborio rice out of the cupboard, some leftover asparagus from the fridge, and a small packet of petit pois from the freezer. As she slowly stirred her risotto she wondered whether she should ask Ellis to dinner. But only if the invitation to the opera was forthcoming, otherwise it would appear rather forward, wouldn't it? He certainly seemed very charming – terribly good-looking – and she missed a man at supper time. Since her divorce two years ago she had been out a few times with a widower, fifteen years older than herself, who had shared her love of ballet, but this had been no more than companionable. He was a retired judge, whom she'd met at a Conservative party fund-raising event. It was pleasant to go out accompanied by an interesting and intelligent man, even if he was the wrong side of seventy. But most of the time she just saw her women friends, either divorced, like her, or now into their third or fourth decade of marriage, and resigned to incompatibility and irritating habits. She was lucky, really: she had enough money to lead a comfortable life, and her children, compared with most of her friends' offspring, were surprisingly undemanding. And her ex-husband was now married to the woman he had decided he had preferred to her, and appeared to be no happier now than before. It was all most satisfactory. She would think about the American, and think about dinner. But not now.

But Ellis moved fast. An invitation from an American is really quite different from an English one: it is made with a degree of sincerity, to be remembered and acted upon. When Geraldine returned home with Bolly the following day, after a walk in the park, there was a letter on the door mat, delivered by hand. It was a thick, cream envelope, lined with dark green tissue, with a note inside, engraved at the top with 'E.V.H.C.'. It must have been responsible for the felling of several trees. Geraldine particularly liked good stationery. The thicker the card, and the deeper the engraving, the better. She ran her finger over the back to check it wasn't merely embossed. No, she could feel the indentation of the engraver's mark. It had her thorough approval. In a large confident hand, in black ink, she read: 'Turn of the Screw', Covent Garden, January 3. Merry Christmas! Ellis.' At the bottom he had written a telephone number. She put it on the mantelpiece and thought about it for a while.

Tomorrow was Christmas Eve. Her children would be with her for supper. On Christmas Day she was lunching with a friend the other side of London, while the children were joining their father and wife number two in their mansion flat in Battersea, the wrong side of the river. She looked at her diary. She had no engagements on January 3rd, and after further consideration she picked up the phone and dialled the number.

Geraldine awoke the morning of the opera outing with a slight sensation of excitement. It wasn't the excitement one had in one's youth – that Saturday-night-it's-a-party jumping up and down thrill that starts somewhere in the pit of the stomach, and ends up as a sort of tingling sensation in one's head – no, it was a more sedate, quietly considered feeling.

Pleasantly anticipatory, that is how I feel, thought Geraldine, enjoying the prospect of spending an inclement winter's afternoon contemplating her

wardrobe, deciding what to wear, and carefully apply-
ing make-up. And then there would be the delight of
entering the grandeur of the Royal Opera House and
being greeted by a handsome man.

They had agreed to meet in the Crush Room at 6
pm. Ellis would be coming straight from work, and
he had booked a table there for supper. Geraldine
remembered the first time she'd been taken to Covent
Garden, as a child, with her parents and her sister:
a Christmas treat to see a matinée performance of
the Nutcracker. In the interval, they had gone to the
Crush Room for refreshments. She had thought it
wonderful, all red plush and huge gilt-framed portraits and mirrors, and smartly dressed people talking loudly to each other. The whole afternoon had
seemed impossibly lovely to a ten year-old girl, wearing a velvet pinafore and patent leather shoes. She
had hoped the other ballet-goers would realise she
too was a ballerina, as she stuck her toes out into first
position, and sipped her lemonade. She thought of
that long-ago outing now as she rummaged through
her perfectly arranged wardrobe.

Bolly sat on the bed and watched as Geraldine
pulled out dresses and scrutinised them. He was quite
certain this activity betokened a solitary evening for
a young poodle, and he was disgruntled. After what
seemed like an orgy of non-decision, a black dress,

one of many, was selected. An even lengthier interlude ensued, with the application of make-up, the choosing of jewellery, and finally, as Bolly had anticipated, a short walk for him in the mews, ending with a rawhide bone in his bowl, and the radio blaring in the background. Quite why Geraldine should think he liked Radio 3 was inexplicable: he hated evenings like these.

In contrast, Geraldine was positively perky. She slipped out, hoping Bolly wouldn't notice her absence, and walked briskly to the end of the mews, where her minicab was waiting. A small pitiful bark – more of a howl – could be heard, but she was not to be daunted. She was going to enjoy the evening.

In the car she suffered that momentary anxiety that all who think too much about their appearance endure. Was everything quite as it should be? She peered into her little mirror, worrying whether her lipstick was the right colour, her subtle eye make-up unsmudged. It was impossible to see clearly in the gloom of a January night in the back of a Japanese car, and she closed her compact resolutely. I shall be absolutely relaxed, she said to herself, with only the merest glimmer of conviction, sudden nervousness overtaking her.

She ascended the wide, red-carpeted stairs of the opera house slowly and carefully and stood momentarily at the entrance to the Crush Room. He was already there at the table. He got up and walked towards her, smiling broadly.

"Geraldine. Happy New year! Wonderful to see you! You look stunning."

"Thank you. And it's lovely to see you too." And it was. He stood before her, a tall slim man, in an impeccably tailored pinstriped double-breasted suit. His dark foulard silk tie was Windsor knotted, his blue shirt starched. He was immaculate. He kissed her lightly on the cheek and guided her over to their table. A bottle of champagne in an ice bucket and a plate of delicate canapés awaited them. Two red glossy programmes had already been purchased.

"I have been so looking forward to this evening," he said, pulling out her chair. She sat down as he waved to the waiter to pour the champagne.

"Yes, me too," she replied, disconcerted by the length of time he held her gaze. But it was, she thought afterwards, a lovely evening. Delicious food and wine, punctuated by wonderful singing. Geraldine had sat on the edge of her seat, gripped by the ghostly story. Was the governess merely mad, or was she spectrally harassed? There was certainly much to think about, what with phantoms on the stage and a heart-throb alongside her. It was very much in contrast to her outing there a few months ago with the retired judge.

She couldn't even remember what they'd seen. The judge had been a little slow on his feet after a knee replacement, and had tripped twice on the stairs. And he had never suggested dinner in the intervals. They had queued at the bar for glasses of the cheapest white wine. This, thought Geraldine, has been an altogether different experience, and one that fully justified her silk black dress and her godmother's ruby necklace.

A car had been waiting for them outside at the end of the opera, and had sped them back to St John's Wood. Boldly, Geraldine had asked Ellis in for a drink and he had accepted. They sat in her little drawing room, she with a cup of herbal tea, he with a brandy, and had spent a companionable half-hour discussing the opera. Looking back on this, months later, Geraldine began to wonder whether this wasn't the longest, most sustained conversation they had ever had. Bolly had ignored him, which was unusual. He tended either to despise – and therefore bark or bite – or passionately adore people, and jump all over them. As Geraldine washed up her delicately painted cup and saucer that night, she had no sense other than of having had a marvellous evening.

The pattern for the next few months was set. The trip to the opera was followed by dinners in elegant restaurants, outings to the theatre, and the occasional Sunday lunch at her little house. It was, felt

Geraldine, and as she told her friends, awfully civilised. Sex appeared to be low on Ellis's agenda, which suited Geraldine perfectly. There was the odd chaste kiss, cautious embraces, and once, even, a tentative but definite fumbling of her left breast while helping her with her coat. They had not, as Geraldine's robust sister Phoebe would have put it, gone the whole hog.

When Ellis mentioned to Geraldine that he would be returning to America for most of July and part of August, she felt no pang of sadness, no pulling of her heart strings. She merely smiled and expressed the hope that he should have a wonderful time. She herself would be joining friends at their house in Normandy, and Bolly, armed with his pet passport, would be accompanying her.

The day before he left for America, Geraldine asked Ellis to dinner – just the two of them – at her house. She spent the afternoon preparing the food, arranging flowers, cutting back the dead blooms in the tiny garden. At seven o'clock, everything ready, she poured herself a glass of wine, and sat in her drawing room, music softly playing in the background, to wait the arrival of Ellis. As she often did, she gazed around the room with pleasure. The French marble fireplace, with the two cream sofas either side, had been a tremendous find when she had first bought the house. It had been lovely to choose things on her own, without the interference of her husband, who had a tendency to dwell on practicalities. She rather pitied wife number two, battling against Formica and wipe-clean floor tiles. The Aubusson rug, inherited from her godmother, had faded over the years to a watery pink, and the vase of lilies wafted their scent through the warm summer air. Really, it was a shame anyone had to intrude on this loveliness. She and Bolly could have had an enjoyable evening to themselves, sitting in the garden in the descending rays of the sun. The bell rang, and Bolly jumped off his toile-covered chair to rush to the front door, barking excitedly. He stopped when he saw it was Ellis, standing there, in pale chinos and a blue open necked shirt, holding a bouquet, a bottle of champagne and a small carrier bag elaborately festooned with ribbons.

"I wanted you to miss me while I'm gone," he said, expansively, as she took him through to the kitchen, poured him a drink and placed the flowers in water. Back in the drawing room, they sat facing each other on the sofas. The sun caught little flecks of gold in Geraldine's hair as she carefully undid the ribbons on the box inside the carrier bag. "I thought it was very you," he said, as he watched her unknotting the bows. She opened the box, and squealed in delight when she saw the green Limoges frog. "Oh, that is so sweet," she exclaimed. "Open up the frog," Ellis urged. The frog was hinged at the back, and on his chest displayed a tiny bee clasp. She carefully lifted it, to reveal inside a golden crown. "He's a frog prince", said Ellis, "just waiting for the right princess to come along and restore him to his human status with a kiss."

Geraldine was startled at this remark. Was she supposed to jump up and lock lips with him? That would have been difficult, since the small space between the two sofas was occupied by a needle-point footstool, on top of which was a découpage tray with two glasses precariously perched. She remained seated, turning the frog over in her hands. "Thank you SO much. What a lovely present. You've been very kind to me." She faltered. "I've really appreciated everything – all the wonderful dinners and outings… really appreciated them. It's all been deliciously spoil-ing." She turned her head, embarrassed. He looked at her appraisingly.

"Wow," he said, "you make it sound like I'm off forever. I'm only away for six weeks. Then I'll be back. Which reminds me," he shifted his position and crossed his legs, "what do you think about American football?"

"I'm not sure I have any opinion whatsoever," Geraldine replied, with surprise. She screwed up her eyes, and pictured very large men in helmets and padding, running up and down a pitch, while girls in skimpy bright costumes raised their legs in perfect time and whooped. "No, I've honestly never given it a thought."

"Great!" Ellis exclaimed. "And how are you fixed for September 4?"

Geraldine hesitated, seeing that a trip to Wembley, or some other place where sporting events took place, might be beckoning. She imagined sitting in a draughty arena, having the minutiae of the game explained to her, while she politely feigned interest.

Ellis smiled. "Let me tell you the plan. My old college, All Saints, way out there in the mid-west, in Indiana, is big on football. I try and go back every year, stay with chums, make a weekend of it, go to the game, party... you're getting the picture? It's a great getaway. We'll catch a ride with a guy that's got a plane – none of all that hassle with intrusive security – and just have fun. Am I tempting you?" He asked quizzically.

Geraldine considered the invitation. Not a lot of it appealed. She was always cautious about staying in other people's houses, since she was usually more comfortable in her own. She tried to imagine what his friends would be like. Would they be as urbane as Ellis, or would they be less sophisticated, less travelled? And would she have to stand on a cold damp touch line, as she had for so many years when her son was still a schoolboy, shouting encouragement with false enthusiasm? None of this was very alluring. But it was the phrase 'guy with a plane' that had stirred within her a response. That seemed to elevate the weekend into a world she had merely dreamed of. And while Geraldine hated the idea of one-upmanship – really, could one be bothered? – there was nothing wrong in letting slip to one's friends that one had just been to America for the weekend. In a private plane.

"How intriguing and wonderful this sounds. I think as long as I can find someone to take care of Bolly for a few days it would be fine. Lovely! Thank you!" She raised her glass to him. "And of course, as long as your friends wouldn't mind a stranger in their midst."

"Oh they're going to love you, I know it," he replied. He raised his glass to hers. "Go All Saints!"

That night the bed, purchased two years ago, with the cane headboard and the embroidered pillowcases, creaked for the first time. It was a discreet creak, the smallest of movements, whilst Bolly glowered malevolently from under the pink pashmina in his bedroom basket. Later, in the early hours, Ellis quietly removed himself from the mews, to prepare for his morning flight, and later still, Geraldine flung all the sheets from her bed into the drum of the washing machine, and turned the dial to 'Hot'.

The following Sunday, Geraldine had invited her sister Phoebe for lunch. This was an unusual occurrence, but not issued without thought. Phoebe lived in Chiswick, in a small terraced house with her partner Eileen, and their two pugs, Jasper and Archie. Phoebe was two years older than Geraldine, and a lesbian of the traditional type. She favoured a masculine cut to her clothes, short, somewhat spikey hair and affected a certain swagger. For many years she had been the producer on the BBC radio programme, 'All Things Must Pass', a potpourri of homilies, home-spun truisms, and bad-luck stories with uplifting conclusions, broadcast on Sunday mornings for those who preferred to worship in the comfort of their own home. Phoebe was an atheist, and had taken tremendous delight at being part of the religious affairs team. But a year ago the programme had been axed, and Phoebe now had to produce a quiz show, hosted by a male journalist whom she particularly disliked, with a rotating panel of unappealing comedians and celebrity chefs. Still, as she often remarked, she was lucky to have a job. Eileen, who was in special effects, had been shunted round various projects like a passenger-less train, and now worked part-time at Pinewood Studios, facing an anxious commute on her moped, her wispy hair flying from her helmet, as she waited, terrified, at every junction and traffic light, convinced that she'd be flattened

by a juggernaut. Alas, Eileen's hours were unpredictable, and at the very moment Phoebe was downing her
first tumbler of pre-lunch Famous Grouse, Eileen's
attention was fixed to a screen, eliminating digitally
any evidence of acne from the well-known face of a
Hollywood actress.

Phoebe and Geraldine were unlikely siblings.
Phoebe always maintained that her father had wanted
a boy for his first born, but Geraldine could see no
evidence of that. Their father had been in the Foreign
Office, and was mainly away from home. On his
returns he never showed any inclination of wanting
any children of any sex, preferring to shut himself
in the garage and make things out of wood – never
anything very practical, nor indeed decorative, but
his wife always claimed it was 'therapeutic' for him.
He had had a Bad War. The badness was sometimes
alluded to, but its exact nature never discussed. All
was left to the imagination, and after the passage of
years, it seemed perfectly reasonable to forget about
it. Occasionally, some random trigger could engender
a strange response – a sudden twitch, or violent jerk, a
shout or rant out of all proportion to the provocation.
Before – and indeed, after – his death, the two sisters
had discussed what really might have happened all
those years ago. Geraldine had pictured the depriva-
tion and squalor of the trenches, but, apparently that

was the wrong war. Phoebe thought it more likely that a remark she had once overheard, about her father accidentally wearing the shoes of a dead Japanese prisoner of war, was the cause of his problems. If nothing else, it would account for his chronic athlete's foot. Geraldine's mother, in contrast, was madly social, partial to a gin and tonic, and kept up the myth that they lived in Richmond, not the less glamorous East Sheen, which confused delivery drivers until the advent of accurate postcodes.

This was nearly, but not quite, all that Geraldine and Phoebe had in common, and so their rare meetings were usually punctuated by a lot of sentences beginning 'do you remember'. Phoebe felt the full force of irony that her sister, who from an early age wanted nothing more than to prance in a pink tutu or borrow her mother's makeup, should be called Geraldine, and that she, Phoebe, should be landed with a ridiculous name, entirely unsuitable for a woman who would have looked comfortable smoking a pipe, had the BBC permitted the use of tobacco on its premises. Her middle name was Jacqueline, and at university she had attempted a campaign to be known as Jack. This had not been successful, so she had dropped it, returning to the familiar, if inappropriate, Phoebe. Feeble Phoebe, she sometimes thought, in her bitterest moments.

Geraldine eyed her combat-trousered sister lolling on the cream sofa. Her motive for the lunch invitation was to secure a dog-sitter for Bolly for her weekend trip to the States. She always felt that she knew far more about Phoebe's life than her sister knew of hers, but, then, there was probably little to know, particularly since the divorce. Phoebe and Jonty, Geraldine's ex-husband, had never really hit it off. At the time of his promotion to colonel Phoebe had expressed astonishment that the army had become so desperate for recruits to the higher ranks, particularly when a dear old school friend of hers, Anthea – very capable in possession of a Chieftain tank – had never even made Major. If Geraldine had needed a shoulder to cry on when the divorce was proceeding, Phoebe's would not have been especially comforting. But she had always been a kind aunt, as had Eileen, to the children, Hugo and Cassie. They often referred to their 'bonkers aunt' and her 'barking girlfriend' in tones almost approaching affection.

Perhaps the real common denominator was the love of all things canine. Both sisters had grown up with dogs – their mother had a series of irascible West Highland terriers. And although Phoebe considered Bolly to be ridiculous, and Geraldine thought the pugs dribbly and snorty, dogs were, at least, a bond between them. Of course Phoebe was happy to take in Bolly – with reservations about his pashmina collection and his yapping – but she wanted to know more about the trip abroad, and in particular about Geraldine's companion. Geraldine had told several friends about Ellis, but really, there had not been much to tell. They had listened to the accounts of expensive outings, and dinners mainly involving champagne, lobsters, and soufflés. They had heard of the excesses of flowers, but, frankly, without the banging of headboards in sexual frenzy against walls, it wasn't terribly interesting, was it? Of course, felt Geraldine, all that had changed now, with – how should she put this? – the consummation of their friendship, and their projected weekend away. Together.

"Well, G, you're looking good," said Phoebe over lunch. "Spring in your step and all that. Go on, tell your old sis what he's like. First one since Jonty, I do believe." Heartiness was the natural element of Phoebe.

Geraldine paused to take a sip of wine. "He's very good-looking, in an American sort of way – you know what I mean. He's a widower with a son in his early thirties, although he doesn't talk much about him. He's a banker. Um… pretty loaded, actually. Very generous."

"And the whole hog? What's that like, eh?"

"Really Phoebe," said Geraldine, affecting embarrassment, and hoping she might exhibit the faintest shade of a blush, "How can you ask things like that? Honestly. Yes, well, all that's fine… yes, great, really." She looked out of the window, over her tiny patch of pots of rosemary, lollipop topiaried bays, and climbing white roses. She thought about that night.

That one night. To be quite accurate, she didn't really remember much, not because of an excess of Puligny Montrachet, but because there wasn't much to remember. It was all over so very, very quickly.

Phoebe broke the silence. "Are you going to bone up on American footers? You know, astound him with all your knowledge and that sort of thing?"

"I hadn't really thought. I suppose I should google it or something. I think Hugo went to watch a match once in Hyde Park. I could ask him about it. Or that might have been Australian football. Perhaps they're the same?"

They both looked at each other, then laughed. "Do you remember…" said Phoebe – "that rugby match at Twickenham…" interjected Geraldine – "that Pa took us too?" finished Phoebe. They dissolved into hiccupping giggles. They were as one, youthful again, recapturing the memory: their father, stuck in a turn-stile – his trouser turn-up caught inextricably in the mechanism – and enraged at the incompetence of the man on the gate, while a crowd of people built up, angrily, behind him.

Chapter Two

Bolly and Geraldine passed a delightful two weeks in France. They motored through Kent, endured the Euro Tunnel, and spent a comfortable night in Boulogne, where poodle and mistress dined alongside each other at a charming restaurant overlooking the port. How civilised the French are, thought Geraldine, in their attitude towards dogs. Next morning they rose early, and drove through empty roads, stopping occasionally to admire the view or cock a leg. They arrived at their destination in time for lunch.

The days drifted by happily. Occasionally Geraldine received texts on her mobile phone from Ellis. They were brief and of limited literary or emotional content. He was at the office in New York, he was week-ending in Maine, he was travelling to Chicago to see his cousin, he had an appointment in Washington. It gave Geraldine an opportunity to smile at her phone mysteriously, with a small, knowing look, while reading his mainly geographical, and somewhat prosaic, jottings. Of course her hostess was fascinated, and imagined deep, heartfelt sentiments winging their way through the ether: passion reduced to a few well-chosen words, its force enhanced by its brevity.

Her host, Giles, had been in the army with Jonty, and had known Geraldine since she had first married. His wife, Phyllida, though not an intimate friend, was a sensible, organised sort of woman. Phyllida found Geraldine intriguing, with her perfectly groomed appearance, and her reluctance to talk much about herself. Perhaps she was even a little envious of Geraldine's post-divorce life, which seemed all the more alluring for its curious lack of detail. Their old timbered holiday house, purchased many years ago, was just outside of Deauville, on the road to Honfleur. It was big enough for several guests and a short stroll from the sea. This was the second time Geraldine had stayed with them, but the invitation this year had not been issued without careful thought.

"Well, she's no trouble," Phyllida had remarked to Giles, back in their comfortable home, somewhere near Salisbury Plain. "On her last visit she spent most of her time cleaning."

"Yes, but it makes it difficult with Jonty, doesn't it?"

"I don't see why. He's the one that left her."

"Do you think we should ask him as well? The following week, maybe?"

"But we can't ask him without Sally."

"Perhaps he'd like a break from her?" asked Giles, hopefully.

"They've been married for less than a year. You don't need a break from your wife after so short a time. And anyway, it's not as if there's anything wrong with Sally. It's just that she's so…"

"Boring?" suggested Giles.

"Yes,… boring, dull, somewhat unappealing." They sat in silence, contemplating Sally's singular lack of verve and vivacity. Phyllida knew they were about to re-tread over old familiar ground.

"I shall never understand it," said Giles, not for the first time. "Why Jonty had to go off like that, leaving Geraldine in the lurch, as it were. Cannot understand for the life of me why he didn't just stay put. And I often think," – yes, I know, thought Phyllida affectionately – "If only Jonty had taken my advice and moved down here when he left the army, like we did, none of this would ever have happened."

Phyllida sighed. "But you retired completely, darling. Jonty didn't. Think of him having to commute from Salisbury every day to the MoD. The train service is ghastly. At least he didn't have to face that, living in London."

"He was living in Fulham," exploded Giles. "That's not what I call London. Probably took him as long on the Tube as it would have done from here."

Phyllida removed her reading glasses from the top of her head and placed them back on her nose. "None of this solves the question of whether we ask Geraldine this year," she said, consulting her diary, "and we've got to bear in mind that we will have your mother with us for a month."

"Ah," said Giles, thoughtfully.

"Think how good Geraldine was with her last year. She took her at least twice to thalassotherapy in Deauville. Even drove her there. And she actually seemed to enjoy talking about hats. No one else can do that, not sustainedly. Particularly not me."

"Well, that seems final, then. Ask her." Giles would have liked to spend the summer in their holiday home on their own. But that never seemed to be an option. Phyllida always wanted to fill the place up with guests. Really, retirement was far more exhausting than work had ever been. Sometimes, Giles envied Jonty's Whitehall desk job. But not, he added to himself, his dull and boring new wife.

Phyllida did not believe in idle days, and planned the time for her guests well: there were always trips to gardens, markets, the casino in Deauville, cafés and bars. Other guests came and went, and Giles's mother claimed Geraldine was the only person who really listened to her. Geraldine occupied the same bedroom as last year, nestling in the eaves, a dormer window view of the sea. The polished oak floor smelt of beeswax, and Bolly slid delightedly over its undulating surface. He was back home here, he felt, a poodle returned to his roots, surrounded by fading pink toile and antique lace. The fortnight passed most agreeably, and Geraldine and Bolly drove back happily to London, the one a little tanned, the other a little wistful. They might even have criss-crossed on the motorway to Calais with Jonty and Sally, who were – unbeknown to Geraldine and quite unexpectedly – heading for a night with Giles and Phyllida, en route to a holiday in Brittany. Jonty had telephoned Giles a couple of days before: it was all, apparently, a rather last-minute vacation, as Sally couldn't see the point of holidays, and Jonty had never organised one in his life before, but they'd been offered a house by a friend, near Dinard, and wondered if they might break the journey with Giles and Phyllida. Awful cheek, and all that, Jonty had declared, but it would be nice to have a bit of a chin wag and a catch up. That never seemed to happen much these days.

"It's only a night," Giles had said to his wife, "I could hardly say 'no' to one of my oldest pals."

"But Rupert is arriving just after Geraldine leaves. I'd rather hoped I'd have him to myself for a couple of days. And then we've got two of his old school friends coming on Tuesday. I'll be washing sheets all weekend."

Giles thought of their only son, at present doing a month's drama course in London, having finished his first year at university. A spell in the army would do him no harm.

"Tell you what, I'll take mother for a run in the car into Deauville, and I'll buy more sheets. Would that help?"

Phyllida sighed. It would help to have her mother-in-law out of her way for a couple of hours, but could she entrust Giles with the purchase of sheets?

"They must be white, 100% cotton, and perfectly plain. And don't go anywhere too expensive."

Giles saluted. "Message understood!"

Jonty arrived with his bride before lunch. They had spent the previous night in an unsatisfactory hotel in Le Touquet. The bed had felt lumpy and the sheets a little damp. He had tried to recall where the lovely little restaurant was that he and Geraldine had found several years before. He and wife number two had walked around for half an hour, Jonty convinced that at any moment they would stumble across the bistro with the navy gingham table cloths. It was only when they had passed the same statue of an unknown duke three times that Sally suggested they give up, and that they should go to the place she had noticed twenty minutes ago. This had not been a success. It was now after 9 o'clock, and *le patron* appeared to have run out of everything except pigs' trotters and duck legs. This suited Jonty, but Sally was not much of a meat eater, and pushed her food round her plate in what her husband considered to be a highly irritating manner.

The car journey the following morning was passed in comparative silence. Sally was map-reading, in order to prevent Jonty shouting at the Sat Nav system. She looked unbearably crestfallen every time he made a marked comment about a missed exit or a wrong turning. What was it, Jonty wondered, with women and maps? Of course, Geraldine had been quite unable to read a map, too, and yet somehow she'd always approached her incompetence with a certain degree of humour.

And why was it, he thought, as they battled down the motorway, past cars pulling caravans at very slow speeds, that one only realises what one's first wife is like when one has acquired a second? Did all much married people feel the same? He had always thought Geraldine neurotic, with her constant tidying, cleaning and re-arranging. He was all for making life simple. If you don't have clutter in the first place, you don't have anything to dust. And the hours she'd take to get ready to go out! It was amazing they had ever arrived anywhere on time. Colour-coding her wardrobe was, he recalled, a particular nightmare, practised by her regularly and with every appearance of enjoyment on her part. And yet, he had to admit, she was surprisingly calm in the face of crises. She had seemed undaunted by the demands of elderly parents, or childish illnesses and accidents. And even when he had told her he was leaving her, she remained controlled. Odd really. But she could drop one of her ruddy bibelots and cry for an hour.

When he'd first met Sally he had found her attitude towards newspapers being left on the floor and towels flung over the bath tub refreshingly relaxed. Her flat, with its mismatched furniture and quirky home-made pottery, seemed so tranquil. One could sit and read for hours, untroubled by the noise of the Hoover in one's ear. But there were, thought Jonty, darkly, disloyally, as he tried to operate the automatic toll machine on the motorway, downsides to this. Downsides that perhaps he did not really want to address while anticipating a jolly night with his old chum. But they lurked, nevertheless, somewhere deep inside, all the time. Enraged by the machine, he turned to Sally. "Do you know how to get the bloody ticket out?" He asked her, crossly. She shook her head and looked miserably into her lap, twisting her handkerchief in her hands. No wonder she didn't like holidays, she thought, they always bring out the worst in everyone.

And of course another disadvantage of his new wife, considered Jonty, as he banged the recalcitrant machine in despair, was that she had never learnt to drive. Geraldine liked being behind the wheel, and long journeys had always been shared. And she had got the car cleaned regularly. He looked at the accumulating sweet wrappers and paper tissues on the floor beneath him with annoyance. Must snap out of this, he said to himself, the ticket finally emerging and the barrier rising. You make your bed, and you damn well lie on it.

Phyllida had wondered whether to say anything to her mother-in-law – something along the lines that it would be diplomatic not to talk about Geraldine too much, but had decided this would merely incite rather than subdue. Rupert's arrival the previous afternoon had already inflamed his father, as their son had emerged from his battered hatchback with his hair tied into a little top knot ("looks like that bloody poodle"), and a strange tattoo on his left arm, which apparently meant something in Buddhist.

It had started to rain. Giles's mother had spent most of the morning complaining how bored she was. Phyllida was frazzled in the kitchen, but had spurned all offers of help. Rupert had yet to emerge from his bedroom, where he could be heard shouting and shrieking as he practised an audition piece for his return to university. He was hoping to take the lead in *Charley's Aunt*, although apprehensive – should he secure the role – at his father's attitude to cross-dressing. Giles, meanwhile, looked out of the sitting-room window onto the sodden terrace. He had forgotten to put the sun umbrella down, and it sagged under the weight of rainwater. Jonty and Sally standing on the doorstep had done nothing to revive his spirits. Jonty looked tense and Sally looked glum. She was wearing a sleeveless flowered dress – unsuitable for the slight drop in temperature – over which she had flung a depressing-looking cardigan. Her hair was flattened by the rain, her glasses smeared with watery droplets. But they all greeted each other warmly. Giles took them up the winding pinewood stairs to their room, which they pronounced delightful. "I'll leave you to sort yourselves out," said their host. "Drinks are downstairs whenever you are ready."

Phyllida had emerged from the kitchen, and was mixing a gin and tonic for her mother-in-law.

"The same for me, darling," said Giles, flinging himself down on the sofa, "I can feel we're in for a long afternoon."

"It's so dreary here," announced his mother, "I don't know why you couldn't have found somewhere on the Riviera."

"Because we couldn't afford it, mother," replied Giles.

Jonty entered the room, followed by Sally, who had changed into a pair of bright blue trousers and a striped top. Both were slightly too tight for her.

"You're looking very nautical, Sally," said Phyllida, greeting her guest with a kiss on the cheek.

"Yes, well, this holiday was all so last-minute. I'm not really geared up for going away. I think I've managed to pack all the wrong clothes."

"Nonsense," said Phyllida, briskly.

Giles's mother glared at Sally, who was trying to decide, with remarkable difficulty, what she would like to drink, but was diverted by the entrance of Rupert, resplendent in a pair of incredibly skinny jeans and a sleeveless vest, revealing his tattoo. His top knot was still in place, and he wore a pair of Italian style loafers with elaborate tassels and no socks.

"Aren't you cold, darling?" asked his mother.

"Rupert, you look perfectly ghastly," barked his grandmother.

"Thanks Gran," he said cheerfully.

"My other grandson is in his last year at medical school, you know. My daughter Antonia's boy," she said, to no one in particular. "He's hoping to be a heart surgeon. Frightfully clever."

"Shame about the coke," said Rupert.

"I have never seen Casper with a glass of Coca-Cola," exploded his grandmother, reprovingly. "I am quite certain he would never touch the stuff. He's very health conscious."

"I think lunch is ready," said Phyllida, with determination. "Let's go through to the dining room."

They sat down at the long oak table, in the low, heavily beamed room. Giles's mother unfolded her napkin with deliberation, before helping herself to bread.

"Do pass that round," shouted Giles, from the other end of the table.

"Would you like tomato salad?" said Phyllida to Sally, who was sitting in silence while Giles and Jonty recalled moments in their joint military careers of no possible interest to anyone else.

"And then he got his head stuck in the water butt!" Giles spluttered, as Jonty wiped tears of laughter from his face with his handkerchief.

"Giles!" bellowed his mother, "do stop wittering on about your blasted army days and pour me a glass of wine."

"Right ho, mother," said Giles, getting up from the table and taking a bottle from the sideboard.

"It's a long time since I've seen you, Monica, but you're looking tremendously well," remarked Jonty, as he gratefully accepted a glass of red, and raised it in salutation to Giles's mother, who replied, briskly, "It's quite difficult looking well at eighty-seven. It's a frightful effort every morning." She paused. "That's why it was so nice having Geraldine here." She looked around the table, defiantly. "She helped me every morning with my maquillage. She's a wonderful girl," she said, addressing Sally, who had a mouth full of bread.

"Hardly a girl," remarked Rupert, "she must be pushing sixty."

"She's nearly fifty-six, actually," said Jonty, regretting the utterance as soon as he said it. His wife gave him a sharp look.

"Well, she looks marvellous, however old she is," continued Giles's mother. "Really, Geraldine has been the highlight of my holiday here. I miss her dreadfully. And of course there's her dear little dog, who's really more human than canine. One almost feels he can talk."

"Pity he never asked where the bathroom was on the first night, then, eh?" remarked Giles jovially.

His mother continued, ignoring him, her glass replenished. She was in full flow. "And of course she was quite wonderful at taking me out. Do you know," she said, with enormous indignation, "in all the years I have been coming here, no one has once suggested taking me to Lisieux? It's quite incredible. Not until last week, when Geraldine kindly asked me if I would like to go. What a fabulous day that was!"

Phyllida started clearing the first course. Giles sighed.

"Of course I am not a Catholic." She emphasised the 'O'.

"No one says, 'CathOlic,' Gran," said Rupert, exasperatedly.

"I am not a CathOlic," she continued, "but I have always had leanings. Are you a CathOlic?" she asked Sally, temporarily forgetting her name. Sally confessed she wasn't and had been brought up as a Methodist, although she was nothing in particular now.

Monica ploughed on, quite uninterested in Sally's religious upbringing. "Geraldine has leanings too, and is especially fond of St Thérèse of Lisieux. Hence our outing. Geraldine says she often talks to St Thérèse, particularly when she is trying to find a parking space."

"Dear God," muttered Giles.

"Geraldine has always had her little eccentricities," said Jonty, uncomfortably. Sally picked at the duck cassoulet in front of her.

"So we motored off to Lisieux, with dear little Bolly in his seat in the back. It really isn't very far away. I cannot understand how I haven't been taken there before."

"You've already said that, mother," remarked Giles, "perhaps no one realised about your leanings."

52

Rupert tittered – an unnecessarily high-pitched utterance, thought Giles.

"We went to the Basilica, which was most interesting. Poor St Thérèse was no age at all when she died, but she came from a very good family."

"That must have made all the difference to her on her deathbed," remarked Rupert, speaking and eating at the same time.

"Please don't talk with your mouth full," said his mother, wondering how many years she had said this, and how many more years she would continue to say it.

The account of the life of St Thérèse resumed. "She used to play on the beach at Trouville as a child, although even then she was terribly spiritual. Then she went into a convent. Her sisters were already there."

"Well, her parents must have saved a lot of money on weddings," said Jonty, thinking, as the father of a daughter, there was much to be said for nuns.

"Her message was that it's those little acts of kindness that make all the difference. It's the tiny day to day actions which can be life changing. I found that a most interesting thought."

"Fascinating, Gran," said Rupert, "when are you going to start on these little acts of kindness? It's never too late."

"Would you be quiet while I am talking, Rupert? Your cousin Casper never interrupts me."

"Probably because he's stoned most of the time."

"Rupert!" said his mother, sharply.

"I have no idea what you're talking about," said his grandmother, "I find the things the young say nowadays utterly baffling."

"I couldn't agree with you more, Monica," interjected Sally, desperate to be included in the conversation.

Giles's mother regarded her as one might a large slug.

"There were the most fascinating photographs of St Thérèse in a side chapel. 'Mrs Acton-Payne,' Geraldine said to me – I have begged her to call me Monica, but she has such charmingly old-fashioned manners – 'do come and look at these pictures. The clothes are an absolute hoot.'"

"Well, thank you for that potted history, mother," said Giles, anxious to move the conversation on. But there was to be no such movement.

"And there was a frightfully good shop next to the Basilica, with the most surprisingly tasteful things. I was able to get something for Pamela Anstruther's 90th. Then Geraldine – who really is so competent at everything – managed to find the most charming tea room where we had an excellent cup of Earl Grey, with the water properly boiled, and some delicious little cakes. Of course Geraldine speaks very good French... do you speak French?" she asked Sally, who had to admit that no, she didn't, but her German was passable.

"Such an ugly language, German," remarked Monica. She continued. "Geraldine said she felt the tea room was terribly Proustian. Wasn't that clever of her? We had such an interesting chat about Proust. We both agreed that all that lying around in a darkened room was no good for anyone. Afterwards we found a tiny little shop selling vintage Hermès scarves for practically nothing. We came home positively laden!" She finished triumphantly.

"Yes, it was thrilling," said Giles, drily, opening another bottle.

"The following day..."

Phyllida started making discreet distress signs at Giles, who merely shrugged his shoulders.

"The following day," Monica continued, "Geraldine and I took little Bolly into Honfleur to a dog-washing parlour. Geraldine thought it would be nice for a French poodle to have a proper blow job in France."

Rupert descended into screams of laughter. Phyllida wondered whether they should skip pudding and move to another room. Jonty took a large gulp of wine. Sally merely sat, looking down into her lap, twisting her gold band round her wedding-ring finger.

Mrs Acton-Payne abhorred gaps in conversation, and felt her account required a decent conclusion. "Yes, all in all, it was wonderful having her here. We are going to meet for lunch in London next month, and Geraldine is going to help me choose a dress for Pamela's 90th. Marvellous dress sense, that girl." She turned to Jonty. "You must miss her so much."

The room fell silent. "Right!" said Phyllida loudly. "Let's move for coffee. I do believe it's brightening up a bit. Anyone for a walk?"

Chapter Three

The day after driving back from Normandy, Geraldine tripped across the mews to take a small box of marrons glacés to Mrs Mankowitz, knowing her neighbour to have a particular fondness for that confection.

"Come in, dear," said Mrs Mankowitz, cheerily. "I've got a new helper from the agency. This girl's from Yugoslavia."

"Surely not?" murmured Geraldine.

"Well, maybe not Yugoslavia. Somewhere over there." She indicated the exact geography with a wild fling of her hand. "She's just about to serve me my morning coffee. I hope you'll join me."

The old lady and Geraldine arranged themselves comfortably on the sofas in the long reception room in eager anticipation. Clattering sounds emitted from the kitchen. Gertie sat on her own in a small chair. "Otto's upstairs having one of his black dog days. He won't be down till lunchtime," remarked Mrs Mankowitz, excusing his absence. She turned her head kitchen-wards and shouted: "How long does it take to boil a kettle? Kristina, I ask you, is it a banquet for twenty or coffee for two?"

"I come, Mitzie," said a large blonde, wielding a trolley though the doorway.

"Mitzie? Do you mind! Nobody calls me Mitzie except my dear late husband. I am Mrs Mankowitz to you."

"I sorry, Mrs… is on your notes, that name, and the agency say to make the ol' ladies comfortable, you use the first name."

"Well, you certainly do not use the first name with me, girl," said Mrs Mankowitz, her blue rinse shaking in anger.

"My friend, Mrs Acton-Payne, is exactly the same," remarked Geraldine, "she says there's far too much informality these days."

"She is absolutely right, dear. I should like to meet your friend one day."

"Yes, I shall arrange lunch for the two of you," Geraldine said, vaguely, wondering if she could cope with quite such a combination of elderly energy in one room.

"Kristina, stop standing there like a great lump and pour the coffee. I like mine milky, two sugars and my friend has hers black, no sugar. Did you bring in the biscuits?"

"Yes, Mrs..., I bring in the custard cream and the 'ob Nob. Now I go and lay the bed," she said, carefully distributing the cups and saucers.

"What do you think, dear, will she do?"

Geraldine took a sip of the dark liquid from her cup. It tasted bitter and wasn't hot enough. "Coffee's not bad at all," she remarked, thinking of the endless numbers of morning helpers who had passed through Mrs Mankowitz's door, and the difficult task they all shared in pleasing the old lady.

"That I've come to this," Mrs Mankowitz declaimed, dramatically. "What Binky thinks I cannot imagine. Poles one week, Bulgarians another, Yugoslavians the next. It's an ethnic trauma, I tell you. When I remember our housekeeper Mrs Macdonald... lovely woman, and always called me Madam. Meticulous, she was! Of course she's long dead. Terrible lungs, she had, dreadfully troubled by phlegm..."

"Did I tell you," said Geraldine, quickly changing the subject, "I am off to Indiana shortly for a weekend with Ellis?"

"Oh yes, the American."

"Yes, the one I met at your party. You played Cupid, Mrs Mankowitz!" said Geraldine, playfully.

"Well, I suppose I did. And it's better than getting a date off the inter world web, or whatever it's called. It was funny that, really."

"What was?" enquired Geraldine, breaking a biscuit in half and feeding it to Gertie.

"The American. How he came to be at the party. I told you, didn't I?"

"No," said Geraldine, "you didn't tell me anything."

"Oh!" said Mrs Mankowitz. "I must have just told Binky. Yes, what happened was, I was in the newsagent one morning, about a week before the party, it was a Saturday... Or was it a Friday? No,... it was definitely a Saturday. And there was this man in front of me asking Mr Patel if he knew who the French lady was with the little poodle whom he'd seen in the fishmongers the previous day. Well, obviously I had to say something. I said, 'She's not French, she's as English as anything. She lives in my mews.' And he turned to me and said he'd stood behind her whilst she was purchasing a turbot, and thought how very lovely she was. Those were his exact words dear, he thought you were very lovely. So of course I had to ask him to my party."

"But Mrs Mankowitz," said Geraldine, quite wondering how to express her alarm over this revelation. It was almost akin to having a stalker. It was most irregular and unsettling. Of course, it's perfectly fine to be considered to be French, one couldn't object to that. Flattering, really. And to be described as lovely,... well, that was most delightful, too. Nevertheless, it was all a little disturbing. She tried to recollect what she had been wearing that day. She screwed up her eyes in an attempt to remember. She could normally recall everything she had ever worn, and where and when – it was a natural facility of hers, she guessed. But why hadn't she noticed HIM? What had he been purchasing? It was too maddening, and, really, far, far too much to think about. She extracted herself from these anxious thoughts. "But, Mrs Mankowitz, you didn't know him. You knew nothing about him. And you asked him into your home."

"Well, dear, he seemed like a perfectly nice gentleman, and he was buying the *Daily Telegraph* at the time. I wouldn't have asked him if it was the *Guardian* or the *Mirror*. And I thought, to be quite honest, dear, that at your age it isn't easy to find a man. I was really only trying to help."

"Yes, well, yes, I suppose so," said Geraldine, acceptingly. It isn't easy to find a man, she considered, thinking of the efforts some of her single friends had made to procure male company. And she hadn't even been looking. Really, most women of my age would be thrilled to have a man as handsome as Ellis. I should be grateful for one – as it were – landing in my lap. She thought for a moment. "Does Binky have an opinion of him?"

"Oh. of course, dear, Binky has an opinion on everyone. He's very partial to YOU. Yes, he said the American was too good to be true. But he's never liked Americans. As you know, he's ten years older than me, and fought in the war. Italy, he was in. I can't remember quite where. I think he moved around a bit. He always said, what with them coming in late and claiming all the credit, and handing out nylon stockings here, there and everywhere and getting off with our girls, and giving sweeties to the kiddies – not to mention their great big ugly cars – he had no time for the Yanks. But I'm much more broad-minded."

Geraldine digested this information. She was never quite sure about Binky. He seemed to have great wisdom in many areas, but so far had failed to come up with the correct numbers for the National Lottery. "He never had a head for figures," said Mrs Mankowitz, by way of explanation.

"And what do YOU think of Ellis, Mrs Mankowitz?"

The old lady paused for a while, then said, "Well, dear, if you want my honest opinion, I think there's something a bit unreal about him." She addressed the wing armchair: "wouldn't you agree, Binky?"

In the last week of August, Ellis returned. Geraldine heard the phone ring as she planted late-flowering annuals in her garden. "I'm back," he roared, like some conquering hero. "Did you miss me?"

"Of course," she murmured, looking in the mirror, wondering whether she did.

"Can I come round?" he asked, "Now?"

She looked in the mirror again. She hadn't really been expecting him back so soon. Surely he had said tomorrow? Her hair had been washed that morning. The house was, as ever, immaculate. She required two minutes with her make-up bag. "Yes, of course," she said. "Do!"

Half an hour later they were sitting in the garden with a glass of Dom Pérignon, brought ready chilled by Ellis. He had stood on the doorstep, more bronzed than ever, his eyes pale, appraising. "You look great, my love." Had he ever called her 'my love' before? She didn't think so, and she wasn't sure she liked it. Jonty had always called her 'old thing', or 'darling' in front of other people. Wasn't 'love' what greengrocers and taxi drivers called their customers? Or perhaps that was 'luv'. Did the prefix of 'my' make a difference? At any rate, she bristled slightly, and wondered if he'd noticed.

Half way down her glass of Dom Pérignon the doorbell rang shrilly, and Bolly swirled into a yapping mass of apricot fluff. Phoebe stepped over the threshold. She was carrying a small rucksack, and her face was streaked with tears. Geraldine could not think of a single occasion in her adult life when Phoebe had turned up unannounced.

"She's left me, G. She's left me. After fifteen fucking years. She's left me and taken the boys. She's gone off with a make-up woman at Pinewood."

Phoebe descended into hot, raging sobs, in Geraldine's tiny hall, her short, chopped, spikey, hair reflected in the fruitwood mirror, as her body racked with rage and sadness. The door to the kitchen opened, and Ellis stood, surveying the scene, an eyebrow – as ever – quizzically raised. The wailing desisted as Phoebe noted his presence. She rallied. She wiped her soggy face, and proffered a damp, pudgy hand in his direction. "I'm Phoebe. The goddess's sister. Sorry. I'm all over the place. Bit of an upset."

The hall, built to accommodate a slim woman and her small dog, began to feel dangerously cramped, and with one move, Geraldine pushed Phoebe into the drawing room, and her rucksack under the stairs. She sat her down on a cream sofa. "I'm going to make you a herbal tea."

"I'd prefer a whisky. Plenty of soda. Feel a bit dehydrated."

Geraldine went back into the kitchen. Ellis was standing by the sink, glass in hand. Would he not think of leaving, she wondered. Surely he could see this was a delicate family moment, requiring tact and diplomacy? His presence was unnecessary, unsettling. Could she ask him to go? "I'm just getting my sister a drink," she said. "I should probably make her a sandwich too. She's had rather an emotional shock. Her partner's left her."

"Difficult to imagine you're sisters. Must have been quite a wide gene pool."

"I take after my mother, and Phoebe looks like my father," she replied, briskly. Really, is this a time for a discussion about family features? She found ice, whisky, soda, and rummaged in the fridge for cheese, butter and tomatoes. With some difficulty, as Ellis remained resolutely lounging by the sink, and the kitchen was very small, she managed to make a couple of rounds of sandwiches. "Mmm, that's good," said Ellis, as he peeled off the top triangle of bread, cheese and tomato from the prettily patterned plate. Geraldine squeezed past him with a tray, to find Phoebe clutching Bolly to her breast, like a treasured teddy bear. "Could I stay tonight, G? I can't go back to the house, not on my own, not at the moment."

Geraldine inwardly balked. Of course the spare bedroom, with its wash-basin set in an old marble-topped chest of drawers, its bedside table stacked with tissues, rose-scented hand cream and carefully selected hardback novels, its bed made up with fine embroidered linen, was always ready for instant deployment. That was not to say, however, that anyone was expected – or indeed, welcome – to stay there.

Geraldine swallowed and took a deep breath. "Bolly and I would love to have you. For the night." Phoebe subsided into a watery mess of gratitude, while nevertheless managing to eat a sandwich.

"Thanks, G," she spluttered, crumbs spraying in a projectile curve over the Aubusson.

On returning to the kitchen to replenish Phoebe's glass, Geraldine was surprised that Ellis was still in almost exactly the same position by the sink. Only the smallest movement had been necessary for him to reach for a top-up of Dom Pérignon. She was finding him irritating. There was something inappropriate about his height, his insouciance, and his beverage, and as he lent into the taps while she negotiated the fridge door again, she had a strong desire to hit him. Instead she smiled – a brittle, resigned, martyr-ish sort of smile. He smiled back, encouraged.

"Shall we go out to eat, my love?" he asked, a relaxed man, ready for a nice evening.

Geraldine seethed. She wanted to say, "Bugger off and stop calling me 'my love'." Instead, she smiled again and said, "I think that's a bit tricky." How calm and English she sounded. "My sister's in rather a state and is going to stay here."

"Oh… oh," he said, evidently put out. "I was hoping to try the new French place in Blenheim Avenue. It's supposed to be great."

"Another time, I'm afraid…"

"Right,… right," he said thoughtfully. "Say, do you know if the delicatessen on the High Street will still be open? I'm famished."

"It's open till eight. I'm really sorry about this. It's all most unexpected. Now, if you'll excuse me, I'd like to get to the fridge."

Slowly, and with an exaggerated air of disappointment, Ellis held up the champagne bottle to see how much was left, and feeling the remaining two inches were hardly worth bothering with, put it back by the sink, smiled ruefully, and walked towards the hall. "Don't forget the weekend." He made a roar, danced a little jig and punched the air. "Oh, when the saints go marchin' in," he sang, with an out-of-tune growl. "You're going to love it. East Cork, All Saints, my old friends. It'll be great." He kissed her lightly on top of her head, and whistled cheerfully down the mews.

After more whisky, a large bowl of pasta, a mug of hot chocolate and several biscuits, Phoebe ascended the stairs towards bed. Geraldine heaved a sigh of relief and poured – the now flat – remainder of the Dom Pérignon into a glass. She wondered whether she should phone Ellis. Had she been a little sharp with him tonight? After all it wasn't his fault that Phoebe's woman had left her. It was strange, she thought, but apart from the texts she had received from him when he had been back in the States, they had never been in the habit of making contact. Perhaps that was because they usually saw each other once a week, and arranged the next outing then and there. A sort of continuous cycle which cut out the need for calls. She had never thought about what he might be doing when he wasn't with her, and had certainly never felt the need to telephone him for a chat.

She took Bolly out for his last perambulation before settling down for the night. Each lamp post was sniffed at as if for the very first time. He trod his territory, defying any marauding schnauzer or dachshund to stand in his way. Satisfied, he indicated he wanted to turn homewards. Geraldine glanced up the road as they turned back into the mews. She could just see a light in the bay window of Ellis's flat. What would happen, now, if she tapped on his window, hoping to be let in like some lost soul in the dark? Would it tweak the relationship a notch higher? Would he exclaim "my love" for the third time that day? And was that what she wanted? She hadn't ever thought much about what she wanted, other than to be in perfect bijou surroundings with a small dog, untroubled by upset. Perhaps, with this wholly unexpected, and unknown, visitation from Phoebe, this was the time to act boldly. She looked at Bolly, slightly shivering at the end of his lead, and without thinking further, headed up the street to the lighted window. There was no reason why she should not ring the doorbell, but instead she opened the gate and stood on tip toe to glance through the glass. Anyone walking past at that moment would question her intentions. But as she had no idea why she was doing this, when ringing the doorbell was a perfectly legitimate option, it seemed like an innocent enough undertaking.

She could hear – just – the strains of *La Traviata*. She could see Ellis get up from his chair, walk over to a console table and pick something up. Then he turned his back on her, and she could no longer observe what he was doing. In the pocket of her flowing cashmere cardigan, flung on in haste against the vagaries of a St John's Wood night, she heard her phone, the distinctive sound of the Flight of the Bumblebee ringtone echoing in the empty street. She looked at the screen. It was Ellis. She saw him turn window-wards, as, hearing a noise – the sound, she presumed, of an electronic Rimsky-Korsakov – he peered anxiously out. She instinctively ducked down. Her phone had now stopped ringing. He raised the sash and stuck his head out, as he said into the mouthpiece, leaving a message: "Hi, Geraldine, it's me, Ellis. Really sorry about your sister. Hope you sorted her out. But hey! It's not all bad. The deli was open and I picked up a delicious zucchini salad and some Parma ham…" He looked down at the flowerbed beneath him. Geraldine was crouched amongst shrubs, her hands over Bolly's muzzle to stop him from barking. In haste, she stood up.

"Goodness," she said, "You must think I'm utterly dotty. I couldn't get your door bell to work, so I thought I'd knock on your window, and then I dropped my keys. Luckily I have just found them." She held her set of house keys aloft, triumphantly.

She continued, "I was giving Bolly his last walk of the evening, saw your light on, and thought I'd apologise for tonight. My sister is tucked up in bed now, but it was all a bit unexpected." She felt quite flustered by this garbled account of her actions, but remained, she hoped, outwardly calm.

"Won't you come in, Geraldine? Or do you prefer to linger among the lavender?" He smiled indulgently, as one would at a child.

"Oh, ok, just a couple of minutes, then I must get home. It's quite late."

He disappeared from the window, unlocked doors, and casually, lightly, placed a finger on the door bell. It rang loudly in the quiet of the gloom. He turned to her and raised an eyebrow, quizzically. What was it her grandmother had always told her? 'Never explain; never complain.' Head held high, carrying Bolly, she walked through into the reception room. There were papers strewn over the desk, a small empty coffee pot next to a mug, and through the double doors at the rear she could see his bedroom – a half-unpacked case, and a pile of shirts on the floor. He caught her glance. "Travel, eh? Too much hassle." He pointed towards the desk. "And I'm trying to get stuff ready for the morning. Big day at the office. Crunch time. Again. More heads to roll…" He sighed.

"Well, I absolutely mustn't keep you up any longer," Geraldine said. "Just let me know what the arrangements are for the weekend and I'll be ready."

She stood up, Bolly still in her arms.

"Geraldine," he said, gently. "Do you have any idea what you are like?"

She looked alarmed. "No," she said. "One tries never to think of that sort of thing. Far too unsettling. 'Night Ellis."

She turned and opened the door to go.

"Till the weekend, my love," he called after her, softly.

Phoebe was asleep with the door open to the spare room. She snuffled slightly as Geraldine silently placed a bottle of Badoit next to her bed. The rucksack slouched in the corner, its contents spilling out over the limited amount of floor space. The inlaid Regency chair, which stood under the window, was engulfed with discarded clothes. Faced with this disorder,

Geraldine suffered a moment's breathless panic, but told herself all would be resolved by tomorrow. She showered, covered Bolly with a clean pashmina, and lay stiffly in her bed, quite unable to sleep.

At 7am sharp, Bolly was sniffing in the tiny back garden. He thought it likely that a fox had been in overnight, and a minute investigation was called for. He could see Geraldine at the window, measuring out his biscuits, filling up the kettle. He cocked his leg on a pot of thyme, then asked to be let in. Geraldine was in her nightdress, a long white lacy garment with a frill round the hem and a high neck. Her hair was clipped up loosely, and her face glowed from the morning's exfoliation and layers of expensive cream. She poured coffee into her favourite cup, and nibbled delicately at a madeleine. Bolly crunched his breakfast, then settled into his kitchen bed for a quick nap. Suddenly, the door was flung open, and Phoebe stood, a dishevelled mass in check pyjama bottoms and a greying T shirt, yawning and scratching like a bear.

"Morning, G. Any chance of a nice strong brew?"

"Do you mind Earl Grey?"

"If that's all you've got… I can pick up some builders' tea in Tesco's later."

Geraldine blanched at this implication of an extended stay. Surely Phoebe could return to her own

72

home today? Surely provisions to suit her particular tastes weren't necessary?

"Have you got any bacon, G?" Phoebe continued.

"Oh dear. What a failure I am as a hostess. I'm afraid I never eat bacon. I have some eggs, though. Would you like me to boil one for you?"

"Fried for me, please, and I can do it myself. No problemo!"

Geraldine thought of the oil plastered up the wall and the lingering smell of frying permeating the house. But she remained silent, watching her sister rummage around her tiny kitchen like a great, lumbering animal.

"I have to go into the Beeb at 10 for a bloody meeting, but you're really close here to Portland Place. I can just walk across the park. It'll clear my head. And I thought I'd take you out for dins this evening. I noticed a new bistro-y café on the corner. Quite reliable looking nosh. If it's warm we can sit outside with Bolly." She paused, then turned to face Geraldine. "You know what hurts the most? That she's taken Jasper and Archie. The bloody make-up woman lives in a flat in Kilburn. What sort of a life is that for a pair of pugs, I ask you?"

"Kilburn?" enquired Geraldine. "That's terribly close. Only three stops on the tube. Don't you think perhaps you should go and see Eileen? Try and sort something out? After all, fifteen years of being together is a lot to chuck away."

"Don't tell me that," shouted Phoebe, bashing her mug of Earl Grey down on the granite work top. "I'm not the one that's run off with some trollop in a short skirt. I'm not going grovelling to anyone."

Geraldine would have liked to have enquired further about the make-up artist, but was fearful of provoking more wrath, resulting in the breakage of precious china. She poured herself another cup of coffee and, quite uncharacteristically, helped herself to a second madeleine. Bolly buried himself within his pashmina. Phoebe dribbled her eggy plate under the cold tap, and slammed it on the draining board. THAT would have to be washed again, observed Geraldine to herself.

"What are your plans for today, G?" asked Phoebe, as she swirled washing-up liquid into the frying pan, and left it sitting in the sink.

"Well," said Geraldine carefully, "I have to go to the dry cleaners, then I have a Pilates class, and the plumber's coming at three to look at the dripping tap in the bathroom."

Phoebe looked at her askance. "Busy day, then, G?"

Geraldine ignored this and continued, "And of course I'm off on Thursday with Ellis. To East Cork, Indiana. For the weekend."

"Ah yes. Ellis. Bit difficult to take it all in last night, what with everything going on and not feeling quite myself. Where's that heading, then?"

"What do you mean?"

"Well, is he really your type?"

"I don't know whether I have ever had a type. I only had a couple of boyfriends before Jonty. I don't think I've decided what my type actually is yet."

"Well, G, I can tell you for free, I can guarantee your type is nothing like Ellis."

"Why not? He's kind, he's generous, he's good-looking, he's intelligent…"

Phoebe smiled what was supposed to be a knowing smile. "Whatever," she said, annoyingly.

"And whatever to you too. I have to get dressed. Get on. With my busy day."

"Yeah, G. Catch you later."

Bolly emerged from his kitchen bed to follow Geraldine up the stairs. The bathroom was scattered with wet towels, and condensation dripped down the mirror. Geraldine opened the window and folded the towels neatly over the rail. She cleaned the bath and put the top back on the toothpaste. Of course, it was a pleasant change, in a way, to have someone to clear up after. Like having Jonty back, she mused. She dressed, applied her make-up, combed her hair and felt quite cheery as she made her bed and tidied the room. She looked at her phone on the chest of drawers. One missed call. From her daughter, Cassie.

Cassie only ever rang in the early evening, and never more than once a week. An earlyish morning call bade ill. She had left no message, but Geraldine felt obliged to ring back.

"Mummy," wailed Cassie.

"What's wrong, darling?" asked Geraldine, alarmed.

"Can I come and stay with you? Now? I've rung in sick, and it's only three and a half hours on the train. I could be with you by the afternoon."

Geraldine sat on the bed to catch her breath. "Darling, you're ill?" There were muffled sobs on the line.

"Oh Mummy. James and I have split up."

"But everything was fine when we spoke last week. Hasn't he just started in gynaecology?"

"Yes, and there I am in midwifery. Obs and gynae are in the same building. We could meet for lunch. It was all so perfect. And then, and then…" There were more sobs. "This bloody girl started in A & E. She saw James and she just sort of engulfed him. Like a whale."

"Is she very large, then?" asked Geraldine, interestedly.

"No! She's about a size four with long blonde hair. I said 'whale' because it's like she's consumed him. Maybe it's more like a boa constrictor. I don't

76

know… It's almost as if he's become a different person. He kept talking about her, how she's such a brilliant doctor blah blah blah. I should have guessed. And then yesterday evening it was my night off, and he said he was working late and couldn't meet me. So I asked Dede – you know, the girl whose parents live in Maida Vale – if she'd like to go for a drink, and she said had I tried this new bar near the Infirmary, and there they were. All over each other. I actually thought I'd faint. And all he said was, 'Sorry', like he'd spilt a glass of water or something. I thought we were practically engaged. I didn't get any sleep last night and I feel sick. I'm getting the 11.30 from Waverley and I'm coming straight to you, Mummy. I'll die if I stay here a moment longer, I really will."

Geraldine felt the life forces draining from her body. With Phoebe staying the only option was for Cassie to share Geraldine's bed. Cassie, although of slender build, was 5 feet 10 inches tall and clumsy. It was always an enormous surprise to Geraldine that someone who was incapable of holding a cup and saucer without breaking it was an excellent nurse and was now training to be a midwife. There was no help for it but to be a brave mother.

"Get a taxi darling when you arrive at Euston, and Bolly and I will be here to meet you. Dear old Phoebe is here – Eileen's left her, so we'll be quite a merry band of single women." She tried to sound bright, but it was requiring some effort. "Chin up, darling, there's plenty more fish in the sea."

"Oh Mummy!" More tears, and the call ended.

Geraldine tapped on the spare room door. Phoebe was already in her habitual work gear of combat trousers, black T-shirt and leather jacket. She seemed cheerier. "Eileen's just called," she said. "She wants to meet me for lunch. We're going to go to the sausage place in the park. Do you know it? It's quite good."

Geraldine expressed regret that she had yet to discover a sausage place in the park, and explained about the arrival of Cassie.

"It'll be like a home for broken hearts here," remarked Phoebe, managing a hint of glee in her voice.

Yes, a refuge for weeping women, thought Geraldine, remembering her own secret tears, when her husband had gone. "A broken heart can be mended," she replied, firmly, to her sister.

"Whatever you say, sis, whatever you say," said Phoebe, knowingly.

Chapter Four

Cassie arrived, with a large suitcase which scarcely fitted through the front door, at the same time as the plumber, who expressed regret at not having the right part with him, and promised to return in the morning. Cassie cried copiously and noisily, upsetting the dog, who howled in sympathy. Phoebe came back to the mews at tea time with a carrier bag containing PG Tips, streaky bacon, granulated sugar and a six-pack of beer.

Trailing behind her on their double lead were Jasper and Archie, replete from a lunch of sausages. "Kilburn just isn't a suitable place for pugs," explained Phoebe, as they curled themselves up on a cream sofa each.

"And good news from the Beeb meeting," she continued, packet of open biscuits in hand. "They're replacing the presenter of 'Who's That at the Door?' Oliver smarmy-pants-know-it-all has been sacked. Such a relief. No more of his ghastly clever-clever remarks."

"Oh, that's excellent, Phoebe. You must be feeling much better," said Geraldine, brightly. "Who have they replaced the awful Oliver with?"

"Stephen Fry."

At supper time, the evening still warm, the three women and three dogs made their way to the High Street for an al fresco meal. They were an ill-assorted party, impossible to believe that any of them were related, except, perhaps, the two pugs. Cassie picked at a fish cake, feeding most of it to the dogs. Phoebe ate with tremendous relish. Geraldine gazed at her Caesar salad. She had distinctly said, 'No anchovies,' and there, curling over the romaine lettuce, were several, a reminder that everyone, but everyone had scant regard for anything she ever said. She pushed them to one side, but found their silver, slithery presence unsettling.

That night, all was restless. Bolly was a fluff of nerves, his territory truly usurped. Geraldine lay uneasily, forced to the extreme edge of her bed by Cassie, who, when she finally submitted to sleep, tossed, turned and wailed aloud. Noisy snores emitted from the spare room – impossible to know if the sounds belonged to pug or person. Geraldine spent a wakeful night wondering about her trip to America, and what she should pack. Only two days to go.

Surprisingly the plumber returned a little after 8am. The bathroom was fully booked, and he waited patiently downstairs, enjoying for once what he called 'a decent cup of tea'. He checked his watch. The time was ticking over nicely. Geraldine was cleaning walls and surfaces with a lavender-scented organic spray. She scrubbed vigorously at the tiles, although, since Phoebe had yet to descend for a fry-up, it was a singular waste of effort. "Bathroom's free," came a yell from upstairs. Geraldine gave the plumber a meaningful look. "I'll finish me tea first," he said defiantly. Eventually, dogs and humans were breakfasted, the kitchen cleaned again, and the plumber left, his wallet bulging with a wad of cash. It was nearly lunchtime.

Geraldine went into the drawing room. Phoebe and Cassie were sitting together, each looking at photographs of their respective lost loves on their mobile phones. Really, she thought, as she looked at their dark heads close to each other, their pale faces and their long thin noses fixed over the small screens, their colouring and features were surprisingly similar.

Perhaps, she thought wildly to herself, Cassie is not my child. She could barely remember her entry into the world. Jonty had recently returned from a tour of duty in Northern Ireland, and had seemed disappointed that the baby was late. He'd been hoping to miss the birth. He would rather, he had said later in the Officers' Mess, as he and his chums wetted the baby's head with copious amounts of whisky, have gazed down the barrel of a Provo's gun, than have watched the bloodied emergence of his first born. At least you knew where you were with the IRA.

"What's the name of that actor? You know the one I mean," Phoebe appealed to Geraldine. "Cassie's James looks very much like him."

"Tyrone Power," said Geraldine, abstractedly.

"Who on earth is he?" asked Cassie.

"Before your time, Cas," said Phoebe. "I'm racking my brain to think of some films he's been in, the one who looks like James."

"Boris Karloff," muttered Geraldine, and left the room.

The occupants of the sofa exchanged glances. "Do you think Mummy misses Daddy?" Cassie asked her aunt. Phoebe paused to think. She ached for Eileen, and though it seemed inconceivable that anyone should feel similar pangs for a buffoon like Jonty, she had to concede it was possible. "Still," she added, "at least she's got this American now. I s'pose he's company for her. Or something…"

Really, thought Geraldine, as she climbed the stairs, the house looks disgusting. The plumber had left wood shavings all over the bathroom floor, which seemed an unnecessary consequence of a dripping tap. She looked at herself in the mirror. She was tired and her hair needed washing. In her room she picked up

Cassie's clothes in a desultory manner, piling them on top of the opened suitcase. Why did her daughter always wear such trailing, droopy garments, the sleeves always dangling over her bony wrists, her skirts sweeping down to her ankles? Was it a sort of counterbalance to wearing a nurse's uniform much of the time? It's surprising, she thought, that half of her family spent their working lives in a uniform. At least Hugo hadn't become a traffic warden or an airline pilot. And was that why Jonty had always looked so slovenly out of his uniform? Bordering on dishevelled, she remembered, disapprovingly. She instinctively stood up straight and brushed imaginary hairs off her sleeveless cashmere top. There were half-empty glasses of water and screwed-up paper tissues next to the bed, and the blind had been rolled with one end higher than the other. She fiddled with the cord to rectify this, and saw out of the window Ellis walking purposefully towards the house. In a frenzy she combed her hair and applied lipstick and scent and raced down the stairs to a mélange of barking, hysterical dogs. Cassie had let Ellis in and was introducing herself, and Phoebe had yet to arise from the cream sofa, where she was eating a chocolate bar.

The eyebrow was raised.

"I just wanted to touch base over Thursday's arrangements," shouted Ellis over the baying hounds.

"I'll collect you at 10am. It'll be very casual in East Cork. No tiaras!" he joked.

Geraldine smiled faintly at him.

"Can't wait," she said. And looking around her, she actually felt she meant it. She closed the front door behind him and returned to the drawing room.

"It's awfully funny," remarked Cassie, as she flung herself back down on the sofa next to Phoebe, "that old people have boyfriends. I find it a bit disgusting, actually," she said, chattily. "I mean, honestly, what's the point?"

"I am not old and he is not a boyfriend," snapped her mother.

"Well, what is he then?"

"How about gentleman caller?" offered Phoebe, crumpling up her chocolate wrapper, and throwing it overarm style into the fireplace. Geraldine marched across the tiny room and picked it up.

"He is just a friend," she said, somewhat shrilly, "and please put your discarded wrappers in the proper place."

Cassie and Phoebe rolled their eyes at each other. "Mummy's got a boyfriend, Mummy's got a boyfriend," Cassie chanted, annoyingly.

"Really Cassie, sometimes you behave like a three year-old. It's difficult to believe you hold down a responsible job."

"Lighten up, G. Chillax, as they say."

"I am perfectly relaxed, thank you very much," Geraldine shouted. "And I am now going to go and finish cleaning the bathroom. Again. Someone has to."

"A tidy home is a wasted life, G. Think about that!" Geraldine slammed the door.

Wednesday dawned, and Geraldine was conscious that she had to assemble her wardrobe for the weekend. She was a methodical packer, and would usually lay clothes on the spare room bed a few days in advance of travelling. In this way she would put outfits together, accessorising them with shoes and jewellery, and discard anything that was extraneous. The garments would then be wrapped in tissue paper, the shoes placed in monogrammed bags. This was not now an option. She had taken advantage of her temporarily feminine household to ask advice on what Americans would wear to such an occasion. Phoebe had once visited Palm Beach, many years ago, and thought florid sleeveless dresses and costume jewellery appropriate. Cassie had recently been to New York – alas, with James, which provoked further snot and tears – and imagined something more cutting-edge, and definitely a pair of Manolo Blahniks, should Geraldine happen to have any lying around. Then they looked at an American football game on YouTube, which provided no inspiration, merely discouragement. Cassie, recovered, had the excellent idea of finding out the weather forecast for East Cork, Indiana, that weekend, and discovered it would be mainly 32 degrees centigrade, with occasional thunderstorms. "I suppose I should pack an umbrella," said Geraldine, regretfully.

In the end she managed to select two pairs of white capri trousers, a floaty pair of harem pants, some silk sleeveless tops, a seersucker skirt, and a couple of polo shirts – "very preppy," opined Cassie of the latter two. At the last minute she put in a smart dress for evening, a pair of espadrilles and a flowery waterproof poncho that she'd bought some years ago for an opera evening at Glyndebourne. She had a pashmina in her hand luggage for warmth, a new hardback novel, and some little presents for her hosts.

On Wednesday evening, emboldened by two glasses of Sauvignon Blanc, she asked Cassie and Phoebe about their plans. They both looked surprised. "Don't worry, Mummy," said Cassie. "I'll still be here for ages. The Infirmary has given me a week's compassionate leave."

"And I'll be holding the fort too, old girl. The dogs and I will be keeping the home fires burning. You mustn't worry about a thing while you're away. All will be tickety-boo and just how you left it on your return – when did you say? Monday morning?"

Phoebe paused. "You know the trouble with you, G, is you fuss about stuff all the time. Everything will be fine, won't it, Cas?"

"'Course it will, Mummy. You shouldn't worry so much. Oooh! I forgot to tell you. Hugo's coming down on Saturday. With the ghastly girlfriend. He texted me earlier."

Geraldine visibly blanched. "But where are you all going to sleep?"

"It's cool!" Said Cassie. "Hugo and Abi are going to have your bed, and I'm going to doss down here in the drawing room."

Geraldine rose to her feet. She felt a little wobbly. "I'm just going to check on supper."

She went into the kitchen, poured herself a third glass of wine, and held on to the granite work surface for support. She took deep breaths, intermingled with gulps of restoring alcohol. She looked in the oven. The fish pie was crisping nicely. She tossed the salad, and placed it on the table. The kitchen seemed to spin a little, and she opened the back door for air.

"Supper's ready," she called, as, somewhat calmer, she placed the steaming plates of pie on the table.

"Thank God!" said Phoebe, wandering in with a can of lager in her hand. "I'm starving." Cassie followed, preceded by the dogs, who all sat in Bolly's kitchen bed, looking expectant.

Phoebe, true to form, ate with the appetite of a starved wolf cub. Cassie picked up a prawn on her fork in a desultory way and eyed it with distaste.

"I say," said Phoebe to Cassie "you're not becoming dyslexic?"

"No," replied Cassie, "I can still read. I just can't eat."

Geraldine poured more wine, and looked at the pile of washing-up in the sink. In fourteen hours she would be gone. She'd be sitting in a private plane, champagne glass in hand, handsome man by her side, executive leather caressing her moisturised, Pilates-toned body. All she had to do was wait.

Another sleepless night next to her daughter loomed. Cassie slept more profoundly this time, but it was still impossible for Geraldine to secure relaxation, especially as Bolly, who hated the appearance of suitcases, knowing full well it might betoken the absence of his loved one, insisted on lying on top of Geraldine's chest – a dead weight draped in a manner calculated to prevent breathing. At six o' clock she rose from her sleepless bed, showered and washed her hair, and took Bolly for a walk. She was dressed and ready, with her suitcase by the door, just after seven. Apart from Bolly, who had returned to his kitchen bed, she was the only one to have ventured forth. Even the pugs slumbered. The hours ahead weighed heavily upon her. She made a list of household tasks that would be required to be done once the various inmates had vacated the premises. She tried not to think about the visitation, in her absence, of her son and his girlfriend.

Hugo had been an undergraduate at Cambridge, reading some sort of combination of economics and a foreign language, and had managed to secure himself a job in administration in one of the many science parks which lurk on the outskirts of that city. His girlfriend, Abi, did something called logistics. Geraldine had no idea what that was. Abi came from Basildon, held her knife and fork in a funny way, was permanently orange, and applied make-up with the subtlety of a drag queen. It wasn't, thought Geraldine, that she was being snobbish about the girl, no, she just felt her quiet, expensively educated son – kind and well-mannered – deserved a little better. Of course she had never expressed an opinion on this, although she had once ventured the phrase 'not quite out of the same bottle', to which Cassie had screamed with laughter. The one thing Hugo lacked was dynamism. He seemed to have fallen into this unsuitable attachment by his inability to withstand the force of Abi, who had an assertive, abrasive personality. Should Hugo choose to spend his life with her, Geraldine was quite certain that family get-togethers would be a thing of the past.

Yet, she supposed, as she attempted to straighten her hair, family gatherings were already a thing of the past. The divorce had rather sealed that one.

Geraldine wasn't entirely sure why the relationship between number two wife and Jonty had begun. He had left the Army, and had started at the Ministry of Defence in Whitehall. It was such a shame, thought Geraldine, that just when she had settled into her own house, with a husband who set off at eight in the morning and was home by six in the evening, it had to fall apart. She supposed it must have been her fault, but to this day, she didn't know why. It had not been easy being married to an Army officer, with all the moving around that the job entailed. The best advice she had ever been given about military marriages was from the Brigadier's wife, a large, bossy woman, who had told her, "Always keep the oven spotless. You never know when you'll have to move on." And she'd kept the oven and everything else in pristine condition, and she'd never complained when she'd had to move for the third time in a year. Nor when the children had wept at having to change schools yet again. The only time she'd really cried was when finally the children were sent to boarding school. She had hated it so much herself, and yet, after the initial settling-in period, they had loved their life away from home, and thrived. And there she had been, finally, settled in the house they actually owned outright, mortgage-less, in Fulham, all their furniture out of storage, her father's inheritance invested securely, when Jonty came back one evening and said, "I've met someone else."

Geraldine didn't scream or cry in his presence. She listened patiently to the story of Jonty, travelling on the Tube every morning, always sitting opposite the same woman, until one day they had talked. The woman had asked him if he had finished with his *Metro*, as all the copies had been taken at Putney Bridge that morning. From this unpromising start among missing sheets of free newsprint, a conversation had cautiously advanced, until one day Jonty had boldly suggested they meet in Sloane Square later for a drink.

She was a librarian at the London Library, and made shapeless pottery items in her spare time. It was rather like her own father, Geraldine had thought, with his formless lumps of wood, only in this case, it was clay.

Eventually, perhaps inevitably, an affair had started. Geraldine listened to the details as if she had heard it all before – and indeed, she had, for in some communal, osmosis sort of way, it is a commonplace tale, told by so many spouses on so many occasions, and from the Gorbals to Godalming, Totnes to Tunbridge Wells, it is very much the same story: only the names and locations change. It seemed incredible. Of all the disasters Geraldine had imagined befalling her, she had never envisaged this one, and yet thinking about it, why ever not? Jonty was male – that fact alone already made it a distinct possibility – he still had most of his hair and all of his teeth, and only wore his spectacles for reading. He had many advantages compared with others of his sex. Yet she'd spent night after night worrying about house fires, child molesters, dog nappers and burglaries. And all the while she had been living alongside this brooding, burning hulk, crazed with testosterone and manly impulses. If only she'd realised.

She had wondered where these moments of passion had taken place. She couldn't imagine Jonty booking a hotel – she had always booked everything for him. She supposed that all those trips on a Saturday morning to the wine emporium, which had taken so long, and had usually resulted in a modest Chilean red – easily purchased at the local petrol station – must have been when the couplings had occurred. Only once had she queried why it took three hours to buy a bottle of Casillero del Diablo. Jonty had always been a man of regular habits, and even his transgressions were timetabled. The librarian's flat was a ten-minute walk away, near the river, and he found it a pleasant stroll. Later he had wondered, had this happened in November, with a chill in the air, and the prospect of months of winter ahead, would he have enjoyed it quite so much?

When he had finally decided he would rather be with one than the other – and he was never quite sure why – it was with the utmost sadness that he broke the news to his wife.

Hugo and Cassie were already into their university and nursing careers, and Sally, the woman on the Tube, was childless and long divorced. No one much was hurt by anything. Bolly was but a pup. Geraldine was wracked with the thought of a custody battle. She had read about that sort of thing in the *Daily Mail* – high court judges settling the habitation of chihuahuas, visiting rights negotiated for labradoodles. But it turned out the other woman kept cats, and Jonty confessed he had always been more of a retriever man. How little we know the people we love, thought Geraldine sadly, as she stood at their bedroom door, watching him pack his bags.

Sometimes, in the dark and often lonely hours of the night, Geraldine had asked herself if she should have put up more of a fight, protested, sought out this Sally woman – a surprisingly mild, slightly dumpy blonde – and reasoned with her. But what would one have said? I would really rather you didn't take my husband? Can we come to some arrangement, perhaps we could share him on alternate weeks? But always she managed to persuade herself of the same conclusion: that she was better off now where she was, mistress of her day, devoted owner of Bolly, and – sometimes – useful mother and sister.

At 9.30 precisely pugs and people began to stir in the tiny, recently over-stuffed house in St John's Wood. Dogs snuffled round the garden. Yawning people boiled kettles and drank milk and orange juice straight from the carton. Geraldine sat rigidly in Bolly's toile armchair in the drawing room. Her jeans had been steam pressed at the dry cleaners. Her Cartier watch had been polished last night with a cloth, as had her diamond tennis bracelet and her platinum earrings with the little South Sea pearls, while she sat at her dressing table. She was private jet-ready in a white T-shirt and navy Ralph Lauren blazer. At five minutes before ten, a black cab stopped in the mews, and a waving Ellis emerged.

"I'm off," shouted Geraldine, to anyone that might hear, but the only one who was interested was a disconsolate Bolly. Phoebe emerged briefly with a thick piece of toast clamped between her teeth, and Cassie hung over the balustrade, her wet hair dripping down the stair carpet.

"Bye!" They called loudly and in unison, as Geraldine closed the front door, her luggage whisked in to the cab by an attentive Ellis.

She breathed a sigh of relief as she settled back in the seat.

"I'm guessing the last few days have been a trial for you," he said. "You're not really geared-up for multiple occupancy."

"You are so right, Ellis. I'm just looking forward to having access to a bathroom."

"Well, America leads the way in plumbing, as in so many other things."

What a reassuring thought, mused Geraldine.

Chapter Five

Her tranquil moment was short-lived, as they made their way down the High Street. It struck her that she had been so busy the last few days she'd given little time to thinking about their prospective three nights together. After all, they had only once spent a night together and that hardly counted as sharing a room with him, to say nothing of a bathroom. This was a whole aspect of the trip that had been entirely overlooked. Although Pilates classes had done a little to halt the passage of time, she was very aware of the gravitational pull on her body. She had not considered the possible hazard of dressing and undressing with a comparative stranger, not to mention all those other little acts of intimacy. She froze in panic.

She looked out of the window of the taxi. They were now speeding westwards on the A40. She suddenly realised she had no idea which airport they were flying from. Her travel arrangements were usually meticulously under her control. She liked to have a print-out of her itinerary in her bag, next to her passport. Why had she allowed herself to accept the invitation? She felt a tightening in her throat, and her heartbeat increasing. As calmly as possible she asked, "Where are we flying from?"

"Chip is swinging by from Brussels, where he's been at a meeting. He started up CrocAir down in Florida a while ago. You know? The budget airline? He's big in aviation. He should be touching down at Northolt now, re-fuelling, then we're off."

Geraldine relaxed slightly. Northolt was only a few miles away. She'd driven past it many times. Didn't the RAF fly from there? She was reassured at the thought of men in uniform, dependable, as Jonty once had been. And wasn't it where the mortal remains of Diana, Princess of Wales, had touched down after the Parisian accident? Clearly a suitable place from which to arrive or depart. She lowered her tightly clenched shoulders. Soon she'd be in a private plane – presumably there would be an air hostess, or perhaps Chip's PA? – and they'd be over the Atlantic having luxurious little nibbles and vintage champagne. This was the life! She smiled as she looked out of the window. It had started to rain. At least it would be warm – if a little wet – in East Cork. She'd looked it up in the big atlas she had in the bookcase on the landing. It was a little to the Southeast of Lake Michigan, on a bend in a river. Perhaps like a small Cambridge. Did they punt there too, she wondered?

The taxi deposited them in a car park overlooking a runway. A small plane was skidding along the tarmac as it braked to a halt. Ellis carried the luggage over to a portacabin-style building, and Geraldine trailed behind, a feeling of apprehension once more stealing over her. She assessed his retreating rear view: tall, rangy, he was dressed this morning in a navy blazer, white shirt without a tie, and jeans with a crease in them. He stopped, and turning round to smile at her, remarked, "I forgot to say, Geraldine, we're looking very matchy matchy today."

Matchy matchy! Exclaimed Geraldine to herself. What a ridiculous remark! Why was it, she thought, that there are certain words or phrases that just instantly ignite one's irritation?

She remembered reading an article in a woman's magazine last year when she was having a pedicure. It was entitled 'Dating Deal Breakers', and was all about the little things men on a romantic encounter had said or done – or just happened to have, in the case of ear wax – that had instantly soured, nay, destroyed the relationship. One woman interviewed had peremptorily ditched her lover when he had – in an intimate setting – used the word 'panties'. It was not that she was shocked by his reference to her underwear, vulgar though that might have been, but that he had used That Word. Ghastly, Geraldine had thought, inwardly squirming while the beautician scraped at the hard skin on her heels. And then another woman had extracted herself from an entanglement with a man because of his habit of reading signs out aloud – car journeys had assumed nightmare proportions, as every visible written word was carefully enunciated. Imagine: one is driving along, and one's companion is intoning 'Church Street', 'No Through Road', 'Halal Meat and Groceries', 'Post Office', 'Keep Left' – Geraldine had shuddered at the thought. It would be like being trapped with an overactive navigational system. Very grating on the ears. But these things were nothing to what some of our sisterhood had endured: pigeon toes, man bags, white socks, prolonged wind – the list seemed endless. Geraldine could scarcely even contemplate ear wax without wanting to retch, and indeed she had been obliged to forsake her place in a queue for a cash machine, so prolific was the yellow lava spewing from the gentleman's ear in front of her. While reading that article, Geraldine had congratulated herself on being on her own, and being entirely untouched by these dreadful nuisances. And yet here she was now, no longer quite single, and – even worse – being told she was 'matchy matchy'. It could really only bode ill for the weekend.

"Can I get your passport, Sweetheart?" Ellis then asked. Sweetheart! No one had ever called her that. This really had to stop. "I'll get the formalities dealt with," he said, as she handed the document over in its beige calf-leather folder. "Chip's here already. I guess he's in the bathroom."

A moment later a short, fat, red-faced man in a too tight shirt, stretched to bursting over his stomach, walked towards them.

"Ellis, man! Great to see you!"

"You too, Chip. Long time, long time…" They high-fived, then bear-hugged. After a few minutes of slapping each other playfully and guffawing, Ellis turned to Geraldine. "Here she is, Chip, here she is… Isn't she gorgeous? Geraldine, meet my old friend Chip."

She offered her hand, and Chip looked at Ellis. "Aw, she's great, Ellis. Real great."

"Isn't she? And there she was, just living round the corner in the cutest little house you've ever seen."

Geraldine had the distinct impression she was either not really there, or had suddenly turned in to a very small child.

"Lovely to meet you, too, Chip," she said.

"I can't get enough of that accent, Ellis," Chip said.

An official-looking man walked over, carrying a sheaf of papers. "We've checked the flight plan, Mr

Mutton. Here are your passports. You're all ready to go."

"And have you got the paperwork for the other guy, you know? Is that all in order?"

"Yes, all done, sir, and the... er... freight is loading right now."

"Great! Thanks. Off we go."

The two men led the way, talking all the time. Geraldine wasn't really listening, although she caught something about someone finally going home after a long struggle. She wondered if she'd ever see her own home again, and what sort of condition it would be in. She was tempted to telephone Phoebe to see how everything was, but as she'd only been gone just over three quarters of an hour, she felt it imprudent. She imagined the ribald comments this would provoke. "G's a neurotic mess," she could hear Phoebe telling Cassie.

Suddenly, she was stopped from her domestic meanderings by the most alarming sight ahead of her. A wooden coffin was being loaded onto a plane by four burly men. They were having some difficulty negotiating its bulk up the short flight of steps. Geraldine feared they would drop it, its contents plopping out onto the rain-splashed runway. But worse was to come.

Chip detached himself from Ellis, and ascended the flight of steps at the front of that very plane, heaving his bulk into the cockpit. With some urgency, Geraldine ran to Ellis and tugged at his sleeve. "Please tell me Chip isn't the pilot, and we're not travelling with a coffin... It's not very big, is it?"

"The coffin or the plane?" asked Ellis.

"The bloody plane! And what about Chip?"

"Well, it's his plane, and he flies it. I told you: he's really big in aviation. Started out as a pilot for PanAm before he set up his own airline. There's nothing Chip doesn't know about planes. And anyway, he has a co-pilot. That's him over there."

He pointed to a young man in a uniform walking towards them. He looked like a mannequin. Handsome in a rather obvious way.

"That's Joachim. Flies Jumbos for KLM. Chip's known him for years." Well, he can't have known him for that long, thought Geraldine, he only looks about twelve years old.

"In we go," continued Ellis, "the quicker we take off, the earlier we arrive."

"But what about the coffin?"

"Oh, that's Stevie Bellingham. Poor guy. He was at All Saints same time as us all. Still, at least he's getting back for the weekend. He'd been ill for a while. Died a few days ago at his house in Le Touquet. It's typically generous of Chip to take him back home. At least he's among friends."

Geraldine was speechless. For a moment she considered running back across the tarmac and ringing for a cab.

"Come on, my love," said Ellis, patting her lightly on the bottom, "in you get."

She would really have to say something to Ellis, but for the moment she concentrated on getting herself settled in the cabin.

To be fair, she thought, it wasn't that bad. But it wasn't quite how she'd pictured a private jet. The upholstery was cream leather, certainly, with the seats arranged companionably facing each other. Two seats had been removed in order to accommodate the coffin. It was all a little more cramped than she had imagined. Further back there was a small door, presumably leading to the lavatory, which now could only be reached by climbing over the coffin. Perhaps she would be able to restrain her bladder for the whole of the Atlantic crossing, and avoid unseemly clamberings over the dead. It seemed so strange to be travelling with a corpse. Poor man, she thought, looking over her shoulder at the wooden box. There was also a small galley area with a fridge and a little oven. There was no sign of an air hostess. Access to the cockpit was open, and she was alarmed to see Chip put on a pair of spectacles to look at a map. She had never in her life been a nervous flyer. Until now.

Silently, she strapped herself into her seat. Ellis negotiated the coffin hazard, and pulled a bottle out of the fridge.

"I'm guessing you'd like a glass of bubbly," he said.

She took the brimming champagne flute gratefully, and closed her eyes as she felt the fizzy liquid trickle down her throat. The only way to get through this flight was with alcohol. She just hoped Chip didn't feel the same.

They took off and rapidly gained height. Windsor Castle looked alarmingly close beneath them. She almost felt she could touch the playing fields of Eton. After a while, the wine began to take its effect, like an anaesthetic. She felt her muscles unclenching, her shoulders dropping. She found her eyelids drooping. Ellis was working on some papers, so she put her glass down on the little table between them, and surrendered to sleep.

She was awoken by a jolt. "Are you strapped in, Sweetheart?" Ellis asked solicitously, "Chip says we're in for a bumpy ride."

This was clearly no exaggeration, as the plane was alarmingly buffeted from side to side and up and down. What would seem like the smallest of movements in a commercial jet felt like being inside the drum of a washing machine in a plane this size. Geraldine gripped the armrests and tried to remember a prayer. Any prayer would do. In her head she went through the Lord's Prayer, several times. Then she tried the words of hymns. *Fight the Good Fight* came to mind, followed by *There is a Green Hill Far Away.* I don't want to die, she thought, hysterically. I don't want to die somewhere over the Atlantic in a sardine tin with a man I'm really quite certain I could never love. She thought of Cassie and Phoebe and darling Bolly, and Hugo and his horrible girlfriend. And Mrs Mankowitz and her dachshunds, and Monica Acton-Payne. She had to survive for her – they were going shopping for a dress for a 90th birthday party, and Mrs Acton-Payne would never be able to choose the right garment on her own. I am needed, God, Geraldine said to herself, I am needed, God, by too many people, I must be spared! She even thought of Jonty and Sally in their matrimonial Battersea mansion flat, with the easy clean laminate floors and bulky leather sofas. She loved them all. And she wanted to see them again.

"What are you thinking, my love?" asked Ellis.

She hated it when people asked one that. "Oh, nothing much really."

"You had such a concentrated look on your face. Those two little lines between your eyes were quite furrowed. Like you were thinking something real deep."

"Really? Goodness, I never think anything deep – far too distressing."

"The turbulence is subsiding soon. We'll be making a landing in Halifax as Chip wants to refuel and check stuff out."

"Nothing wrong, I hope?" she enquired nervously.

"Oh, it's Chip being careful. All routine. Nothing to worry about. As I said, he's a very experienced pilot – he's been flying nearly all his life. I think he could fly before he could walk," he chuckled. "And then next stop East Cork. There in time for dinner!"

Geraldine settled down to read a book, slightly cheered by the dwindling of the turbulence and the prospect of delicious food. She dozed on and off. Really, private jets were very boring. Then a shout came through from the cockpit that they were going to be landing in Halifax shortly.

"Will we be getting out, do you think?" she asked Ellis. He looked up from his papers.

"I guess we'll have time to stretch our legs. I don't think we'll be there long."

The plane started its descent. Geraldine looked out of the window and saw a wide river, small wooden houses, charmingly painted, lining its banks, then sky-scrapers, and, before she could observe much else, they were bouncing along the runway before drawing to a stop. Chip poked his head through from the cockpit.

"Hey you guys, how's it going? Bumpy enough for you?"

Geraldine smiled weakly.

"I always put on a bit of a show for newcomers. We'll just be on the tarmac for a short time while we re-fuel, and I want to do a full check. Can't be too careful with your girl on board, hey, Ellis? And we may get an inspection or fumigation on the plane if they've got nothing better to do, but they're generally pretty good here."

Chip got out and talked to some maintenance men dressed in orange overalls, and a tanker slowly made its way towards them. The door to the cabin was left open, and as it was a little cool she rummaged through her bag for a shawl. "I think I'll just stretch my legs for a minute," said Ellis.

Geraldine continued reading. She could see, out of the corner of her eye, Ellis performing some rather ostentatious exercises at the bottom of the steps. That could definitely be a dating deal-breaker, she thought, as she looked at him twisting his upper torso round from side to side, his hands clasped behind his neck. He'll probably put his back out, she thought, unkindly. A small vehicle drew up, occupied by two men in dark uniforms and peaked caps. They spoke briefly to Ellis, then mounted the steps to the cabin.

"Hello there, ma'am, we're just going to step inside,

if you don't mind," they said to Geraldine, slightly ominously, she thought.

"Oh please do," she said, most graciously.

Their eyes alighted upon the coffin at the back. Geraldine had almost forgotten about it. "What's that?" they asked her.

"It's a coffin."

"A coffin?"

Geraldine wondered whether this was one of those odd language differences, like the words nappy and diaper, or dustbin and trash can, or roundabout and rotary. Clearly it required translation.

"Yes," she replied. "It's a large box that you put dead people in."

"We know what a coffin is, ma'am... Where's the paperwork for this?"

"It must be with Chip. He owns and pilots the plane. He's just getting something checked, but I am sure he'll be back soon."

One of the men was poking around the box, trying to push it. "It's not secured properly. This could slide down the cabin."

"Well, we had a lot of turbulence earlier. I didn't notice anything sliding," said Geraldine, helpfully.

"Could have had a fatality mid-air. This could have been a real dangerous situation."

"Goodness," said Geraldine, "what a terrible irony

it would be to be killed by a coffin in mid-air. One would never expect that."

The two men eyed her cautiously. "We really do need the paperwork."

They looked at each other, then walked through to the cockpit. The young co-pilot was sitting there, studying his laptop. He removed his headphones. After another, more technical, exchange, he produced a file from a document case.

They took their time going through everything. They all seemed surprisingly chatty under the circumstances. Did they even laugh at one point in the conversation? Geraldine caught a few words here and there. 'Ghana' seemed to crop up several times, then she thought she heard the word 'infectious'. It was at the utterance of 'ebola' that she lost all reason. She instantly looked through her bag for antiseptic wipes. Really, today was a nightmare, and she hadn't even arrived in East Cork. She half-wondered if she could get out and try and book herself on a flight back to London, then, horrified, realised Ellis had not returned her passport. She felt panicky.

The men walked through the cabin. "Bye ma'am. All in order. Have a pleasant flight. And go heaven!"

Go heaven? What could they mean? Why would one say that to someone about to take off in what was little more than a tin can. Here I am, she thought, contemplating the possibility of death by coffin, with little expectation of a safe arrival at my destination, and they say 'Go heaven'. Were they trying to alarm her unduly? Surely they could see she was of a highly sensitive disposition? There were so very many unresolved questions. She sat quite still in her seat, taking deep breaths, counting to seven on exhalation. It made not a bit of difference. Another man entered the cabin with a roll of webbing, which he started elaborately to tie round the coffin, like a Christmas present. Geraldine, in her heightened state of impending hysterics, forgot to either inhale or exhale and found herself gasping for air. Her eyes watered, and she coughed long and loudly.

The official with the webbing stopped his weaving, took off his cap and said, "I'm very sorry for your loss, ma'am." Geraldine was unable to reply, what with the lack of breathing, the coughing, and the added problem of now wanting to giggle at the thought of her presumed widowhood. Ellis returned at that point, looked at her in horror, and asked her in a meaningful way if she was All Right. She nodded, incapable of speech.

Chip heaved himself up into the cockpit, the official left, doors were closed, and shortly they took off again. Geraldine cast backward glances at the coffin, wondering if she could detect it moving. Was it now adequately secured? And what about that half-overheard conversation? Ghana? Infectious? Ebola? She looked at Ellis, heavily immersed in *The Economist*, and wondered whether it was polite in the presence of the deceased to enquire about their cause of death. *Debrett's* probably had an answer, but she felt distinctly uncomfortable about discussing the box at the back of the plane. Once they'd reached full height, Ellis opened another bottle of champagne. Chip had now swapped seats with the co-pilot. "Pass me a glass, Ellis," he called through from the cockpit.

Ellis raised an eyebrow at Geraldine. Was it always the same eyebrow, or did it change? She'd have to watch more carefully. "And you think he's joking," he said, deadpan.

Geraldine downed her glass unnecessarily quickly, hoping for oblivion. No such luck, merely a trip to the restroom beckoned, with all the complications of negotiating the coffin. When she finally got back to her seat she closed her eyes and tried to dispel all negative thoughts.

She dropped off yet again, to be woken with the assurances that they would be landing in East Cork within an hour. She inwardly cheered.

She looked out of the window. She could see water – it could almost be the sea, but she assumed it was a vast lake. She saw yellow fields, and tiny houses dotted randomly. As they descended further, she could make out railway tracks, and a huge warehouse-style building, stuck right in the middle of nothingness. Then she saw a glint of gold, a dome. "All Saints," shouted Ellis, punching the air with excitement. They skimmed over ecclesiastical-looking buildings, several quadrangles and a sports arena. Minutes later they were bumping along a runway. They had arrived.

Formalities were few. The coffin was removed and placed in an unmarked van, and a large black car skimmed towards them, coming to rest a few feet away. This, thought Geraldine, beats arrivals at Heathrow. It was 5pm local time as the car purred towards security gates and out into the wilds of East Cork.

Ellis seemed both hyperactive and enthused, like a small boy at Christmas.

"Wow, you know every time I come back it's like I'm eighteen all over again. I love this place." He looked longingly at the passing landscape. Houses, apartment blocks, trees... It was difficult, thought Geraldine, to quite comprehend the attraction.

"Ok, so this is the plan. We're staying in the Hilton downtown overnight, then tomorrow we'll go and settle in with Chuck and Barb. They have this condo right next to the campus, and they'll be flying in early tomorrow – or maybe late tonight – for the game."

"So they don't live here then?"

"Live here?" He sounded surprised. "Why, no – they live in Florida. They just come for the football."

"And," he continued, "even better, another great friend, Bud, and his wife Maryjo, have just bought the condo next to Chuck's and Barb's."

"Just for the football?"

"Yeah, of course, just for the football. They reside in DC. There'll be a group of about 16 of us altogether. You are going to love it!"

Geraldine smiled. It was a fixed, somewhat brittle effort. "Super," she said.

Chip, who had been silent in the front so far, suddenly shouted, "Whoa! Here I am at Chip Towers. Guess I'll catch you later."

They had pulled up outside a capacious bungalow with a copper roof. It was situated on a main thoroughfare, opposite part of the campus. It had a deck in front of it with an assortment of tables and chairs perched in readiness for outside dining. A mighty Wurlitzer of a barbecue sat menacingly on the porch. Four enormous cars were parked on the driveway.

"You see that grass there?" said Ellis in hushed tones. "Chip bought that from the stadium at All Saints when they dug it up and replaced it with AstroTurf."

"Yep," said Chip proudly, "that little bit of front lawn cost more than the house and its contents all put together. But worth every penny. My little bit of heaven, right under my feet. Literally. Whenever I touch down here, I come outside first thing – no socks, no shoes – just to feel the grass between my toes. Whatever the weather."

Geraldine looked out of the car window at the hallowed turf. It was short and green, with a few brownish patches. She tried to think of something to say. "Goodness," she murmured, "how very therapeutic. And I can't thank you enough, Chip, for allowing me to travel with you in your plane. It was lovely, such a treat," she continued, as he raised himself out of the passenger seat.

"Is that English for thanks for the ride?"

She smiled at him as he closed the door. Really, he was rather sweet.

Chapter Six

The Hilton, East Cork, like many other similar establishments, was a large, characterless building with a small drive-in and a selection of potted palms. As they were ushered though to the foyer by a helpful bell-boy, the heat of the sidewalk was replaced by the sepulchral chill of air conditioning, turned down too low. The receptionist behind the desk was exceptionally solicitous about their day so far, their general health, and their plans for the evening. Her suggestion that they should not contemplate stirring from the hotel, but rather, should sit in the restaurant and partake of the pre-Fall menu, involving panko-crusted walleye pike, smoked turkey cassoulet and artisan vegetables, was luckily declined by Ellis. Geraldine's relief at his refusal of dinner in the hotel was soon eclipsed when she remembered she had recklessly chosen to spend three nights with him. She stood silently with him in the elevator, wondering what fate lay ahead of her.

Their room was on the ninth floor and overlooked a tree-lined boulevard of six lanes, almost empty of traffic. An open truck with a load of chickens meandered along at a lazy pace, followed by an equally slow school bus. Beyond, was a river, trickling darkly towards a more important destination.

"It's beautiful, isn't it," he said, as he wrapped his arms round her waist, and gazed out of the plate glass window.

"Yes, absolutely lovely." She tried to draw herself away from him. It was difficult to see the attraction of a deserted motorway.

"Now," he said, "to business. To the evening ahead of us, my love. If you're not too tired, I have a table booked at Myths, the restaurant on campus. That's for 7 o' clock, so you have plenty of time to freshen up, unpack, relax, whatever. Then off we'll go. You're going to love it."

"Well, I'll fiddle about with my suitcase, and hope everything's not too creased up and crumpled, then I'll take a shower. Would you like to use the bathroom first?" she enquired, solicitously.

He flung back his head theatrically, and laughed. "Man, I love you Brits. Hey, I'll use the bathroom whenever, Geraldine, we're lovers, right? We don't stand on ceremony, do we?"

She visibly blenched. The idea of sharing a bathroom with someone she scarcely knew horrified her. And as for lovers – did one quick romp and a few pecks elevate everything to that status? She tried to remember her early life with Jonty. Had she felt inhibited with him? She remembered her annoyance when she discovered his habit of locking himself in the lavatory for hours with a detective novel. And forgetting to flush. It's funny, she thought, the little things that stick in one's mind.

She did not feel remotely relaxed with Ellis, and as she unpacked, she hummed to promote an impression of casual ease and nonchalance. It didn't fool her.

He was lying on the bed, checking his phone. She took her wash bag, clean underwear, harem pants and a top into the small bathroom and bolted the door. She undressed and turned on the shower. The water restored her, and dressed in clean clothes and made-up, she felt more able to face the evening ahead.

"Wow," he said as she emerged. "All Saints won't know what's hit it. Hey, listen to this, my love, this is going to kill you. Chip's just sent me a joke. I nearly fell off the bed laughing. 'Why are Mexicans cold?'"

She looked suitable blank. She hadn't thought Mexicans would be cold. Wouldn't it be quite hot in Mexico? But she knew how to play the game.

"I don't know. Why are Mexicans cold?"

"Because they have chicken fajitas!"

Geraldine had absolutely no idea why that should amuse. Indeed, it wasn't until the small, wakeful hours of the night that it came to her: chicken for heaters. But she was able to laugh loud and heartily, as in her absence in the bathroom, Ellis had changed into a pair of knee-length shorts and a T-shirt, the body of which was purple. On the front was emblazoned, 'All Saints' in gold, while the back announced, 'Go Heaven'. At least that explained the remark of the customs men in Canada. The sleeves of the T-shirt were golden yellow, and the shorts were yellow, too, with discrete purple piping round the turn-ups. His calves, tanned and hirsute, were neat in ribbed white socks, beribboned at the top with gold. He looked, she thought, bizarrely, like a canary dressed as a bishop.

"Goodness, aren't you jolly," said Geraldine, uncertain of what else she could say. She gazed down at her black harem pants and delicately pleated cream silk top. She surreptitiously removed a bangle or two. "I'm ready whenever you are," she said, with forced cheeriness.

They stood in the elevator again. Geraldine looked at their reflection in the mirror, and remembered Ellis the first time they had been to Covent Garden. The dark pinstriped double-breasted suit, and the Windsor knotted tie, with his height and his well preserved waistline, had enhanced his Cary Grant-ish air. Now he was more like Mickey Rooney. Or even Wayne Rooney, if one knocked off a few years.

She recalled Ellis's lost elegance, wistfully, as the lift reached the ground floor.

A yellow cab sped them away from the river and up a gentle hill. Geraldine could feel Ellis's mounting excitement. It was like the tension in Bolly's body when he knew he was going to be let off his lead in the park. A signpost carved in stone on the corner of two streets proclaimed, 'All Saints University, founded 1886 by Brother Pepe Herring'.

"What an unusual name," remarked Geraldine, peering out of the window.

"The story is that Brother Herring had been travelling by railroad across the States. He'd been given some time out by the Blessed Martyrs Brothers. You see, he'd lost his faith. So, he went on this journey. The train stopped – for absolutely no reason – and Brother Pepe got out. He saw this place, and there was nothing there." Geraldine could easily believe this. "So he looks around, and says to himself, I'm going to build a college here, for people like me, who are lost but want to be found. And he built a college, out of bits of wood and things he could find."

"Goodness!" interjected Geraldine.

He continued, "So he builds this place, virtually on his own, the blood pouring from his hands, the sweat pouring from his brow, and a few local people come, seeking knowledge, and when he's not building, he's teaching, he's exhausted by it all, but the place grows and grows and then…" He paused dramatically. "One evening someone forgets to blow out a candle, and the place burns down. No loss of life, thank God, but everything Brother Herring has built is reduced to ashes."

"How very dispiriting."

"Yeah, but he doesn't let it get him down. He says to himself, this isn't going to get me down. He starts to gather wood, salvage whatever he can from the fire, that kind of thing, and he says to himself, this time I'm going to build it out of stone."

"Oh," interrupted Geraldine again, "it's a bit like the three little pigs' story."

"This time I'm going to build it out of stone…" continued Ellis, ignoring her, "Now it just so happened there was a quarry not far away."

"How very convenient," murmured Geraldine.

"So he goes over to the quarry with his wheelbarrow, and he's collecting stones, and as he raises up a big stone with a shovel, he notices something glinting underneath it. He digs a little more, and it's a metal box. He holds it up. It's heavy and he wonders what can be inside it. Then," another pause, "a bolt of lightning comes from nowhere (it can be pretty thundery round here), and Brother Pepe drops instantly to the ground, and the metal box springs open. He's not dead, just stunned, and when he pulls himself together he sits up and looks at the open box, and you know what's inside? Gold coins, hundreds and hundreds of gold coins. And he thinks, it's a gift from God. I can build a college of stone that will be great and famous. And not only that, all at once he's re-discovered his faith."

"Did he ever find out who actually owned the coins?"

"What do you mean? It's obvious, isn't it? HE did, the college did. You see, it was a gift from God, right?" he explained, patiently.

They were driving through the campus. The quarry must have been exceedingly big, thought Geraldine, looking at the serried ranks of stone buildings. They drew to a halt outside the only edifice not built of stone. It was a sort of large wooden hut, its roof thatched haphazardly with straw, and neon lights proclaiming, in the gathering twilight, 'Myths'.

"This building is almost an exact re-creation of what Brother Pepe's college would have looked like. You're going to love it."

The designer of Myths had clearly wanted to replicate the lack of light that Brother Pepe and his companions would have had to tolerate every evening. It was not, however, dark enough to disguise the fact that the banquette they were taken to was covered in crumbs and something sticky. Geraldine discreetly pulled out an antiseptic wipe and rubbed the seat with it, before carefully sitting down. Ellis looked at her sternly, but said nothing.

A waitress brought menus, and Geraldine peered through the gloom at the selection available. Catfish burgers, moose burgers, bison burgers – all were there, clinging to the frontier spirit.

"Would you like a beer?" asked Ellis, "The local brewery, 'The Devil's Fiddle', does some great little numbers. I'm going to have an Elk Heart. It's a beer made out of corn, and you can't get it anywhere else in the States."

"I'm not awfully good with beer. I think I'll just stick to white wine if I may."

"And to eat?"

She struggled. "Catfish sounds good. Perhaps I could have it with a side salad."

The drinks arrived. The beer was in an enormous tankard, the colour of morning urine, with a thick foamy head. Ellis slurped with relish. "Taste that," he said.

"No really," she demurred.

"Aw, go on try it. You'll have never tried anything like it." He was right. She hadn't.

The food arrived. Ellis was having what was described as Pepe's Medley on the menu. It was the *spécialité de la maison.* It was an excalibur of a dish, a skewer reaching skywards, piercing an array of large hunks of assorted, monstrous meats. Geraldine's catfish was more modest – three boney looking fillets atop a mountain of mash potato. The lettuce was sufficient for three, and awash with salad cream.

"Enjoy!" said Ellis, raising his tankard. It was difficult to think this was the same man, who in the pink gilded boudoir that is the Ritz Restaurant, London, had discussed in detail with the sommelier the merits of a somewhat recherché Mersault.

However much Geraldine tried to eat, the amount before her remained the same. Perhaps this was a gift from Brother Herring, a sort of unending miracle, a two-loaves-and-fishes job? Or perhaps even, she speculated wildly, eyeing the never-ending pile of mash, it was a scene from a horror movie, where eventually the heroine is engulfed by malevolent red-skinned potatoes.

She placed her knife and fork together, exhausted. "Would you like that in a doggy bag?" The waitress asked helpfully.

"No thank you, regretfully, my dog is back in London," said Geraldine sadly, thinking of Bolly snuggled in toile.

Ellis paid the bill and asked the waitress to phone for a cab. This, thought Geraldine, is getting to the really difficult bit. As if this day hasn't been difficult enough.

She sat quietly in the taxi, steeling herself for the inevitable. They arrived at the hotel, ascended in the elevator, and entered the bedroom. The sheets were turned down and chocolates placed on the pillow-cases. Geraldine wondered how many weary travellers had awoken in the morning, to find themselves smothered in dark minty goo.

Ellis started to remove his clothes. First his trainers, their soles capable of any activity from scaling the Eiger to walking to the North Pole. The white socks remained on. Then he removed his T-shirt. Geraldine realised that in their single brief conjoining the lights had been out. She looked in astonishment at the long scar that slashed through his tanned chest. He caught her gaze, and pointed proudly. "Quadruple bypass, 2006. Never felt better since." Geraldine felt quite queasy. Jonty had had an operation for haemorrhoids that very year, and had spent his recuperation sitting on endless packets of frozen peas.

Ellis folded up his T-shirt and placed it on the armchair. Next, the plaid shorts were removed, and put in the trouser press. He was now down to just boxers and white socks. The underwear had little fishes, swimming hopefully towards the crotch. "Herrings," he explained, "in honour of Brother Pepe."

Geraldine took her Liberty nightgown into the bathroom and leaned heavily against the door. She quickly undressed and pulled the gown over her head. She cleaned her teeth. There was a knock.

"Hey, any chance of using the facilities? I'm desperate," shouted Ellis.

The ensuing cacophony suggested that the gaseous elements of Elk Heart could be prolonged in their affect.

She sat on the bed mournfully. Then she realised she had never turned off 'airplane mode' on her phone. Perhaps she would discover an urgent summons home that would require her immediate return to London. The phone bleeped. Three text messages. From Phoebe it said, 'Bolly and Archie had a bit of a bust up. All fine now as ear has stopped bleeding. Pxx.' Next message said, 'Mummy! Guess! James has dumped A&E tart! He can't live without ME!!!!!!XXXXXX.' The final message said, 'J has arrived here with roses! Zoomed down on the 3.35! Hugo is here with Abi! P is making her special chili con carne! Super fun here! Will send pic! Cxxxxxx.'

Geraldine rested her head on the pillow, careful to remove the chocolate. She thought of minced meat, reddened by tomatoes and chili, oozing down the kitchen walls. She thought of Bolly, his soft little apricot ears caked with blood. She thought of her tiny bijou house, its walls groaning outwards with the gathering crowds. And she thought of the whizzbang noises still coming from the bathroom, and the fishy pants and the horrible white socks, and she wanted very much to scream.

The noises stopped. There was the sound of rushing water, and the door was flung open. Ellis emerged in nothing but his white socks, the contents of the now discarded herring pants bobbing jauntily at half mast, a big flashy grin on his tanned face.

He advanced towards her, like a beast of the jungle. He crawled onto the bed and placed himself on top of her, simultaneously raising the prettily sprigged nightie. There was a succession of grunts, loud and feral, and seconds later he had rolled onto his back next to her. "Wow," he said dramatically, raising his hand to his sweating forehead. "Wow, wow and more wows." He turned his head and looked at her. "How was that for you my love?"

She regarded her nightdress, somewhere askew around her abdomen, and her thighs, dripping with lakes of what looked like the salad cream from the unmanageable lettuce.

"Super," she murmured, "absolutely super."

He turned off the light, and in moments, almost as quick as his sexual performance, he was asleep, his mouth apparently agape as snores emanated from somewhere deep within, loudly, and with satisfaction.

Geraldine lay there, wondering if she could creep to the bathroom to remove the salad cream and properly cleanse her face. She remembered she'd never ask about Ghana or 'infectious' or 'ebola'. She drifted eventually into a twilight zone of dozing and wakefulness, till the pale dawn glowered at her through the plate glass windows.

Somehow she must have dropped off again, for she woke to find the full sun beating on the bedspread, and Ellis, in the same clothes as the night before, packing his bag.

"Up you get my love. We have to get off to Chuck's and Barb's. It's already 10.30. Do you want breakfast? They do a great buffet here. It stops at eleven."

"I'm not much of a breakfast person. You go down and I'll get ready."

"Don't be long," he said, wagging a finger at her, "we don't want to miss valuable beer-time!" He closed the door. Geraldine lay on the bed, trying to summon the strength to get up and shower. The dried salad cream on her thighs was like an overnight face pack, a greying, cracked reminder, and even worse, a promise of more to come.

She dressed, with no expectation of looking the part, whatever the part was, in white capri trousers, which skimmed her calf, a black cotton T-shirt and pale pink ballet pumps. She packed her bag, and sat, waiting apprehensively for his return.

"Did you miss something down there or did you miss something? You'd have loved it," he announced, striding through the door.

"I'm not really a breakfast person," she said again, weakly, as they stood in the lift for the final time. He paid the bill, a car was called, and they were off again, up the gentle hill and past the stone sign. The sun was beaming, and Geraldine allowed herself to feel a little hopeful in the warm rays.

"Chuck and Barb are right opposite the road to the stadium. They couldn't be closer to the action if they tried. It's a great place. You'll love it."

They drew up outside a row of pale brick houses, six storeys tall. There was an entanglement of large cars depositing people with bags, golf clubs and cool boxes.

"This is it, 54347," said Ellis, ringing the bell. A dismembered voice floated through from the entry phone. 'I'll buzz you in,' it said. Ellis pushed the heavy front door, and they entered a ceramic floored hall, the walls painted in horizontal purple and yellow stripes. "All Saints colours," Ellis pointed out, proudly.

There was a small, domestic-sized lift, which they took to the sixth floor. The doors spread open, to reveal a huge room, dedicated to dining, cooking and living. It must have been forty feet long or more, and at the other end, wide sliding windows opened onto a broad balcony. There was, it appeared to Geraldine, a crowd of people, all different, yet curiously somehow the same. Both men and women were dressed in variations of shorts and All Saints tops. Some wore baseball caps. A skinny woman and a large man detached themselves from the group. There were cries of "Ellis!", "Chuck!", "Barb!". There was high fiving. There was a funny little dance, a sort of abbreviated lederhosen slapping of thighs, and raucous cheers from the others. They all looked at Geraldine with interest. "She's great, Ellis," they said. "I knew you'd love her," he said. They advanced, as one, on her. "This is for you," they said, holding aloft a purple and gold T shirt. "Gosh thanks," she exclaimed, her voice, disembodied, as if it was coming from very, very far away.

Beer was poured ("No, no, not for me. I'm more of a white wine girl," she heard herself intone). Barb took charge of her, placing a claw-like heavily be-ringed hand on her arm.

"I'll show you to your room," Barb said, picking up one of Geraldine's bags, then added, as she summoned the elevator, "but I have to apologise, as you two guys are the last to arrive, so you're in the basement. It's a got a full bathroom and everything, and a real comfortable bed, but there's no windows. I hope that doesn't bother you."

"No, of course not," said Geraldine, trying to erase from her mind her claustrophobic tendencies.

They entered a corridor, somewhere beneath the garage, hung with All Saints memorabilia. There were several doors. Behind one belched forth similar noises to the wind-filled bathroom last night. "That's the furnace," indicated Barb, a little uncertainly. "I think it turns itself off at night. I don't come down here very often, except to store luggage." She opened the door at the end of the corridor. The room was painted a light mauve, a sort of feminine version of All Saints purple. It had a large double bed, over which hung a moose or elk's head – Geraldine wasn't sure which, but its antlers looked suitable for hat-hanging. There was a commodious wardrobe, largely filled with Louis Vuitton suitcases, and shelves containing many different books about All Saints. Geraldine was already beginning to feel the oppression of being without a window.

"Here's the bathroom," said Barb. It was as big as the bedroom, and contained a pine cupboard. "The sauna," indicated Barb, "don't get up to anything I wouldn't do," she said, attempting a wink. Quite difficult, Geraldine thought, when her eyelids seemed to be raised so very much higher than her eyes.

"Now I'm going to leave you to sort yourself out. But remember, you're not allowed out of this room without the All Saints shirt on. It's illegal!" She trilled.

Geraldine looked sadly at the top. It was at least two sizes too big, and purple had never suited her ("Makes you look jaundiced," her mother had always helpfully remarked). She put it on and looked in the full length mirror in the bathroom. Her face was drained of all colour, and the shirt trailed down towards her knees. She looked like a deflated purple balloon.

She brushed her hair, and applied lipstick and scent to try and rally herself. She checked her phone for more harrowing messages. No reception. She supposed there wouldn't be any in the bowels of the earth. She left the room, pleased to be heading upwards towards some natural light. She entered the small elevator. She pressed '6' and nothing moved, so she pressed 'open door', thinking there must be a staircase. Nothing opened.

It seemed, she thought, after about ten minutes of polite 'excuse me-s', followed by louder 'helps', that even if no one could hear her, someone would want to use the elevator eventually, and would realise that it was stuck. But on the sixth floor, beer bottles raised, old times remembered, no one needed access to another floor, or wondered about the whereabouts of the English woman. Not even Ellis.

About an hour later, Chick or Bud or Rick remembered they'd found an old photograph of all of them, together, back in their All Saints student days, in the lumber room in Connecticut, or DC or New Jersey, and they'd packed it in their suitcase. They wanted to go and look for it in their bedroom below.

"Aw," said Barb, pushing the summoning button, "the damned elevator's stuck again. Chuck! What is it you have to do?"

"How many times have I told you, Barb, you just have to press the button twice, then hold it down for ten seconds, and then it all re-boots."

"You do it, Chuck, I've just had my nails done."

Chuck posted a podgy digit over the button, and performed the magic ritual. A whirring sound stirred somewhere in the basement, and Geraldine stood up from her crouched position, hearing the sound and hopeful at last of an exit. She had a few seconds to pull herself together before being revealed to the sixth-floor assemblage. And pull herself together she would, she intoned bravely. With knobs on.

She stepped out, smiling, blinking in the daylight.

"How long were you in there, sweetheart?" said Ellis, affecting extreme concern.

"Oh only a few minutes," she lied.

"You look like you could do with a beer," said Chuck, advancing with a bottle.

"No really," she repeated, "I'm more of a white wine girl," wearily, hopefully.

"Give her a Bloody Mary, Chuck. Plenty of Tabasco. She looks pale." Remarked Barb, with concern.

"No really, white wine would be just great, thank you."

Chuck was sent down to the wine room, somewhere next to the furnace, to find bottles of white, and Chick or Bud or Al or Rick went to retrieve the photo.

Chapter Seven

Glass in hand, claustrophobia held at bay, shirt reconciled to, Geraldine began to feel happier. She was able to talk knowledgeably about the Royal Family, popular British television serials involving large country houses and a butler, and the fog in London. She expressed regret at not knowing many of their friends based in different cities in England, whom they were quite sure she would have come across. Thus all conceptions held by the English about the Americans were delightfully confirmed.

At about 4 o'clock, vast amounts of food and drink having been consumed, Chuck ding-dinged on his beer bottle. The company fell silent.

"Have I got a treat for you folks. You are going to love this." There was a murmur, a buzz. Cries of, "What, Chuck? What?" He cleared his throat and paused.

"I have only got Johnny Dalglino to come in and give us a pre-game talk."

The gathered crowd clapped their hands and exclaimed in astonishment. "It's unbelievable," they shouted. Someone said, in awe, and everyone agreed, that it was well known Johnny Dalglino never went out for forty-eight hours before a game.

"Well, let's just say," said Chuck, above the noise and hullabaloo, "we may just be seeing the Chuck and Barb Training Facility at All Saints sometime soon."

Caps were thrown in the air, Barb nodded in proud assent, beer bottles were waggled and raised aloft dangerously. Ellis ting-tinged on his glass. Everyone was silent. "This calls for the Saintly Sling-Off!" he shouted. "The Saintly Sling-Off," they echoed, the wives moving wall-wards respectfully to give them room. Geraldine obediently followed.

"Come on guys," said one. "Get moving!" They stood in a line, one behind the other, hands on the shoulders in front. Slowly, allowing for hip replacements, they raised their knees, first right then left, and made a slow, swaying progress round the room. Once a rhythm was established, a low humming noise started in the backs of their throats, like some ancient machinery returning to life. The humming grew, as they encircled the room. And then it stopped. They all stopped, and with different heights and levels of success, raised their arms in a kind of star jump.

"Where do Saints go?" they shouted.

"They go to Heaven!" they answered themselves.

"Where do All Saints go? All the way!"

This was repeated several times, as the men became increasingly red in the face and breathless, until they stopped, hanging their heads down and clutching their knees, as if they had run some distance.

"Hank, do you want your inhaler?" A large woman in tiny shorts called out.

"Nah, Gloria, I'm good."

There was the sound of the doorbell, and everyone looked at each other. "It's Johnny, it's Johnny." Geraldine glanced out of the window. A car, bigger than all the others, was parked on the driveway. People were gathering round it, peering and poking at it, as if it was a precious relic. Small children touched the chrome bumpers, tentatively, like clutching at the vestments of a Pope. Those who'd left their phones indoors rushed to gather them for a surfeit of selfies. The anticipation in the room as the whirring of the elevator kicked in was palpable. Bet HE doesn't get stuck in the lift, thought Geraldine to herself.

To thunderous applause, the elevator doors parted, and Johnny Dalglino, hero, god, icon – famous far beyond the railroads of East Cork, known beyond Indiana, revered throughout the mid-west – stood in all his five feet five inch-glory, his wavy toupé a little askew, his smile as broad as a husk of corn. The coach of All Saints football team was in the building.

It took a little while for the level of excitement to ease, and as there was nowhere to sit, they all stood around while Johnny occupied a large armchair, which had thoughtfully been placed for him in the middle of the room. It was an odd set-up, thought Geraldine, as she leaned against the wall, narrowly avoiding hitting her head on a plasma television screen.

Johnny ran through the line-up for tomorrow's game. It was a detailed summary, noting the height and weight of every player, and their form so far. Geraldine confidently expected bowel movements to be mentioned.

"And we have Elijah Tizer. Sophomore quarter-back, at 220 pounds and 6 feet 3 inches. In his first road start Tizer went 19-for-35 for 321 yards and two scores." The audience nodded sagely at each other. Geraldine looked puzzled, then stifled a yawn. "However," the coach continued, "we have to agree that no matter how well Tizer played last time out, his receivers have to avoid dropping balls. Which takes me to junior receiver Sheldon Shumate. 215 pounds and 6 feet 1 inch. He dropped a deep ball that could have been a big touchdown and a crucial 2-point conversion…" His voice droned on, its timbre a little nasal, a little high. He might have been speaking Ancient Greek. Or Klingon, thought Geraldine – a language, she had heard, many Americans had mastered. She glanced round the room. Her companions' faces gazed with an almost seraphic reverence at the little coach. And what could it be like, she speculated, for this small man among giants? She imagined the great bulk of the football team, all gathered round Johnny, a leprechaun look-alike, for their pre-game pep talk.

"And finally," Johnny Dalglino intoned (Thank Goodness, thought Geraldine, surreptitiously looking at her watch: he'd been talking for forty minutes), "and finally we come to Justin Bloom. Now, we had a lacklustre performance with him last week at Tulsa." What I could tell you about lacklustre performances, thought Geraldine, laughing to herself. And of course, Tulsa, she'd heard of that – what was the old song? "I was only 24 hours from Tulsa." That was it. How far away would that be? Could East Cork be 24 hours' drive away from Tulsa? Or was it even further away? It certainly felt like a million miles from home.

"But he still ranks impressively high in both yards per game (13th) and yards per carry (7th) nationally."

There were appreciative murmurs. Johnny looked at his large be-diamonded watch, its face catching the early evening rays. "That's all, folks," he said, getting up.

Cries of thanks, and remarks on the awesome-ness of the occasion rose up as Chuck escorted him down to his car.

"Wow," said Ellis, coming over to Geraldine. "That was something else."

"It certainly was," agreed Geraldine. "But tell me – and I realise this may be totally heretical – isn't he rather small to have been a footballer? My impression is they're always quite large."

"Geraldine, let me tell you something. Johnny was never a player. Nah, he was too clever for that. What he did was, from the age of about five, he just studied every game. If he couldn't go to a game (and he came from a poor Italian family in the Bronx), then he'd pore over newspaper reports, memorising every detail. He knew the stats for every game played in every state, he knew the details of every player. That was his life. Right from the get go. It was like he was born to be a coach, just through sheer, methodical, organised dedication and hard work."

"Perhaps he has Asperger's syndrome – it sounds like rather obsessive behaviour. Like being a plane spotter," Geraldine suggested.

Ellis looked at her, askance. "We're talking about one of the greatest men alive, Geraldine. We're not talking about a guy with a syndrome: we're talking about a genius. Man, I can hardly believe he was in this room. Sitting in that chair. That was something."

He looked misty eyed at the thought of being in such a presence.

There now seemed to be a hiatus in the programme of activities, before dinner at Myths. Ellis imagined Geraldine was thrilled to be going there two nights running. He and three of his friends went on to the communal lawn outside the condos, conveniently equipped with a couple of golf holes, to practice their swings. Others, exhausted by the eating, the drinking and the excitement of the day so far, went to their rooms for a short, restorative nap. Geraldine did not have that option, owing to a lack of windows in her basement bedroom, so decided she would take herself on a little tour around the condo, as far as it was possible to explore.

The top floor was entirely devoted to entertainment and partying. The kitchen area contained a fridge the size of her own kitchen back home, and the cooker was as big as the oven in a crematorium. Every picture on the wall was of some aspect of life at All Saints – teams of various different sports ranging from ice hockey to ping pong; triumphant photos of men in tweeds, elk hunting; dinners at arcane clubs: the Moose Wranglers, the Sinners, The Angelic Tribe – the latter was particularly sinister, with its scrubbed face aryan-looking members in high-collared jackets and long shorts. Geraldine prowled round the enormous room with great interest, noting, too, the glass dome-covered reconstruction of the original wooden shack, hewn by Brother Pepe, given pride of place under the giant plasma television screen.

She tentatively opened a door next to the elevator, and found, with some relief, it led to a roof-lit landing with an elaborate ironwork staircase. She descended to the next floor, where there was another, more formal reception area. Several men were listening with rapt concentration to a sports programme on the radio. A glazed door led from there into a smaller, book-lined, room, furnished with curlicued French-style sofas. Two wives sat, one doing needlepoint, the other filing her nails.

"Come on in and join us," they said to Geraldine, cheerily, "this is the game-free zone!"

Geraldine promised she would be back shortly, once she had been to her room to retrieve her bag. She continued her prowling. There were a couple of doors that she assumed led to bedrooms, then she descended further. Curiously, the stairs led down two more flights without ingress to any rooms, and she concluded that, sandwiched on the fourth and third floor, was another, lesser condo. The second floor appeared to contain more bedrooms, and a small kitchen – presumably for the preparation of midnight and early morning snacks. And the first floor – of course, what one thinks of as the ground floor – was mainly taken up with a garage, big enough for several cars, golf buggies and assorted gym equipment, gathering dust.

She reached the basement, collected her book, her bag, and her phone, and despite the many flights of stairs to regain the fifth floor, decided it was worth the climb to avoid the possibility of getting stuck in the lift again. As she emerged from the basement her phone regained life. Two messages. 'Mummy! P's chilli con carne gave everyone runs!!! J roasting lama!! Will send pic!!! Xxx'

Geraldine puzzled over the roasting lama, but assumed, eventually, it must be lamb. But who knew. Really, she began to feel anything might happen. The second text was from Jonty. This was most surprising. She didn't think she had ever received a text from him, even when they were married. Had he even had a mobile phone? She couldn't remember. It read: 'What's all this the kids say you are in the States with Cary Grant lookalike for football match. Have you gone mad? How long are you there for? J' Geraldine paused to read this several times. Was it proper for him to enquire about her whereabouts, her companion, or her sanity? And should she reply? She would like to come up with something terribly witty and pithy, but settled merely for being irritating: 'only here for weekend. Came in private jet. CG super. This is the life. G'

She pressed 'Send'. It felt rather satisfying. And although Ellis was certainly sub-super, and the plane had been ghastly, and if this WAS the life, she would probably welcome death, there was no need to let anyone know. Particularly not her ex-husband.

She opened the glazed door. There were now three wives retreating from game talk. One was Gloria, who had been so solicitous about her husband's inhaler; the needlepointer, a thin, mahogany-tanned blond called Pat; and the third was Maryjo, a sporty looking woman of muscular build, her dark hair short in a sensible bob. They looked at her with the eagerness of television presenters embarking on an interview with a particularly reclusive celebrity.

"Well," started Gloria, getting straight in, "so you're with Ellis. How long has that been?"

"Ohhh… since about Christmas time."

"Did you get him off the internet?" asked Pat, bluntly.

"No," said Geraldine, a little shrill. "No. I met him at a party. He lives near me, actually, so it's very convenient." Geraldine paused. She realised she'd made him sound like a corner shop. "We go to the ballet a lot," she added, irrelevantly.

"That's nice," said Pat. "Ellis's wife loves ballet. Well of course, she used to…"

Geraldine sat up in her chair. The present tense

had been used. The other women noticed her barely contained surprise, and smiled knowingly.

"It's so sad, isn't it?" said Maryjo.

"Yes, yes it is," said Geraldine, not wishing to show her ignorance of the situation, "it's terribly sad." She added, boldly, "and terribly sad for Ellis."

They all nodded and sighed. "Terribly, terribly sad for him," they muttered in unison.

The room went a little quiet, then Gloria piped up. "But it's good he got her blessing – when she was still able to give it – it sort of released him, you know," she paused, "otherwise YOU wouldn't be here!" she remarked, cheerfully.

"Or the others," added Pat.

Geraldine attempted to retain her composure. It was, she felt, one of her few accomplishments. She looked around, hoping no one detected her discomfort. She tried to think of something further to say.

"Yes, when he first told me, you know, about it all," she hesitated, "I immediately thought of Mr Rochester. Something nasty in the attic, and all that."

The women looked at her, blankly.

"And of course," she continued, rather too quickly, "a man as good-looking as Ellis is bound to have lots of… lady friends." She beamed, pleased with her mature response.

144

"Nowadays," remarked Maryjo, enigmatically, "anything goes."

"That's so true," agreed Pat "we've got friends in Florida who've been in and out like a cuckoo in a clock."

Geraldine felt her smile fix itself into a sort of muscular spasm. Was she quite understanding this conversation?

Her phone bleeped. "I'm so sorry," she said, "I must just check this. You know what it's like when you're away from home. They can't do without you!" she trilled.

A reply from Jonty. 'Good luck. Can't stand Americans myself. Awful accents. You must be mad. Sorry. Already said that. J'

Further communication seemed unnecessary, so Geraldine snapped the phone shut and put it back in her bag.

"All ok?" asked Pat, solicitously.

"Yes, fine," Geraldine replied. "It was my ex-husband, actually." Again they looked knowingly at each other.

"Don't talk to me about exes," said Pat. "I have two. Both were pains in the butt. The first gave me nothing. He was an associate professor on the East Coast at a swanky private college. Went off with a grad student whilst I was pregnant. Second one died just as we were in the throes of divorce. Dropped dead in front of the refrigerator. Couldn't open it for hours. And now Chick…"

"Aw," said Maryjo "he's a keeper, that one. You know, I think these All Saints guys, they're, like, forever men."

"Most of them," said Gloria, looking at Geraldine.

Pat got up, casting her needlepoint aside. "I better go get myself looking beautiful for Myths," she said. The others felt they should follow suit, so Geraldine reluctantly headed basement-wards, pondering over the conversations.

Ellis was clearly still perfecting his swing. Or swinging, thought Geraldine ruefully. Was that even the right word? And, really, did she care? She felt a little hurt that he'd been somewhat economical with the truth over his wife. Or had he? She tried to remember what exactly he'd said. Had he said 'no longer with us'? And as for the reference to 'others', well, she supposed a single (or near single) man in possession of a fortune was quite at liberty to do what he wanted, with whom he wanted. Which brought her to the cuckoo clock remark. It was all too much, she thought, as she changed out of her hideous huge shirt, racing to exit the oppressive basement bedroom.

She ascended the stairs yet again, in kitten heels and a sleeveless cream shift dress. No doubt the wrong attire, but there was nothing she could do about it

146

with her limited wardrobe. She assumed everyone would foregather in the party room, and by the time she reached the half landing before the sixth floor she paused to recover her breath. She could just see into the room. No one appeared to have changed. But hadn't the women in the French boudoir talked of making themselves beautiful?

All was clear as she walked towards Pat and Barb – the former clutching a martini glass in her mahogany hand, the latter sticking to her customary glass of water. Their make-up would have suited the back row of a chorus line. And the jewels – whether they were paste copies or just out of the safe – Geraldine inwardly gasped at the rocks around Barb's skinny little neck.

"Cute dress," remarked Pat, "you're going to show us all up!"

Hardly, thought Geraldine. Pat's rings could have been used to guide in a deep-sea trawler on a foggy night.

Geraldine was sporting nothing more than a pair of pearl earrings and her Cartier watch. She was tired, overwrought, and would never, she hoped, ever see any of these people again. She allowed herself a sweet smile, and a feeling of nonchalance that, once more, she looked and felt totally out of place. I really don't care, she said to herself, as she gratefully accepted a glass of white wine. "I've got your number on the booze front," said Chuck, wagging a finger at her playfully. There was much discussion about the distribution of passengers in the fleet of cars, ready at the door to make the three-minute drive to Myths.

It had started to rain heavily, and Geraldine felt the linen of her dress cling wetly to her back as she dashed to her designated vehicle. She found herself sitting in the front passenger seat next to Hank, with two newcomers – condo neighbours – sitting in the rear.

Hank spent most of the very short ride mistaking Geraldine's knee for the gear stick, which she tolerated with good humour, until she realised on leaving the car for the brief, wet dash to the doors of Myths, that it was automatic transmission.

She gave a little inward growl as she stood in the foyer, attempting in vain to smooth the creases out of her frock. The party assembled from their respective vehicles, and they were ushered not into the restaurant, but a private dining room at the rear of the shack. This was a long, wood-clad room, with a table down the middle laid for twenty guests. Barb clapped her hands and shouted, "There is a table plan," pointing to a small easel. "Find where you are and sit down."

Geraldine found her place, then sat down, noticing that everyone else remained standing behind their chairs. She rapidly stood up again.

"Father Hessian will say grace," said Chuck, reverently.

A youngish man, moon-faced, bespectacled – a flash of white at his neck the only clue to his vocation – stood at the head of the table.

"Thank you, God, for our privilege and our honour. Give us your grace to do good, to exercise humility, to serve, to love our fellow men and women, and to enable us to spread our faith further. And bless this table, especially our hosts, Chuck and Barb, and let us give thanks for their generosity. Let us think of the poor, the sick and the needy, the oppressed, the disabled and the maimed, as we sit down and enjoy the feast before us. And let us not forget the homeless and the dispossessed. In the name of the Father, the Son and the Holy Spirit, be with us Lord and remain with us to our dying day. Amen."

That just about covered everything, thought Geraldine, as she resumed her seat and placed her napkin on her lap.

"I hear you travelled out with Stevie Bellingham," said Bud, as he helped himself to a wholemeal roll.

Geraldine was momentarily blank, until she remembered the coffin on board the plane. "Yes," she said, "did you know him well?"

"We all did. All of us All Sainters here, wow, we go back a long way. Stevie was one of us. Not the first to go, and certainly not the last, but he'll very much missed." He shook his head sadly. "Very much missed indeed."

Geraldine broke a breadstick in half. This was her opportunity to find out more. "Had he been ill for long?" she enquired solicitously.

"Well, he got the Big C back in the 90s, but he fought it off. Boy, was he a fighter. Came back again, different place, 2004. Then it was just on and off, on and off. He went to the Mayo Clinic, he went to Mount Sinai in New York, he went to some swanky private hospital in London. He lost a lung, half a kidney and his pancreas."

Geraldine gazed uneasily at the hors d'oeuvre of cold meats and pâtés placed before her.

Bud continued on his grizzly tale of human reduction. "He had his right leg amputated, part of his nose removed, and his tongue out. He re-learnt how to talk by manipulating his uvula." He paused in this lengthy medical history. "Then he went to some out of the way place up a mountain in Austria. They made him run up and down it every morning" (with one leg, wondered Geraldine). "He lived on a diet of raw goat's milk yogurt and wheat grass, and he had coffee enemas every morning. And you know what, he phoned me up at the end of it all, and he says 'Bud, I've never felt better. I feel like I'm eighteen again." So he goes back to New York, and his doctors give him the all-clear. Not a cancerous cell in his whole body. He says to his wife, Lana, 'Lana, let's get ourselves over to France and ENJOY life.' They have this great place in Le Touquet."

"Oh! I know Le Touquet well," interjected Geraldine.

Bud looked at her, then continued. "Their house belonged to some British duke back in the old days. You probably know him. Now, every year there they give this big garden party – a sort of fête for all the locals. And you can imagine these locals are real grateful to be asked up to this lovely big ducal home." Yes, Geraldine was quite sure she could picture the look of gratitude on those locals' faces.

"So Lana says, 'This year, Stevie, let's do a tombola and give the proceeds to the old folks' facility down the road.' 'Great idea' says Stevie. So on the day, there's Stevie, at the tombola table, and suddenly there's this wasp, and it stings him right on what's left of his nose. He thinks nothing of it, and continues with the tombola." Bud took a big gulp of wine. This narrative was exhausting. "Within the hour he was as bloated as a balloon full of water. Infected from head to toe with wasp venom. Died the next day in his bed, which, incidentally, Lana had picked up in Paris the previous year at Sotheby's. It had belonged to Marie Antoinette." He sighed. "But you know what, Stevie lived the dream. Born in Trentham, New Jersey. Son of a hot-dog seller. Scholarship to All Saints. Went to work for Ford. Started his own company with a hundred-dollar loan from the bank, and ended up with billions, dying in a French queen's bed in an English duke's house. That's America for you. Couldn't happen anywhere else."

Geraldine nodded in full agreement. It certainly couldn't happen anywhere else. Still, with some relief, she realised she'd travelled with a body free of infection from ebola contracted in Ghana. Perhaps she should have a hearing test, or, she thought, draining her glass rapidly, a herring test, in homage to Brother Pepe.

She returned to the difficult business of tackling the giant steak that lay before, hewn from the flank of a beast so vast it must have galloped from East Coast to West. There was the familiar sound of the ting-ting of the glass. Not more football stats, she hoped.

Every man in the room, in succession, rose to his feet and commended the hosts, the present company, the absent company, the university, and, in particular, the football team. There were cheers and hurrahs and many shouts of 'Go heaven'. Eventually the room calmed down. Geraldine looked around. It was surprising that no woman had got up.

Emboldened by at least eight hours of drinking, she was testing Pinot Grigio positive. She stood up tentatively. All eyes rested on her.

"I would just like to say..." Her voice sounded high pitched and very British. Rather like Queen Elizabeth, she thought, as she wondered what on earth she was doing. "I'd just like to say," she repeated, "how wonderful it is to be here at All Saints, and how terribly grateful I am for all your boundless hospitality and kindness." There – that was quite good, she thought. She saw Ellis look approvingly at her from the other end of the table. "And I raise my glass to All Saints," – applause – "and, and... the President of the United States!" The proverbial pin might have dropped. She sat down. Pat leant behind Bud and clasped her on the forearm. "We're all Republicans here, dear."

Chapter Eight

By the end of the evening Geraldine had recovered what she thought of as her usual sang-froid, and had even been persuaded by Bud – or was it Bob? – to sing the first line of the Eton Boating Song. She had surprised herself, as she didn't even remember that she knew it.

Somehow, a little later, not quite knowing how she returned to the condo, she found herself in the windowless bedroom with Ellis.

"You were flying, honey," he said, as he elaborately removed his shorts and folded them carefully along the crease.

"Oh goodness," she groaned. "Was I very embarrassing?"

"No, babe," he said kindly. "It was nice to see you shake off that British reserve. They all loved you."

"Well, the president thing was a bit of a gaff."

"We all make mistakes, Sweetheart. And Father Hessian votes Democrat." Geraldine fell instantly into unconsciousness.

She awoke violently, in the blackened room where it could be any hour of the day or night. There was a sound like the horn of the Titanic, warning of icebergs. It honked several times then stopped. Ah, the furnace – or boiler, as we call it, thought Geraldine, primly. She reached for her phone, using the light as a torch. It was 3am. Ellis was lying naked beside her. Bollock naked, Phoebe would have said. Geraldine averted her eyes. The light faded back to black, and once more she sank into sleep.

"Oh God, Oh Christ, Oh God!" She was awoken yet again, hearing plaintive cries emanating from beyond the room.

Once again she reached for her phone. 4.35am. The bed was empty. The cries were Ellis's, coming from the bathroom.

She got up and pulled her nightgown over her knees, and tentatively knocked on the door. "Are you all right?" she enquired.

"No," came the reply, "I am not fucking all right." Geraldine had never heard Ellis swear before.

"The darn john is blocked, and there's shit everywhere. And it's not even my shit."

Geraldine retreated hastily back to bed and clasped her be-sprigged knees to her chest. She said nothing.

He emerged, blinking in the light of the bedside lamp which she had turned on. He was now dressed

155

in a striped bathrobe, his face ashen, his short hair standing on end.

"Don't, whatever you do, go in there. Under no circumstances. The room is knee deep in crap. It was just coming up, out of the john, like lava out of a volcano. It was like Vesuvius." He placed a chair in front of the door.

Thank goodness it wasn't earwax, thought Geraldine, irrelevantly. "But what shall we do in the morning?" she asked, "Supposing I need to go to the loo or something. Urgently?"

"I'll get Chuck in an hour or two. He's an early riser, come what may. He'll call someone out. Chuck'll get it sorted."

Geraldine settled back in the bed. There was a slight smell. She sprayed herself with Coco Mademoiselle. She lay there, worrying if she could remember if there was a lavatory on the next floor. Perhaps she'd be able to hold on. By about five fifteen she knew she couldn't, and again using her phone as her guiding light, she tiptoed to the door, anxious not to wake the now sleeping Ellis.

She walked along the corridor to the stairs, and quietly took a step at a time, her feet cold on the marble. She opened the door to the front hall, where she was sure there would be a cloakroom.

It was if all the bells of all the churches for miles beyond East Cork rang at once. She had set off the burglar alarm. She could hear shouts and scurrying, the opening and closing of doors, as anxious faces peered, at different levels, over the ironwork bannisters. Chuck appeared, in a purple and gold striped night shirt, brandishing a baseball bat. Barb was close behind,

"I'm awfully sorry," said Geraldine, "it's all my fault." She saw heads turning to each other, exchanging knowing glances. "It's the English woman, again, dear," she heard a male voice say from somewhere aloft. "Go back to bed," the voice wafted, wearily.

"I'm terribly, terribly sorry," continued Geraldine. "We've had a frightful disaster in our bathroom. There's effluence everywhere," she added, discreetly.

Chuck turned to Barb. "I told that goddamed, smart-assed developer there was a problem in the basement the last time it happened. Did you ever ring him back?"

"Aw, Chuck, I forgot. I was in Miami."

Chuck looked at her. "It's not like I ask you to do much, Barb, but as the president of a multinational conglomerate it's sometimes hard for me to remember all the little domestic details."

"I know, Chuck, I know." She looked shamefaced.

"We'll be along in a minute," he said to Geraldine.

He came down the stairs in an All Saints dressing gown and purple and gold slippers. Barb followed, her baby doll pyjamas revealing cocktail stick legs pushed into ostrich feather mules.

Ellis had not stirred in the basement eerie, fast asleep, hermetically sealed from the sounds of the bells. He was spread on top of the bed, still in his bathrobe, one corner casually tossed aside to reveal a pink chipolata, carelessly flung across his hairy scrotum. Barb gasped and gripped Geraldine's arm tightly, in feminine solidarity at the beastliness of men, and glanced away. But worse was to come. Chuck shoved the chair aside and pushed open the bathroom door. Barb screamed aloud, "It's like that trip to India in 1994." Ellis awoke and hastily pulled his robe around him.

Chuck merely took a phone out of his pocket – clearly, he had no problem with reception down here – and dialled a number. "I want you here. Now". This, thought Geraldine, is how you get to be president of multinational conglomerates.

Barb took her upstairs to the 'Hers' bathroom of the Master Suite. Geraldine spent a happy half hour wallowing in scented foam and dressing herself in her voluminous All Saints shirt and white capris. She emerged, cheerful at the all-pervading smell of coffee. She even wondered if she could manage a little breakfast. This was available on a serve yourself basis – silver platters brimming with eggs every which way but loose, and an array of bread and buns that must have cleaned out the local bakery – in the sixth-floor party room. Geraldine eyed the five different jugs of fruit juice, and the other guests eyed Geraldine.

"That was quite a show you put on for us," said Matt. Or was it Mick?

"I am awfully sorry. I should have realised there would be alarms everywhere. It was so silly of me. I do apologise."

"You know," said Maryjo, "I could listen to your accent all day."

There was a murmuring of polite assent amongst the breakfasters. "Gosh, thank you," said Geraldine, selecting the smallest pastry she could find. "Just don't wake us all up again," said Bud, wagging a finger at her as he departed.

"Have you seen the programme for the day?" asked Pat. "It was put under the bedroom doors this morning."

"Er, I think I must have missed it, what with one thing and another."

Pat handed her a sheet of A4 paper. It read:

Saturday, September 4

7.30 – 9.30   Breakfast available in the Great Room

9.30 onwards	Cars available for trips to Brother Pepe's Grotto
	Or Golf Course
	Or Shopping Mall
11.30.	Hot dogs and beer available in the Great Room
	Golf buggies available for transportation to campus for tailgate
5 pm.	THE GAME

Note: on campus entertainment –

1. A tour of the Football Hall of Fame
2. A talk on Uranus at the Planetarium
3. A lecture by visiting Professor Florian Van Der Vanker on Mesoamerican remains in the Snout Museum
4. Band plays from 1 o'clock onwards

Mass available in the Cathedral at
10am, 12 noon and 3 o'clock.

Geraldine studied this with interest, wondering how to plan her day. She thought Brother Pepe's Grotto would amuse, and a trip to the shopping mall was a must. She could do without hot dogs and beer, and felt Mass could decently be postponed until tomorrow, Sunday.

Ellis entered the room and poured himself some coffee. He looked more his old self, thought Geraldine. He peered over her shoulder at the programme.

"Am I going to give you a day, Sweet Dream. We're going to take a tour of the campus, see my old dorm, check out the refectory, walk along the lake…"

"Could I go to the shopping mall?"

He furrowed his brows. "Whatever for, my love? You can shop anywhere, but there's only one All Saints. This is the opportunity of a lifetime!"

Geraldine sighed, then smiled up at him, resolutely. "Super!" she said.

"Now," Ellis continued, "we're going to have to move bedrooms, as Chuck is getting in a team to sort out the problem in the basement. Barb isn't sure what room she's putting us in tonight, so could you go and pack up your bag now, and just leave it for when we come back from the game? We've got a golf buggy to get round campus, and then we'll meet everyone at the tailgate. Does that sound like a plan or does that sound like a plan?" He seemed pleased with his manly decisiveness.

Geraldine returned to the basement. Several Latino-esque men in hard hats and hi-viz jerkins were wielding bags of cement and assorted tools. The corridor was lined with ferocious-looking digging equipment. She quickly packed her bag and left it by the wardrobe door, out of the way of the bathroom. She tried to think of all the things she might need during the course of what was clearly going to be a long day. She decided her espadrilles would be the most comfortable footwear. And her Glyndebourne rain poncho might be prudent. Antiseptic wipes were a must. She brushed her hair, and left the room, chirping, rather successfully she thought, "Buenos días," to the gathering workmen.

Ellis was waiting outside, sitting in the driving seat of a golf buggy, his hands clasped to the wheel, his face a rictus of gleaming white teeth.

"Oh could I drive it?" asked Geraldine, "It looks such fun."

Ellis looked at her in horror, "I don't think so, my love. What would the insurance implications be?"

Geraldine wondered, envisaging a scenario where a vehicle of very small proportions, painted in regulation livery of purple and gold, travelling at a speed less than the average walking pace, mowed through seething crowds, squashing and maiming in its wake, before knocking down the entire football stadium with its own momentum. She sat meekly at his side.

They drove sedately across the road to the campus. This, apologised Ellis, was not the main entrance, but apparently would give Geraldine a good idea of the magnificence of it all, since so far she had only seen a little bit of it under cover of darkness. There were already hundreds of people swarming in a controlled manner along sidewalks, bordered by grass verges planted with measured regularity. They passed the tennis courts, where Ellis had played a particularly triumphant match in 1973, then a large stone building – apparently the department of Geophysical Activity ("They can predict a tornado in that building a year before it arrives," boasted Ellis), then more large stone buildings. Many, many large stone buildings. Eventually, after meandering for a while they entered a wooded area, which cleared to reveal a small lake. Ellis stopped the buggy, breathing in the air, taking in the view. "It's fabulous, isn't it?" he said. "Yes, lovely," agreed Geraldine.

"Brother Pepe's Grotto is over the other side, so we're going to leave the buggy here and walk round the lake." Others had had the same idea, and so they proceeded along the path that bordered the lake en masse, as if in pilgrimage – which I suppose is exactly what they are doing, thought Geraldine. It was already very warm, and a little humid. Tiny black flies circled menacingly. Geraldine thought of Lyme's disease. There had been a programme on Radio 4 the previous week about its devastating effects. She had listened to it while ironing. How timely, she thought. And how she wished she had worn ankle-hugging trousers instead of calf length capris.

"Are there ticks here?" she called after Ellis, who was striding ahead purposefully. He appeared not to hear, but a woman walking behind her assured her that ticks weren't a problem in these parts, but the racoons could give a nasty nip.

The lake was actually larger than it had originally appeared, and by the time they had reached the other side Geraldine was feeling hot and sweaty, and her espadrilles were rubbing her heel. Ahead of them, two piles of stones marked a clearing in the wood. A narrow path, really only accessible in single file, wound through the trees. After about fifty yards they came to a clearing. There were more piles of stones, this time shaped into a semi-circle, like a collapsed wall. Amongst the stones were little niches, with candles flickering in purple lanterns. A small hut next to the stone half-circle had a notice by its door:

'Votives $3. No responsibility taken for accidents. Take care lighting candles. Remember fire kills.'

These warnings appeared not to discourage, and a line of potential arsonists were queuing to buy their lethal weapons. "I have to light a candle," Ellis whispered. He went off to buy one. Geraldine watched a small child being lifted up tenderly by his father, so that he could light a candle.

"Brother Pepe was a very good man," she heard the father explain.

"Did he have a gun?" the child asked cheerfully.

"No, he did not have a gun. He was a real gentle man. He did not need a gun."

"Well, why does Grandpoppy need a gun then? Is that because he isn't a good man?"

The father looked round. Geraldine smiled encouragingly at him. He rolled his eyes. "Kids, huh? They ask the darnedest questions."

He turned to his son, "Let's just get this candle lit, then we'll go and have a burger." Ellis returned with two candles in purple jars, and gave one to Geraldine.

"I'm going to light this for Bolly," she said.

"You can't light a candle for a dog," protested Ellis.

"Why ever not? He's one of God's creatures. And he's very kind."

Ellis shook his head, lit his candle, and closed his eyes solemnly for a minute or two.

A large family group moved, and, to her surprise, Geraldine noticed a life-size, wooden cut-out, depicting Brother Pepe, leaning against the wall. He was portrayed as a small, round man with a benign, smiling face. His right hand was raised, presumably in benediction, though there was a touch of the Nazi salute about it, she thought. She wouldn't mention that.

She wondered what happened to him at night. Presumably he was put back each evening, smiling, into the little hut. Did one have to be specially trained or selected to handle him? Perhaps he had been occasionally kidnapped by students and taken to parties. Geraldine tried to recall details of a story she had read in the newspaper about a garden gnome who had been stolen from his suburban rockery. His captors had taken him on a world tour, occasionally sending postcards to his home from exotic climes. Possibly Brother Pepe would like to travel? Surely he deserved some rest and relaxation away from the rigours of East Cork. Geraldine found her mind – as it so often did – wandering. Perhaps, like Sooty the glove puppet, there was more than one of him. Maybe at the back of the small hut there was a stack of Brother Pepe cut-outs, used strictly in rotation to ensure he always appeared pristine and bandbox fresh.

Ellis remained deep in thought by his lit candle. Then he crossed himself, and strolled over to her.

"This place really gets to me," he said. "It's so peaceful". Geraldine looked round. A small girl was screaming for ice cream. An old man in a wheel chair was asking loudly for directions to the bathroom. A morbidly obese dwarf, wearing a T shirt proclaiming she was 'living the dream', rocked rhythmically to the bass beat emerging from her headphones.

Peace, Geraldine decided, was truly relative.

They walked to a stone archway marked 'Exit', along a dank earth path that smelt slightly of urine, to a paved area surrounded by posts, upon which were pinned messages. Small floral tributes lay at the foot of the posts. It reminded Geraldine of those roadside displays where some poor unfortunate has been mown down. They paused. The messages ranged from 'Car repossessed tomorrow. Help', to 'Timmy age 3 has been diagnosed with a brain tumour. Please pray.' Ellis laid a hand on Geraldine's shoulder. "People have been hoping for years that Brother Pepe would be beatified, but there has never been a miracle that can be properly verified." Ellis shook his head sadly.

"Perhaps after all that building in wood, only to see it burnt down, and then having to build all over again in stone, poor old Brother Pepe was absolutely knackered and just wanted a good rest once he'd died? Perhaps he gets fed up being asked all the time to help people – I know I would," suggested Geraldine.

Ellis looked shocked. "Do you always have to make a joke out of everything? This really means something."

Geraldine walked on. Luckily, the planners at All Saints had devised an efficient one-way system to and from the Grotto, and so they strolled, with others, along the other side of the lake.

Did she make a joke out of everything? Geraldine wondered. Existence, on the whole – and even for a comfortably off, middle-aged woman, who had so far been spared many of life's tragedies – could really be quite difficult. Wasn't that how one got through this journey of ours, she thought, by making light of everything? How else would one cope? She remembered her darkest moment, when Jonty had left her – the endless sleeplessness in the early hours, mulling over all the things she should have done, the things she shouldn't have done, raging at the unfairness of it all. Had she joked then? She certainly hadn't written any little messages and posted them on trees in the hope of the miraculous return of her husband. Rather, she had got on with it, made lists of what she had to do: ring lawyers, estate agents, removal firms. The divorce process had taken several months.

There had been days when she did little more than cry, but poor Bolly had been so upset at the sight of her tears she had had to moderate her emotions. Crying was then reserved for the shower only. What she had hated more than anything was the pity from her friends, and the knowledge that, as soon as she left a room, gossip ensued. Everybody loves the tittle-tattle that a wronged wife provokes. Geraldine remembered the endless effort of putting on a brave face and assuring everyone that, yes, all was fine, just fine. Of course she bloody made a joke of everything, she thought crossly, as she followed Ellis back to the buggy, slapping at the black haze of tiny insects buzzing around her. She sat down and surveyed her bitten ankles. Ellis, she noted, despite being clad in knee length shorts, appeared to be without a blemish. "Gosh," she remarked, "flies don't seem to like you the way they like me." She pointed ruefully at her ankles.

"Didn't you put any insect repellent on this morning?" asked Ellis. "I smothered myself with the stuff."

Geraldine inwardly seethed. "Well, it hadn't occurred to me it might be necessary. No one told me. Have you got any of it with you?"

"Gee, honey, I'm sorry. It's back at the condo. I just thought you'd know."

Geraldine stared fixedly in front of her. She was usually a person of mild sensibilities, but she felt utterly enraged and exasperated. She had been maimed and disfigured by an onslaught of insects. She could see her ankles swelling, and she could hear the blood pounding through her ears. She felt every muscle in her assaulted body clench. Right, she thought, let's go for it. Let's just go for it.

"I understand from talking to Maryjo and her friends that your wife is still alive. I thought you said she was dead."

Emergency stops in vehicles proceeding at walking pace are not generally dramatic, but nevertheless, Geraldine felt herself propelled forward.

"My God," said Ellis, resuming control of the buggy. "You women. Chuck warned me that room you all sit in is something else. Yabber, yabber, yabber…"

"In fairness to myself," replied Geraldine, "I have been in m'lady's boudoir only once, and since I was apparently the centre of attention, my scope for yabbering was limited."

"Well," said Ellis, evenly, "I apologise for that. And I honestly didn't mean to mislead you over my marital status. I think I told you that my wife is no longer with us. That is entirely correct. Eight years ago, just after her fiftieth birthday, she was diagnosed with early onset Alzheimer's. She's been in a home in Santa Barbara for the last six years. She doesn't know her name, she doesn't know who I am, she doesn't know where she is. Can you imagine what that is like for me?"

"It can't be great for her, either," replied Geraldine, tartly. Ellis pursed his lips and paused.

"She's in diapers now. Do you know what it's like to have your wife in diapers? Can you even get your head round what that must be like for me?"

"Clearly not. But how very unpleasant for her."

He stopped the buggy, and, reaching into his pocket, drew out his wallet. "Look at this." He pulled out a creased photograph. "This is her on our honeymoon. Switzerland, 1978. She was 21." He handed it to her.

Geraldine looked at the image before her. The colour had faded somewhat, a metaphor, perhaps, for the diminishing creature depicted – a wispy woman with long blonde curls, a child-like woman, with big doe eyes smiling helplessly up at the camera.

"She was very pretty," Geraldine said.

"She still is. She's still got all that long mermaid hair. They wash it every other day at the home. And her big, big blue eyes look at me and there's just nothing there. No light on and no one at home. I cannot begin to describe what it's like to be in this situation."

"I don't really understand why you didn't tell me about this before – after all we're…" Geraldine struggled, trying to think what they, the two of them, actually were, "we're friends, aren't we?"

Ellis returned the photo carefully to his wallet and started up the buggy.

"I didn't want to tell you because if I don't talk about it, I can sometimes forget about it. And you're so different from her. You're so… so tough and strong!"

Tough and strong, thought Geraldine. That makes me sound like a rugby fullback or a heavyweight boxer, or an advertisement for lavatory roll.

"I don't mean the way you look," said Ellis, realising suddenly he had stepped into a verbal minefield.

"Well," he floundered, "you look perfectly healthy, of course. But not large. Obviously. But you've got that sort of inner resilience… I mean, Candy never had much resilience, even before her diagnosis. You know, like, she couldn't drive, couldn't fly on her own, couldn't pay bills. Always felt tired. She was… I guess you'd say, a little woman – in everything. She's tiny, too. Barely five feet tall and 90 pounds. She's like a teenie weenie fairy. You could pick her up with one hand." Ellis's eyes glistened. Geraldine sat in silence, contemplating this fairy-like being in some far-off home for the wealthy and bemused.

"Do you see her often?" she asked.

"Two or three times a year I go over there. There's almost no point. She has not the remotest idea of who I am. I phone the home every week and they give me an update. But there's nothing anyone can do except keep her clean and comfortable. It's just a question of waiting."

"And what about your son?" Geraldine felt she was now in a no-questions barred situation. There was almost another emergency stop, but this time Ellis exerted more control.

"He's not able to see her," he said, tight lipped. "Wow!" he exclaimed, pointing to a large stone build-ing. "That's the new Business School. Isn't that some-thing else?"

Yes, thought, Geraldine, something else, yet somehow exactly the same. And how interesting he should change the subject so very, very quickly.

"Does the university always use the same architect?" she asked.

"Yup, pretty much – as you probably know, All Saints is at the vanguard of the Palladian-Goth Stone Revival movement. This place is a byword in architecture."

He pulled up outside a large stone building. "This is the refectory. They still have the table where I carved my initials." They entered a double-height foyer, a pervading smell of fried food wafting unattractively in the air. They walked through to a huge hall, its walls lined with commemorative boards, the long tables and wooden benches gleaming in the sunshine as it streamed through the stained glass windows. It was a refectory that could have been found anywhere in the western world in a place of privilege and learning.

"Now, let's see," said Ellis, theatrically, "where did I used to sit?"

They walked down the rows of tables, until Ellis shouted and threw himself down on the floor, underneath a bench. "There!" He called from a prone position, pointing upward. "'E.V.H.C. September 1972' – yay! It's still here. Wanna see it?"

Geraldine crouched down politely and craned her neck. "Yes, I can see it."

"Quite something, huh? Leaving one's mark."

Rather like Bolly, thought Geraldine, then wished she hadn't, as she wondered how her apricot ball of fluff was at that precise moment. She stood up, the sudden rush of blood to her head making the stained glass light darken. She suddenly felt horribly sad and homesick, just like when she was back at school. She bit her lip.

"What are you thinking my love? Is all this a bit too overwhelming for you?"

She looked at him, momentarily speechless. Yes, of course all this is overwhelming, she thought, ironically, for an Anglo-Saxon cave dweller like me, deprived of educational institutes, stone buildings, and proper fucking plumbing. She gathered herself. "Not a bit," she replied sweetly, "it reminds me very much of St Millicent's, where I spent seven happy years as a schoolgirl."

"Was it as big as this?" asked Ellis.

"Bigger, I would say."

"How about we go to the shop now," said Ellis. "I bet your St Millicent's didn't have a shop."

"No, it didn't," agreed Geraldine, "but the uniforms came from Harrods." She was being ridiculously childish for a mature woman, she knew, but somehow it made her feel better.

"Aw, but I've just remembered, you haven't seen my dorm. You've gotta see that."

"But do we have time? We mustn't be late for the tailgate party, and I must buy some presents to take home." Ellis reluctantly agreed that what with the crowds and the advancing of the hour, a visit to the dorm would have to be postponed.

"Till another occasion," sighed Ellis.

I very much doubt that, thought Geraldine.

They returned to the parked buggy. By now the crowds were thickening fast, a sea of purple and gold. In the distance, a brass band could be heard, tootling and banging.

"Ah, the band," said Ellis, stopping in his tracks. He started to sing, "'All Sainters, Come to the fold, All Sainters, We are so bold, We're the ones that God did choose, And we shall never lose.' You'll be hearing a lot of that over the next few hours. It's the Flight Song."

"Super," remarked Geraldine.

It was now almost impossible to proceed with the golf buggy, what with the crowds and all the other golf buggies. There was much tooting and good-natured shouting as they made a snail's pace progress past more large stone buildings to the shop – a huge edifice of department store proportions. They managed to park, then elbowed their way in through the wide-open doors. "If we lose each other, Sweet Pea, we'll meet back at the buggy in twenty minutes."

All and everything was devoted to All Saints. Clothing, baby wear, dog collars; crockery, umbrellas, stationery; garden furniture, artwork, wallpaper. All was a miasma of purple and gold. There was a desk where one could order customised purple and gold vehicles, from perambulators to Range Rovers. There were queues forming in long crocodile lines for book signings by All Saints authors – an alumnus who was now a famous crime writer had a line so long it wound out of the door into the car park. An All Saints professor was less popular, with a modest dozen waiting to have their volumes signed. Geraldine picked up the book: 'A Foot in the Mouth: a History of Misunderstanding'. Catchy, she thought, putting it back down. The tills were alive with the sound of dollars, and when she eventually emerged clutching her carrier bag of assorted presents – an American football for Bolly, pens for Hugo and Phoebe, soap for Cassie – she felt bruised by the crowds and itchy with bites. She could do with a drink, she thought.

Ellis was already in the buggy, his ear to his mobile. "Ok, that sounds simple. We'll see you soon," he said into the mouthpiece.

176

"Hey, Sweetheart. Looks like you found some things to buy. That was Chuck. They're all set up at the tailgate, so let's go find them."

They set off again, so slowly an elderly man on a Zimmer frame overtook them. "We're heading towards the Angel's Gate, which is just about the swankiest place to have your tailgate. It's right outside the Press Box, where we'll be sitting for the game."

The stadium loomed ahead of them, a vast oval of brutal stone and steel, encircled with flag poles. It took over half an hour to negotiate the few hundred yards to the building. The Angel's Gate was on the other side, so a further twenty minutes was spent circumnavigating. Eventually, Geraldine could see golden gates, elaborately decorated, and in front of them an array of purple and gold gazebos. There was a small parking area for golf buggies.

Every gazebo sheltered an assorted number of people in All Saints clothing. Geraldine imagined it could be very difficult to identify the right party. She thought of the car park at Royal Ascot, and the be-hatted race-goers popping champagne corks a-dozen. This, she felt, was not quite like that. She noted, horrified, a man drinking what looked like a glass of milk. Others had their mouths wide open to engulf foot long hot dogs. There was a smell of onions. She wondered what the less-smart picnicking areas were like. Shouts of "Hey Ellis, you guys," alerted them to the right gazebo, where, much to Geraldine's relief, she was offered white wine. "I remembered you're a bit of a wino," said Chuck, winking.

A young man in a chef's apron was grilling over a barbecue. Geraldine had noticed him washing up in the kitchen at the condo yesterday, and he'd been flipping eggs this morning. He was good-looking, tall and muscular with blond curls and chiselled cheek bones. Had he not had so vacant a look about him he might have resembled a Greek god.

There were mountains of steaks and sausages and chicken legs, piled next to a vast array of bread. Geraldine thought briefly of salmonella, but then returned to the more pressing problem of the bites on her ankles. She noticed an improvised bar, with what looked like ready mixed dry martinis in small plastic glasses. With tremendous enterprise, she helped herself to a glass, removed the olive and the cocktail stick, and, dipping her hanky in the glass, dabbed her bites. It felt cooling, less itchy, the throbbing ceased... and of course alcohol is a tremendous disinfectant, she thought. She closed her eyes for a blissful moment.

"Say, are you ok?" asked Gloria, quizzically.

"Gosh, yes, fine. I just got horribly bitten at the lake and was resorting to some rather unconventional first aid."

"Have you not got any insect repellant?" Gloria enquired. "No, no one mentioned it," said Geraldine, "unfortunately…"

"That's a real shame," interjected Maryjo. "The Indiana midges are an absolute pain. Those bites," she said, indicating Geraldine's gin-soaked ankles, "will be the size of golf balls tomorrow."

"Well, I'll just have to pray," said Geraldine, brightly, downing her wine glass.

Ellis came over with a plate piled with hot dogs and salad. At least he's got me something to eat, thought Geraldine.

"Say," he said, waving a bun at her, "you better go get yourself something. The salads are going down pretty quick." And with that he sat down at the trestle picnic table with his loaded lunch and joined in a hearty conversation about the prospects for the afternoon's game.

Bugger the lot of them, thought Geraldine, as she disconsolately helped herself to a tomato, a grilled slice of aubergine and a sausage.

"Why do you women always have to be on diets?" said Bud, surveying her meagre selection.

"Because you men eat up all the food," she snapped.

She sat down next to Ellis, who was explaining a complicated sporting tactic with the aid of a paper napkin, a plastic fork and a chicken bone. She munched broodingly on her grilled aubergine, wondering what was going on at home. It would be after seven in London. She imagined sitting in her drawing room, her apricot poodle at her side, a sliver of something lovely awaiting her for supper, a scented candle wafting on the découpage table, her slim ankles devoid of insect invasion. She stared mutinously into her empty glass, vowing never ever to leave home again. Ever.

"What games do you follow?" asked Bob, who was now seated on her other side, tucking in to a dripping barbecued rib.

"Um, well, my father sometimes took me to the rugby at Twickenham. And of course I live very close to Lords, so I've been there a couple of times."

"Wow! Me and my wife went to Lourdes ten years ago. I didn't know there was a game there as well. We missed that one. What is it?"

"Cricket." Said Geraldine, a little puzzled. "That's what it's famous for."

"You learn something new every day. I never saw any cricket there. Mind you, I wouldn't have understood it."

"It is quite complicated," Geraldine agreed. "but I can't understand how you could have gone to Lords and not seen any cricket."

"I guess we were too busy at the grotto."

Grotto? Are they all totally and utterly bonkers here, she asked herself. She'd had enough of grottoes for one day. In fact she'd had enough of nearly everything. Except wine.

"I wonder if it would be possible to have another glass of white?" she asked Ellis. Wasn't that what men were supposed to do: pour drinks?

"Why sure, honey. It's over there. You just help yourself."

She went over to where Barb was standing, glass of water in hand. "There isn't enough food, is there?" Barb wailed.

"The salads did seem to disappear rather rapidly. But there's still plenty of meat."

"Aw," said Barb, "these game days are a nightmare. I have to organise everything from our home in Florida. I have to email Anthony over there," she indicated the young man in the chef's apron. "And he does the rest. Chuck just doesn't get how difficult it is. He's going to be mad with me later."

"I'm sure he won't. And as I said, there's loads of meat, and also tons of bread. I'm sure he won't mind," said Geraldine soothingly, wondering how difficult it could be to send an email from Florida to East Cork.

"You don't know the half of it," Barb muttered, gulping at her water. "Chuck's gone to meet some guests who've only just arrived in town, and have got lost. Ted and Lulu." She paused, "they're both vegans. What am I going to do?"

Geraldine thought. "Is there a nearby supermarket?"

Barb looked as if she had suddenly found the Holy Grail. "A supermarket? Yes, there's one just behind the condos." She looked at Geraldine with gratitude. "That's real kind of you."

"Well, it was only a suggestion," and an obvious one at that.

"Yes, but offering to go. That really is kind."

Offering to go? She had done no such thing.

Barb was opening her bag. "Here," she said, handing Geraldine a wad of dollar bills, "you know what vegans eat."

Geraldine felt alarmed. "But I don't know where the supermarket is. This is my first time in East Cork." And certainly, she thought, her last.

"Oh, it's just behind the condos. You can't miss it!"

"But…"

"Thank you so much, hun. You are an angel," Barb said, a surprisingly steely tone entering her voice.

Geraldine walked away in a depressed manner. Why couldn't she just say no? Really loudly and firmly. She cast a glance behind her as she dragged her espadrilles across the dusty ground. Already her feet were aching, her blister was weeping, and her heart was heavy.

No one seemed to notice her departure, not even Ellis, who was now illustrating an even more complicated sporting manoeuvre with a bowl of limes. And she hadn't managed to have her second glass of wine. Her bites felt as if they were gnawing into her ankle bones, and she was certain her blister would turn septic. It was murderously hot. She made her way along the road past the tennis courts. This was not easy, as she was going against the crowd, who were still surging on to the campus. How outrageous, she thought, of Barb to expect her to go to the supermarket. It was absolutely invidious. She crossed the road to the condos, and walked over the immaculate lawns, hoping she might find someone to direct her. All appeared to be empty, so she made her way round the back to a small parking area. There was a gate, only about 3 feet high, which separated the condos from a narrow street. Presumably this led to the supermarket. The gate was locked. "Heigh ho," she said to herself, as she swung her left leg over the top and heaved herself up. For the second time that day an alarm went off – not as loud as this morning, but nevertheless loud enough for a man to emerge from his car at the end of the road. He was dressed in a uniform.

"What do you think you're doing, lady?"

"I am trying to get to the supermarket."

"This is unauthorised use of private property. You're trespassing."

"I'm not trespassing. I am staying with friends in one of the condos, and they asked me to go to the supermarket. They never mentioned I would need a key."

"What are the residents' names?"

"Chuck and Barb."

"Chuck and Barb who?"

"I have no idea. We weren't formally introduced."

"I thought you said they were friends."

Geraldine looked at this man with all the hauteur she could manage. "Under what authority are you asking me these questions?"

"Under the authority of East Cork City Police Department."

"That doesn't look like a policeman's uniform."

"That's because it isn't, ma'am. This is my weekend security job. I'm employed by the condo board of management to patrol during the game."

"Well, I would imagine the condo board of management are probably more concerned about people getting in rather than people getting out."

"There's the unauthorised use of private property. You climbed over that gate."

Geraldine took a very deep breath and counted to ten.

"I absolutely appreciate, officer, that you take your job of security very seriously, and I applaud you for that. But the fact remains that my hosts have asked me as a matter of some urgency to go to the supermarket to buy food for vegan guests who are about to arrive at their tailgate party. This is an emergency. Do you understand me? An emergency!"

The man scratched his head, uncertain what part of his brief had prepared him for this.

"Where's the tailgate?" he finally enquired.

"Angel's Gate," Geraldine replied, rather pleased that she should remember this important fact.

"Angel's Gate! Well, why didn't you say so in the first place. That's only for the high rollers. It costs mega bucks to set up there." He was clearly impressed. "I'm going to let you off just this once. Don't climb over the gate again."

"I have no intention of making a habit of it I can assure you, but – if I ever find the supermarket – I'll need to come back through the gate to get to the party."

"No problem. I'm going to take you there myself, then drive you back on to campus."

Geraldine now noticed that the vehicle in question was an East Cork police car, so she assumed she was quite safe getting into it with a stranger. They drove the short way to the supermarket, which was empty-ing of customers, most of whom were weighed down with beer and bags of ice, heading towards the game.

"I'll wait for you," the officer assured her.

She found a trolley, and raced up and down the aisles. Really, she thought, this place made it very easy for picnickers. There were lots of ready prepared platters, hygienically nestling under cellophane wrappers. She managed to procure salads, olives, an enormous pack of guacamole, and delicious looking bread – far more interesting than the bread that had been provided under the gazebo. She staggered out to the car. Her resourcefulness astonished her. She would tell Barb to cancel her email from Florida, and do all her shopping herself.

They drove out onto the main road and headed towards the campus. As they approached the tennis courts, the officer put on his siren, and, as Moses divided the Red Sea, so the crowd parted to allow the speeding police car to approach the stadium. They screeched to a halt outside Angel's Gate. Geraldine warmly thanked her new best friend for all his help.

The assembled tailgaters gazed in astonishment as Geraldine emerged from the police car, weighed down with carrier bags. Barb detached herself from the group. "Hun, you've saved the day. I don't know how you did this, but you did. Chuck!" she called, "get the girl a drink." Ellis accepted many congratulations on the usefulness, resourcefulness and downright heroism of his Englishwoman.

Geraldine was now the object of much interest, as she told the revellers her story. The two pale-faced vegans were introduced to her by Barb.

"This woman is literally your saviour," Barb gushed.

Geraldine beamed. She felt relaxed, as the itching seemed to subside and all thoughts of a blister were gone. Ted and Lulu, though not lively, were pleasant, and told her about their plans for a Mediterranean cruise.

"I love the name Lulu," said Geraldine, now in receipt of her third glass of wine. "It always reminds me of that song. You know the one."

Ted and Lulu politely claimed not to know the song she meant.

"My grandmother used to sing it to me. Now let me see how, did it go? 'You can bring Rose with the turned-up nose, But don't bring Lulu. You can bring Pearl who's a darned nice girl, But don't bring Lulu. She's the kind of smarty Who breaks up every party, Hullabalooloo, Don't bring Lulu. She'll come by herself'." She finished triumphantly. "It was my favourite song when I was a little girl!"

Ted and Lulu looked nervously at each other, and Lulu's pale face turned even more ashen as she clutched her husband's arm. They excused themselves, as Ted helped his wife over to a chair, which she sank into, almost as if on the brink of collapse.

Ellis came over to Geraldine. "Aren't Ted and Lulu great? I knew you'd love them. Lulu's had prolonged health issues. Apparently this is only the second party she's been to since her recovery. Ted really had to persuade her to come."

Barb joined them, glass of water in hand. "Has Ellis been telling you about Lulu?" she asked conspiratorially. "She's had terrible problems. Down there," she whispered. "Everything, and I mean everything, gone. And then she had this really dreadful experience at her step-daughter's wedding. It was just after she'd had the surgery, and she was feeling like death, worse, really. So she says to herself, either I go to this wedding or I lie in bed at home all by myself, waiting to die. She really makes an effort. She puts on the brightest dress she's got – orange it was. Balenciaga – you would not believe what that had cost. She slaps on make-up, and all the while, she's psyching herself up. I can do this, I can do this, she's saying. So she gets to the wedding. She can hardly stand and she's clinging on to Ted. She can barely move without his support. And Ted's ex-wife is standing there in front of the church, a great lump of a woman in a floral dress with orange flowers all over it, and this ex-wife (who it turns out is up to the eyeballs on Valium) screams, 'Orange is MY colour. I'm the mother of the bride and it's my colour. Just get out of here and die!' Well, can you imagine, you're feeling real ill and someone talks like that to you. Lulu managed to stagger back to the car, and she sat there for the next three hours, shaking. That was the last party she's been to. We really weren't sure whether she'd make it today. It's taken all of Ted's energies to get her here." She shook her head.

Geraldine took a sip of wine. 'Hullabalooloo, Don't bring Lulu. She'll come by herself' echoed in her brain. Goodness, I am an idiot, she thought. An utter idiot. I must learn to think before I speak. She took another sip, wondering what it would be like at Cassie's wedding, should it ever happen. Would she be the embarrassing mother of the bride, heaping opprobrium on the hapless Sally? She took a third sip – more of a gulp, really, as she contemplated the horrors of life. It went down the wrong way, and she found herself choking, spluttering and gasping. Barb was rooted to the spot, seemingly unable to do anything helpful. Without thinking, Geraldine grabbed Barb's glass of water from her claw-like hand and took a deep gulp. It burned. It took her breath away. She nearly spat it out. It was neat vodka. Once she had recovered herself she glanced at Barb, who was looking shamefaced at the ground. Geraldine smiled sympathetically, and put her hand on Barb's boney shoulder. Barb shook her head, and mouthed, "Don't," grabbing a tissue from her sleeve.

Chapter Nine

Early Friday morning, back in Battersea – the wrong side of the river – Jonty had received a telephone call from Cassie. It had left him feeling agitated. It wasn't because his daughter's news of her break-up and quick reconciliation unduly worried him. No, it was the knowledge that his wife, or ex-wife, as he should say, was somewhere across the Atlantic, with a man who Cassie claimed was very good looking – 'for an old guy'. Those were her words. Jonty looked at himself in the mirror while shaving, appraisingly. No one, he felt, not even his late mother, could describe him as good-looking. He sat disconsolately staring at his boiled egg, swirling his toast soldiers through the soft yellow yolk. "Do you think I'm good-looking?" he asked Sally, who was stirring honey into porridge. She looked startled. "Um, yes, whatever good-looking means." She paused, then continued, encouragingly, "When I first met you I thought you looked like a teddy bear."

"A teddy bear? You've never said that to me before."

"Well, you haven't asked me before if I think you're good-looking."

"Do you mean I'm good-looking for a teddy bear?"

Sally felt flustered. "Yes. No. I don't know, really. I haven't given it enough thought. But I like teddy bears very much. They're such a comfort aren't they?" She got up from the kitchen table. "I must phone mother before I go to work. She was feeling a little poorly when I talked to her yesterday."

Jonty sighed. He finished his egg and took his breakfast crockery over to the sink. He gazed out of the window. Not bad weather-wise, he thought, not bad at all. He gathered up his briefcase and keys. "I'm off," he shouted. "I may walk a bit of the way." That would clear his head. "Send my regards to your mother."

He arrived in Whitehall twenty minutes late and sweating. "You look a bit flushed, Jonty," said his irritating colleague, Graham. "Hope it's not the menopause!" He laughed heartily. Jonty managed a weak smile as he consulted his diary for the day. He had a meeting in the afternoon, but for now he had merely to catch up on emails. He tapped his pencil impatiently on the desk, waiting for the computer screen to spring into action. He wondered what Geraldine was doing. Indiana – that was where she had gone. Wasn't that what Cassie had said? He looked up time zones. Eastern Standard Time, five hours behind British Summer Time. He glanced at his watch. Just coming up to ten o' clock here, so it would be five there. What would she be doing at five in the morning? Sleeping? Next to her new beau, he thought bitterly. Her very good-looking beau. Or even... No, he couldn't contemplate THAT without breaking out in a further sweat. He wondered what the wretched man was called. At least if he had his name he could google him. Find out about him. No doubt he had some damned stupid name. Most Americans did. He was probably called Marvin Hunkelpfefer III or Art Shradecker or Nat Anglepoise. He passed a half hour or more coming up with ever sillier names, which took him nicely to an earlyish lunch and a stroll along the Embankment. He decided he'd phone Cassie. Do a bit of subtle probing.

"Hi Pops," she screeched, "twice in one day. Are you desperate or something?"

"No...just forgot to ask you this morning if Bolly's all right. You know, without Geraldine."

"You're phoning me to ask if Bolly's all right? I thought you told Mummy he was ridiculous and you preferred retrievers."

"I never said he was ridiculous. Did she tell you that? No, I was just, um, concerned about the little fellow. Thought perhaps his tiny wet nose might have been put out of joint by the advent of this new man on the scene. What did you say he was called?"

"I didn't, Pops. Never mentioned a name. And actually all I know is he's called Ellis. Don't know his surname."

"And what does he do, this Ellis chap?"

"Oh gosh, one of those sorts of jobs where you run things and make a lot of money. I don't really know what. He's got a Porsche, though."

"A porch? Lots of people have them. We had one in Fulham. Over the back door."

Cassie screamed with laughter, "No, Pops. A Porsche. It's a fast German car."

It would be, fumed Jonty as he walked miserably back to the office. A bloody German sports car. Fancy this and fancy that. That's what this Ellis chap would be like. One of those guys with everything. Including my wife. Or ex-wife, he corrected. His meeting passed in a haze. Probably just sent AK47s to Libya, he thought, as he sat on the bus home, trying to remember what he'd put his signature to in the course of the afternoon.

The flat was empty, except for Sally's cat, Tiddlepuss, who was sitting in a shaft of sunlight in the bay window. They eyed each other with mutual dislike. Friday was Sally's pottery club evening, and she wouldn't be home until later. He poured himself a whisky and looked in the fridge. Eggs, milk, butter and some wilting Brussels Sprouts. What was a chap supposed to do with that? He'd never had to cook for himself before he'd met Sally. He'd just passed seamlessly from his mother's cuisine to Geraldine's, with some jolly good nosh in various Officers' Messes in between. He opened a large packet of crisps and sat down with his whisky under the watchful glare of Tiddlepuss. A little later, having flicked through every television station, drunk more whisky and eaten a withered apple, he consulted his phone. He would send a text to Geraldine. That was what he would do. This took some time, since he had only succumbed to mobile ownership in the last couple of years, but he was pleased with his efforts. A little later a message pinged back. "'This is the life!'" he shouted at the cat, enraged by Geraldine's reply. "'This is the life'," he squawked, getting up to pour more whisky. Bloody yanks, he thought, indignantly, quickly putting his phone in his pocket as he heard Sally's key in the door.

"Nice evening, Sal?" he said with forced brightness.

She eyed the nearly empty glass disapprovingly. "Yes, quite interesting really. We're working on spiralised vase wear. It's quite advanced. I bought some fish and chips on the way back from the bus."

They sat at the kitchen table and ate the cooling cod and soggy chips in silence. "I love chips when they're

194

all greasy," said Sally, wiping her mouth with a piece of kitchen towel. There was nothing Jonty could say. "I'm hitting the sack, Sal. Tiring week and all that."

Saturday dawned, bright again. "What's your programme for today?" he said, looking towards her, next to him under the duvet. She yawned. "I must find out how mother is, and then I'm hoping to tackle a rather complicated jug."

Jonty sighed. "I thought I might try and see Hugo later. He's going to be in London. And it's a lovely morning. Might have a bit of a constitutional in the park. Want to come?"

"No thanks." She turned over, her back solidly facing him. No point hanging around here, he thought, I may as well get up. Seize the day. An hour later he was in the park. He walked briskly for ten minutes, breathing deeply, then, seeing an empty bench, sat down. A couple strolled towards him, pushing an old-fashioned pram. The coachwork gleamed in its newly restored splendour, the chrome glinted in the sunshine. This ensemble of prosperous parents, with their traditional-style baby carriage, made a pleasing, nostalgic picture on an early September morning. Jonty thought sadly of when his own children were young. Not that he had ever pushed a pram. But it seemed, sitting on that park bench, such a very happy time, and so very long ago.

The man glanced at Jonty as they passed, smiled, then looked again, more searchingly.

"Good heavens! Colonel!" He said, adding, "I don't suppose you remember me? Harry Robson. Captain Robson as I was then. 2010 it must have been. Caterham." Jonty stood up, his brain momentarily scrolling through the hundreds of young men who had passed before him during his Army days. "Of course I remember you, Harry, good to see you. What are you up to now?"

"Banker, I'm afraid. Sold out to capitalism and all that. This is my wife, Juliet, and this," he said, pointing to the occupant of the pram, "is Fergus. Born three months ago."

Jonty obligingly looked at the baby. It was like all babies, a squashed, grumpy face and slightly pink. "Well done," he said, smiling at Mrs Robson, a pretty blonde in a striped Breton top and cream jeans.

"Are you living round here, sir?" asked Harry.

"Less of the 'sir' stuff, Harry. I'm in civvy street now, pen-pushing at the MoD, for my sins. Quite a change… and yes, I'm in one of those flats over there. What about you?"

"We've just moved into a house off Northcliffe Road. Bit of a whirlwind, the last two years," Harry remarked, "what with leaving the army, starting at Nathan Brothers, getting married, producing a sprog.

And now a new house. We've only been in it a month, but Juliet's got it all under control." He looked at his wife and squeezed her hand. She smiled back at him.

"Gosh, you have been busy," said Jonty, trying to sound jovial.

"And how's your wife? I remember her very well," enquired Harry. "Lovely lady," he added.

"Yes…," said Jonty, confused. "Yes." He paused, an image of Geraldine floating before him, ghostly, tantalisingly. "Yes, she's very well, thank you." And he supposed she was very well, luxuriating States-side, cosseted by and closeted with a good-looking man. This wasn't the time or the place, he thought, to explain the change in his circumstances.

"How are you finding Nathan Brothers? They've hit a bit of trouble, haven't they?" Jonty asked. "I seem to remember reading something in the papers."

"Luckily not my department. I'm in equities. But they flew in some American guy to take over and it's going okay now. He's done a lot of weeding out – bit of a ruthless bastard so I've heard from my colleagues."

"It's the same everywhere," said Jonty. "Look at what they're doing to the Army. And it's even worse with the RAF. Nothing's safe now." He shook his head, sadly.

"Yes, you're absolutely right. We have to enjoy things while we can." Loud cries started to emit from the pram. "Now let me give you my e-mail address. Come and see us," said Harry, looking through his wallet for a card. "We'd better keep moving. This is what happens if we stop," he laughed, pointing at the bawling baby. "But it's been great running into you."

"Good to see you, too," said Jonty. "And I'll be in touch."

He resumed his seat on the bench. He wouldn't see them again. How could he? It would seem peculiar turning up with a different woman. They would wonder why he hadn't mentioned he'd remarried. Oh, but, there's a thing, supposing he was out with Sally, and they bumped into each other? That would be awkward. He'd have to tell them – in front of her – that he'd forgotten to say he was now married to someone else. Difficult situation.

Should he run after them now, and just set the record straight? He glanced down the path. They were quite some way off. No, he'd have to e-mail Harry and explain the changes in his life. He'd give that particular e-mail a bit of thought sometime. Not now, though. He closed his eyes, enjoying the sunshine on his face. But all he could see was a hazy impression of his first wife. When had he last seen her? Must be over a year, at his mother's funeral. He'd worried that it would be difficult for the two wives to finally meet each other, and he knew that Sally had felt anxious.

But it had all been absolutely fine because, well – he had to admit – because of Geraldine. She just took it all in her stride and was charming to Sally. Lovely lady, that was what Harry had said. Would he think the same of Sally? Would he? Jonty hated himself for asking that question. Angered, he smacked his head with his fist, alarming a passing elderly lady with a shopping trolley. I have to snap out of this, he said to himself. I have to get a grip. But he felt wracked by guilt, tormented by sadness, as if for one brief moment he had held happiness in his hands, only to see it disintegrate before him, trickling elusively through his fingers, forever lost.

Jonty didn't much care for self-analysis, but he knew that everything had started to go wrong when he'd left the Army. It had been such a muddling sort of time, what with the new job and the new house. He would have liked to talk about how he felt to Geraldine, but one didn't, did one? And anyway, in that first year in Fulham, Geraldine had been far too busy decorating. She insisted on doing most of it herself. Every wall and skirting board was lovingly stroked with a narrow brush ("You get a much better result," she had said, "even though it takes twice as long"). Surfaces had to be smoothed down laboriously with sand paper, every decorative decision agonised over. She'd repainted the kitchen four times before she'd got the right colour. Yet all the other previous colours had looked the same – a sort of wishy-washy grey. It was difficult, he thought, as a mere man, to appreciate not just the tiny degrees of light or dark in a pigment, but also the subtleties of different paint finishes. No wonder they'd made that film for women, *Fifty Shades of Grey*, probably about interior décor. He felt he'd lived every one of those gradations, back in Fulham. No, he couldn't have talked: he'd never liked men moaning. He'd had enough of claims of post-traumatic stress and Gulf War Syndrome when he was in the Army. A good dose of jollop, that was the answer for most woes and ills, he thought, either that, or a large glass of whisky.

He exhaled loudly. He should resume his walk, but he felt unable to leave the park bench, as if it had temporarily become his home. His thoughts became even bleaker. He'd be sixty soon, his desk job would come to an end, and then what? What the hell would he do? Of course, his father hadn't even reached forty. Not that Jonty had any recollection of him.

When Jonty was a child, grown-ups still talked about the Lewisham train crash. A trip to the sweet shop in the village always resulted in a few extra penny chews being put in the paper bag, as the kindly lady behind the counter whispered to others waiting to be served that he was the poor little lad, you know, who lost his Daddy in that train crash. It happened on a foggy December evening – and just a few weeks before Christmas, too. Terrible for a kiddie.

Jonty doubted anyone remembered the incident now. He'd sat through old Pathé newsreels – a certain distance lent to the tragedy by the grainy black and white images – listening to the clipped accents describing the disaster. His mother, left with three small boys to raise, chose to be brave and resilient, and hardly ever spoke of her loss. It was only in her last days, senile, crippled and bed-ridden in a care home in Sevenoaks, that her old frail voice had murmured, "pea souper, pea souper." The nurse on duty, young and recently arrived from the Far East, had brought the elderly woman a mug of soup, only to have it tossed aside with remarkable ferocity. His mother had died a week later, and, as Jonty had looked through her handbag, stuffed with handkerchiefs, worn-down lipsticks and peppermints, he'd found a black and white photograph of his father. She must have always had it with her, he thought. Oh, all these lives of words unspoken, of thoughts not uttered – what a terrible waste! And now here he was, sitting on a park bench, utterly miserable, and the only woman he had ever really loved had swanned off with a damned American. If only Geraldine had put up a bit more of a fight. But she hadn't even cried when he'd told her about the affair. He'd expected her to beg him to extricate himself from the other woman.

But she'd just sat there, stroking that bloody poodle and listening quietly. Perhaps she'd been pleased he was leaving? Perhaps this American was part of a long line of matinée idols? How was he to know? He wished he knew more about the present situation – was it serious? Supposing Geraldine suddenly went to live on the other side of the Atlantic? What would he do then? A jogger, stopping for a sip from her water bottle, looked at him curiously. Pull yourself together, Jonty, he muttered. You've only yourself to blame.

He wanted to know more about what was going on. But he couldn't keep cross-questioning Cassie – that would be inappropriate. Aha! A bit of inspiration! He could ask Giles and Phyllida if they knew anything. He reached for his phone in his pocket. He would call them.

Chapter Ten

"Time to go," shouted Chuck, examining his watch. "Don't get too excited, but the game begins soon. We need to get ourselves up to that Press Box, because if we miss a single minute, we'll never forgive ourselves. Come on!"

Geraldine looked around for Ellis. He waved at her. "Heart racing, my love, huh?" he said, walking over to her and grabbing her by the hand. "Your first game. What a moment for you! This is something you'll remember for the rest of your life. And have I got good news, or have I got good news?" Geraldine smiled politely. "Now, like Chuck said, we're all supposed to be in the Press Box, right? Which is great, of course. There are people here who would literally kill to be in the Press Box." Geraldine surveyed the crowd with interest, wondering if she could identify any literal killers. "Aw, honey, don't look so worried. Those two little lines are coming back. You know, those little frown lines."

Really, thought Geraldine, there could be many advantages to being disposed of right now. She raised her eyebrows as high as she could and smiled. "That's better, my love. Now, what was I saying? Oh yes, have I got a surprise for you!"

Perhaps, thought Geraldine, a car was coming to take her to a shopping mall, and she would miss the game. That would indeed be a pleasant surprise.

"Now the Press Box," continued Ellis, "to be brutally honest, fantastic as it is, you really don't get the full atmosphere unless you're out there in the stands. So... at the last minute I've been able to get us another pair of tickets! For the stands!" He waved them around, triumphantly. "It's literally unbelievable being there, with everybody. You're going to love it. And after all, here we are, in the greatest democracy on this earth. We don't want to be in the Press Box, with a bunch of rich guys. We want to be with the people," he stretched out his arms, expansively, "sitting next to anybody – a vagrant even."

"But would a vagrant be able to buy a ticket? Wouldn't it be quite expensive for him?" Geraldine asked.

"Aw, my love, you know what I mean. I want this experience to be real. For you. For us!" He bent down and kissed her full on the lips. A little posse of his friends applauded. "Way, hay, hay!" they shouted, "None of that, you two love birds, you wait for later."

Geraldine could taste chicken drumstick and beer in her mouth. She searched for a peppermint in her bag. She was not a person who indulged in public displays of affection, not even in those early days of her courtship with Jonty, and she was certainly not starting now. She must, she decided, while nevertheless acknowledging her need for thinking before speaking, exert full firmness and assertiveness.

"It all sounds absolutely super, but I think I would like to sit in the Press Box AND the stands. After all, for me, both are part of the wonderful new experience of an All Saints game."

Goodness, she thought, she was accomplished at this. "I suggest we spend the first half in the stands and the second in the Press Box." Forty minutes or so in the heat with the unwashed would be just about bearable, she considered, and then the second half could be spent sequestered in comfort with a nice glass of something as the game proceeded to its conclusion.

"Whatever you say, Princess. Let's go, go, go, go. We do not want to miss a second of this."

It seemed to take forever finding the way to their seats. Geraldine sat down, first checking that hers was clean, and then observed her surroundings. She was truly amazed by the size of it. The stadium seemed far bigger inside than out, and the sheer number of spectators – and their noise – was overwhelming. There were endless announcements, adding to the level of decibels, blaring from different speakers, each message equally unintelligible. She glanced at the man next to her, who had just taken his place. Certainly not a vagrant, she observed. She smiled at him. He replied with an encouraging, "Hi." He was about fifty years old or so, attractive, with thick blonde floppy hair, a tanned face and kind brown eyes. A teenage version of himself, less smiley, and engrossed in his programme, sat alongside him. Geraldine felt encouraged. "It's my first game," she said conversationally.

"Wow, you're English, right? I was a Rhodes Scholar at Oxford. Oxfawd, as you Brits say." So much, she thought, for a brush with the people. She laughed, and replied "My aunt lived in Oxford. We used to go there every Christmas when I was a child. And I remember Rhodes House very well. I always used to think it looked like a biscuit barrel."

Ellis was bristling next to her. It was the sort of bristle that Bolly affected when Geraldine stroked another dog. "My love," he said unnecessarily loudly, "any minute now the cheerleaders will be on. You don't want to miss a minute."

There was the distant sound of the band, rising to an explosion of timpani and trumpets as battalions of girls in tiny little sticky-out purple skirts, purple and gold military-style tight jackets, and peaked purple caps with great gold plumes, wafting in the breeze like a field of corn, marched into the stadium. Their smiles would have lit up the night skies, as they raised their legs in perfect time to the marching band. They twirled their batons and tossed them in the air. The music grew louder and louder, as the band streamed on, hundreds and hundreds of purple-suited boys and girls, blowing their bugles and banging their drums. The crowd roared above the marchers and musicians.

"All Sainters, come to the fold.
All Sainters, we are so bold.
We're the ones that God did choose,
And we shall never lose."

Ellis sang along happily with the band, his face bathed with pleasure. Geraldine felt a momentary pang of envy, as she saw his unalloyed joy. Did she ever feel like that? About anything? The green Astro Turf became a swirling mass of purple and gold, the lines of marchers forming themselves by complicated and intricate manoeuvres, into giant letters: *A* and *S*: All Saints. They remained, marching on the spot, in this configuration, as small, pink-clad creatures slithered around, their bodies and arms weaving sinuously. "The herrings," whispered Ellis, in explanation to

Geraldine. "It's a tremendous honour to be asked to be a herring, although it's obligatory that one is under 5'3"." Band, cheerleaders and fish all marched or swam their way down to one end of the stadium, and for a brief moment all was quiet. Then, from the other end, the rival team's entourage emerged. "Wolverhampton College, Utah," said Ellis. "A really strong football school, unfortunately for us. The Wolves!"

"Oh," said Geraldine, as one who has had a revelation. "Like Wolverhampton Wanderers. I believe they're called Wolves, too."

She turned to the erstwhile Rhodes Scholar. "Did you come across Wolverhampton Wanderers at Oxford?" He expressed regret at this omission in his time abroad and became absorbed in a conversation with his son. He was still puzzling over the remark about the biscuit barrel.

Wolverhampton College, Utah, had cheer leaders as numerous but of a less exuberant hue. They were dressed in dark green leggings and white jackets, nipped in at the waist, and extending down at the back into a point, past their *derrières*, and edged in silver. They sported furry tails, which wiggled provocatively as they stamped up and down. Geraldine considered the rival team was in more tasteful attire. Their band, though, seemed subdued compared with All Saints, but perhaps they were feeling the oppression of being away from their home ground. Their college song, a paean of praise to all things vulpine, including a sort of baying chorus, was followed by lots of little wolves scampering onto the pitch. "They must be awfully hot in those fluffy outfits," Geraldine remarked to Ellis.

She wondered what Utah was like. Wasn't that where Mormons lived? And could only Mormons live there, or was it open to anyone? She would have to enquire later. Really, she thought, it was dreadful how snooty British people could be, decrying Americans for not knowing that Manchester is north of London, or that Glasgow's in Scotland, but what do we know of America? Utah could be anything, or anywhere, as far as she knew. Was it a desert, or heavily forested? Or mountainous, or even by the sea? She struggled to recall anything. Yes, she had remembered. Salt Lake City. That was in Utah. So that was probably a sort of sea, although, as she looked down on the stadium, aswirl with the dancing, marching, tooting crowds, she could see no Wolverhampton College equivalents to All Saints herrings. Just as well, with all those wolf-cubs.

The herrings, however, were now sitting cross-legged at the edge of the pitch, and the cheer leaders had segregated themselves into bright blocks of colour. There was a terrific stereophonic rumble, as if from two loud hailers placed very far apart. From each end of the stadium the opposing teams emerged. Everyone roared as these mighty men entered onto the pitch. Even from a distance, one could see they were taller and broader than any normal mortal. Their fearsome armoured appearance, with the padding and the cladding, the tight trousers, the shoulders wide enough to span a river, the helmets catching the light of the sun, made a warrior-like spectacle. It was as if two armies, the one purple and gold, the other green and silver, had been blasted forth out of great, giant cannon, the strength of their presence like a life-giving force that could be plugged into the national grid to energise a nation. Ellis's eyes streamed with tears. "To think they're just boys, really, and yet look at them. They're gods."

Geraldine could not deny their impact, and even she felt a little choked at the concentration of proud, enormous humanity before her. Both bands, united momentarily as a part of something greater, struck up the first bars of the *Star-spangled Banner*. From nowhere, a podium had appeared in the middle of the pitch, and a girl, thin as a needle in a pair of the tiniest purple shorts, started to sing. Ellis nudged Geraldine. "Fletcher Quick," he mouthed. "She's big. Her brother's a sophomore here."

"Really?" Said Geraldine, surprised. Fletcher Quick was Cassie's favourite singer. She must remember to text her daughter later. The solo voice was joined by 80,000 others, clasping their hands to their chests, swaying slightly with emotion, as the strains of the *Star-spangled Banner* spread upwards and outwards, far, far beyond the stadium. Geraldine felt quite wrung out by all this mass of sentiment. But there was more. Two uniformed boys, one All Saints, the other Wolverhampton College, met at the exact centre of the pitch, saluted each other, then smartly turned and walked together to the towering flagpole, and in combination, slowly, and with marked deliberation, raised the Stars and Stripes. The tears ran down Ellis's face as the flag reached its summit and fluttered defiantly in the early evening breeze. "Oh God," he moaned, "this always gets me – here." He thumped his chest, where the long, livid scar slashed through his breast bone.

Geraldine wondered where the coach was. Johnny Dallaglio, that was it, wasn't it? She was pleased at being so well-informed. She looked for him on the pitch. She couldn't see him. Perhaps he was standing amongst a shoal of herrings, never to be seen again. It must be very nerve-wracking, she thought, being a football coach. Terribly bad for one's blood pressure.

The teams appeared to place themselves as if play would commence. At least, Geraldine thought that might be what was happening. She decided to observe very carefully and pick it all up as she went along. She hoped no one was going to attempt to explain the game to her. It would be pointless. She would never understand their explanations. She gazed upwards, vaguely, at the blue sky. Somewhere, a long way in the distance, there was a small black cloud, no bigger than a footballer's clenched fist. It waved and rocked in the atmosphere, like a child's balloon released at a birthday party. It was a carefree, inconsequential cloud, and as whistles were blown, and those great gladiators briefly ran hither and thither, no one much noticed it. The gods ran again, then they stopped. Then they ran, then they stopped. The cloud grew nearer, gathering girth, and still they ran, and still they stopped. The cloud expanded its greying drear until it had completely covered the stadium, like a large saucepan lid. The sudden obliteration of the sun's rays cast an apocalyptic light.

"Whoa!" said the former Rhodes Scholar. "Lake-effect here we come." There was a moment's stillness, and then down came the rain. At first it was gentle, refreshing almost, after the heat. The droplets were polite, falling softly on the crowds. Then, momentum gathered, the shower matured into giant globules, which stung the face and soaked the hair. Geraldine rootled for her Glydebourne flowery poncho. She struggled with it over her head, pulled it on and arranged it to her satisfaction. At least, she thought, this would keep her dry. Everyone else placed their see-through plastic bag-style cover-ups over their already sodden bodies. The play, with its running and stopping, continued much as before, unaffected by the downpour. It was only when the long fingers of lightning appeared, poking their way through the dense black clouds, that Geraldine wondered what the contingency plans were for major storms. She was about to ask Ellis, when she saw to her horror, projected onto the giant screen on the other side of the stadium, a Gulliver-sized marquee of pink and blue roses. It turned as she turned, it raised a hand to its head as she raised a hand to hers. There was a ripple of laughter, above the roar of the elements and the whistles of the referees, as the uniformly clad audience noted the flowery interloper on the screen. It was the briefest of brief moments, but for Geraldine, her five seconds of infamy were mortifying, flesh-wounding.

"Did you see that?" enquired Ellis, laughing. "You were on the big screen, my love. You're a movie star!" Geraldine was about to think of a frighteningly withering, yet witty reply, when a clap of thunder was followed by a bewildering blast of announcements. Apparently, if the storm was nearer than ten miles, the entire stadium would have to be evacuated in the usual way. Geraldine wondered what the usual way involved. This procedure had not been further explained. Perhaps one should hide under one's tip up seat – although for the large of girth that would be an impossibility. Or perhaps, thought Geraldine wildly, this lack of information was some secret means of exterminating poor fools like herself, uneducated in the rituals of football. Yet again she had not been clearly informed. She struggled to follow the continuing announcement, certain she would be the last woman standing, as everyone else, flocking to safety, would leave her, a human conduit for lightning from the sky above. "Where do we take shelter?" she shouted at Ellis, his ears covered in polythene.

"We go into the complex of tunnels under the stadium," he shouted back, "but looking at the weather, I think it's going to clear. At least I hope so!"

She hoped so, too. She had already had enough of being window-lessly enclosed in their basement bedroom, and besides, surely it must be nearly half-time? Press Box, and drinkies, she thought happily, as she observed a piece of blue sky, the size of a footballer's helmet, emerging through the clouds.

The rain tailed off, and she was able to remove her floral disaster, and bundle it under her seat. Why she should be the only one in a crowd of 80,000 not to have the regulation see-through cover-up was quite beyond her. She thought of earlier that day, and the blithe assumption that she would have covered herself with insect repellant. Really, anyone coming to this neck of the woods for the first time should be issued with an instruction sheet. She ran through items for her imaginary pamphlet, then realised that at least twenty minutes had ensued since the storm, and they seemed to be no nearer half-time. She could see, if she craned her neck, the Press Box looming above the hoi-polloi, where probably the glamorous rich were at this minute downing champagne, and she wondered how long it would be until she joined them.

Suddenly, a vibration surged through her body, as if the stadium was about to collapse. More than half of the spectators had risen to their feet. "Touch down," yelled Ellis, excitedly, leaping from his seat, "the Saintly Sling-off." Geraldine stood too, baffled, wondering what could be going to happen. There was the sound of humming, like a huge swarm of angry bees, then thousands upon thousands raised their arms and jumped in the air, and as their feet touched down again, she felt the boarding beneath her wobble and shake. "It's surprising the stands have never col-lapsed," she said to Ellis, amazed at her resolute insou-ciance in what could easily be imminent termination. "Nah," replied Ellis, "as you can imagine, the warp and weft of the Saintly Sling-Off has been factored into the engineering design of the structure. The dynamics of sympathetic vibration have been accounted for.

Nothing is ever overlooked at All Saints, absolutely nothing."

She sighed. She felt quite overlooked. And looked over, too, unable to rid her mind of the image of herself, twenty times her normal size, on a big screen. She returned her thoughts to the game. She observed one large helmet-clad man after another pick up the ball and run. Nothing seemed to change, to progress. This was certainly a different experience to watching, say, a good film. Where, she asked herself, could the interest be? What exactly was she missing? Ellis was animatedly throwing words around like 'penalty' and 'time out' to the fat man on his right. The good-looking blonde man on her left was engaged in a complicated explanation involving pointing and hand signalling with his son. She felt left out of it all and quite bored. The singing and marching and twirling had all been highly entertaining, but now she was ready to go. She wondered if she could quietly slip out and somehow commandeer a taxi to take her to the nearest mall. She looked at Ellis quizzically. Really, she thought, although unsatisfactory in so very many ways, he was most pleasing in profile. His nose was just the right side of big, and had a patrician line. Jonty's nose had been broken the month before they had married. Yes, as he often remarked, he had injured it in the Falklands. Not, as it happened in combat, but, with one too many inside him, he had walked into a door whilst celebrating victory in Port Stanley. At his wedding that July his nose had still been swollen and a little bruised. It was all most unfortunate, thought Geraldine, that her only acceptable wedding photographs were those taken from a distance.

"When will it be half-time?" she enquired of Ellis.

"Not for a while my love. Excited by it all?" He smiled broadly at her while squeezing her knee.

"Oh gosh yes," murmured Geraldine. "Riveted. But how long actually, to be precise, is it until half-time? They seem to be have been playing for ages."

"Each half is a half hour, my love."

"But we've been here for much longer than that. I've been sitting in a puddle of rainwater for at least that long."

"A half hour of playing time, my love."

"But even allowing for the bands, the cheerleaders, the singing and everything, it must be at least an hour already of playing time," she said, a note of panic entering into her voice. She knew that a New York minute was very brief – could an Indiana half hour be very, very long, an eternity even?

"Half an hour of playing time means when the ball is in play, Sweet Pea."

"The actual ball? Being played with?" asked Geraldine.

"Well, I wouldn't put it exactly like that, but yes, that's what it means. It's really difficult to predict how long a game can go on for. It may be three hours, even four. If the lightning comes back again, it could go on indefinitely. That's one of its mysteries. It's like some great story, unfolding before one."

So she could be here forever. With damp feet and a heavy heart. Of course, she thought, many things go on too long. Wagner operas, for example, Shakespeare's plays, car journeys with small children. A life could easily be spent doing things that go on too long, only to find one's days were over. What a terrible irony, she thought. She would just have to try and make the best of it: there was no alternative. She wrestled her attention once more back to the game. It was really rather like rugby, she decided, and not a bit like football. Of course, she remembered, football was called soccer. It was all so complicated. She could barely recollect the rules of Snap, yet alone recall the ins and outs of rugby. I'm just not a team player, she told herself. Did Pilates count as a sport? She was quite certain it wasn't yet part of the Olympics, and, as she wondered when she would next be able to attend a Pilates class in St John's Wood, she engaged her inner core. Yes, that felt very good. She could feel her spine lengthening, her seated posture instantly improving. There was a light tap on her shoulder.

A woman leant over from the seat behind. "You couldn't sit down a little lower, could you, honey? My little boy can't see all the action with your head in the way."

She obligingly slid down her seat. Honestly, what was one supposed to do – decapitate oneself or something? It was too bad, sitting here wasting valuable shopping time, damp, drink-less, humiliated before thousands by a floral ensemble. She wondered what St Thérèse would do under the circumstances. It would certainly be a challenge for her, saint though she was. Perhaps St Thérèse had come across Brother Pepe on the Other Side?

That would be interesting, thought Geraldine, relieved that her little intellectual meanderings could keep her spirits up in very difficult circumstances. She was just idly considering what St Thérèse would have worn to an American Football game when, all of a sudden, it was half-time, and Ellis stood up, stretched, announced he was famished, and that perhaps now was a good time to proceed to the Press Box.

"I couldn't agree more," said Geraldine, delightedly.

They squeezed and squashed their way through people searching for lavatories and refreshment, then, taking a twist here and a turn there, navigated the corridors to their destination. It was a spacious, plate-glassed edifice, half way down the length of the stadium, with long lines of graduated seating. Most of the tailgate party were milling around by the top of the stairs leading to the seating area, clasping polystyrene cups and munching on large sandwiches. Geraldine smiled happily, pleased to be where she felt she nearly belonged.

"Everything is complimentary," explained Ellis, "so I suggest you go right over there to the counter and get whatever you like. Easier than me choosing for you, as I know my Sweet Dream can be a little picky. I'm just going to find the bathroom."

Geraldine wandered over and looked at the sandwiches and cakes piled on silver chargers. She wasn't very hungry, but found herself a plate and helped herself to a delicately sized cheese roll. Two young men in short sleeved white shirts and purple bow ties were busying themselves behind the counter.

"Can I help you, miss?" enquired one.

"Well, it would be fabulous to have some champagne. But if that's not possible, perhaps I could have a glass of white wine? Sauvignon Blanc would be super, but at a pinch a domestic Chardonnay would be fine, as long as it's not too oaky." She smiled sweetly.

The young men looked nervously at each other. "No alcohol here, Miss," said the taller of the two.

"Really?" she said, trying not to convey the shock, panic, and disappointment that had swept over her.

"Perhaps there's a bar somewhere else where I might get a glass of wine?"

The duo exchanged glances again. "No alcohol in the stadium, ma'am," said the other, ageing her instantly.

"No alcohol in the stadium?" she asked incredulously, thinking of Lords, of Goodwood, of Twickenham. The names reeled before her. Except they didn't reel. They merely loitered, teasingly in front of her. She paused. "Not even beer?" Not that she would drink beer, not if it was the last beverage available on this earth.

"No beer. We have sodas, juices, coffee, teas and hot chocolate. No Sprite, though, we're right out of that."

She tried to focus, turning her thoughts to the absence of that soft drink, perhaps brewed by fairies and imbibed by pixies. She attempted to persuade herself of the merits of watery coffee or thick sweet chocolate. But all she could think of was wine, white wine, any wine, and the taste of its sharp, cold dryness on the tongue, its revivification of the flagging soul, its numbing effects on catatonic boredom. How could it be bad to serve wine? Think of the dull people made interesting, the tedious conversations rendered scintillating. And food – who could not forget that beef stew elevated by wine becomes boeuf bourguignon? And what would *coq* be without its *vin*? Wine was the life blood. Look at holy communion, she thought, you couldn't transubstantiate ginger ale. It was all simply outrageous.

"How am I supposed to get through the second half of a football game without wine?" she wailed. The young men looked again at each other. One mouthed silently, questioningly, "Security?"

Ellis returned from his comfort break. "Is this young lady bothering you?" He enquired, most jovially.

"Oh no sir, we were just explaining... er... what was on offer."

"Yes," said Geraldine, recovering her poise. "Can you believe it, Ellis, no Sprite! What's an elf supposed to do?"

* * *

Giles and Phyllida were sitting in the kitchen of their house somewhere near Salisbury Plain, agonising over the *Daily Telegraph* general knowledge crossword.

"I cannot understand," said Giles, exasperatedly, "why every week they have clues relying on one's knowledge of Nobel Prize winners. No one can be expected to have heard of any of them," he finished, crossly, adding more sugar to his coffee.

"I saw that," said Phyllida. "It's supposed to be no more than one teaspoon, remember?"

"You're a hard woman, darling. Sometimes I think you missed your vocation as a prison warden."

"Thank you, Giles. I am merely saving you from yourself."

"But I don't want to be saved. I want to expire in a mountain of sweetness. And cake."

"Have you touched the walnut cake in the larder? You know that's for tea."

"I just tested a slice. To see if it was up to your usual standard."

"Really, Giles," said Phyllida, exasperatedly. "And your mother will be down in a minute. It must be nearly ten thirty. Do you think you should take her some tea?"

"I am not encouraging the old bint. It's bad enough that we've got her till Monday. I don't know why Antonia can't have her more often."

"Well, you know why. It's because Antonia lives in Holland Park, and your mother thinks one shouldn't spend the weekend in London."

"I thought when she moved to that flat in Pimlico…"

"Belgravia, darling, remember it's Belgravia," laughed Phyllida.

"When she moved to Pimlico I thought she'd have more to occupy herself. There was that phase when she went to a concert at the Wigmore Hall every lunchtime."

"That didn't last," interjected Phyllida, "and then there were the watercolour classes."

"Didn't last either."

"And the book club with that woman she knew in St George's Square."

"Disastrous. I'm surprised there weren't legal consequences. And playing Bridge seems to have fallen by the wayside."

"Yup! Quite what one does with an easily bored delinquent eighty-seven year-old is beyond me," said Phyllida.

The kitchen door was flung open. "Are you talking about me?" asked Mrs Acton-Payne accusingly, resplendent in a blue flowered dress with a large brooch.

"Goodness," said Phyllida, "you look awfully smart, Monica."

"One tries to make an effort, even if it is just a tiny house in the country near a railway line."

"Well, Mother, there's always Antonia in her interior-designed, seven-bedroom mansion in Holland Park. You're not obliged to come here."

"Nobody stays in London at the weekend, Giles," his mother said reprovingly. "I once had to go to Fortnum's on a Saturday morning to collect a small basket of glacé fruit, and the doorman was most surprised to see me."

"But Antonia is there. And of course, Geraldine." said Phyllida.

"Geraldine is not there this weekend," said Mrs Acton-Payne, triumphantly. "She has gone to America."

"Really?" said Phyllida, surprised, "What on earth for?"

"She has gone with a man." She was delighted to see she had caused a sensation. "Yes, I know all about it. She told me everything," said Mrs Acton-Payne, with tremendous satisfaction.

"Well!" exclaimed Phyllida. "You never mentioned anything about this when you were with us in France. Of course I remember her receiving all those text messages. But I hadn't realised there was a grand romance in the offing."

"Well, naturally Geraldine confided in me. I am terribly discreet. But, yes, I would say it's quite serious. She showed me a photograph on her phone that a waiter had taken of them both at the Ritz. He practically made one swoon."

"What, the waiter?" interjected Giles.

"Don't be silly. The American. He looked exactly like Cary Grant."

"Isn't he dead?" asked her son.

His mother ignored him. "And he's six feet three and terribly rich and generous. I think it's just what Geraldine needs."

"Talk of the devil," said Giles, looking at his phone vibrating on the table. "Or rather the devil's ex. It's Jonty."

He picked up his mobile. "Jonty, dear boy. How are you?"

Jonty looked across the grass from his park bench to where a pair of teenagers, a girl and a boy, were locked in a passionate embrace. Rather early for that, he thought. "All well here, Giles, just wanted to get a bit of – ah – info. Do you happen to know anything about Geraldine and this new man? According to Cassie they've gone off – would you believe? – in a private plane to watch an American football match. Bonkers. I know I shouldn't be, but quite honestly Giles, I feel concerned about the whole thing."

"Sorry to hear that, Jonty." He put his hand over the phone and mouthed to Phyllida, "He's worried about Geraldine. Going off with this new man."

"Oh," said Mrs Acton-Payne, her voice trained over the years to be heard over several hockey fields, "tell him he has nothing to worry about. Geraldine's gentleman is terribly, terribly good-looking and frightfully rich."

Giles and Phyllida simultaneously glared at the old lady.

"Have you got Monica there?" enquired Jonty, still surveying the over-amorous adolescents. "Does she know anything about it?"

"Hand that thing over to me and I'll talk to Jonty," said Mrs Acton-Payne.

"No need, mother," whispered Giles. "Now look, Jonty. You're not to worry. Geraldine's perfectly capable of looking after herself, and besides," he paused, "she's no longer your wife."

"She's still the mother of my children," said Jonty, lamely. "Grown-up children," responded Giles.

"Let me speak to him," said Phyllida. Giles meekly handed the phone to her.

"Now, Jonty," she said firmly, "Geraldine is perfectly entitled to go wherever she wants with whomever she pleases. That is the inevitable consequence of divorce, and you must accept that, just as she accepted you leaving her." Giles's jaw dropped. "I say, that's a bit harsh, darling."

"I know you're right, Phyllida. But it's hard." Jonty's voice trailed away. The boy and girl were now inextricably entangled with each other on the grass.

"I'm sorry to have bothered you. But one worries," continued Jonty. "It was so nice seeing you all last month." He sounded wistful. "Let me know when you're both up in town again and come and have dinner in Battersea. Sally and I would love to see you."

"That sounds like a good plan, Jonty. We'll look forward to that," said Phyllida, handing the phone back to Giles. It fell from her fingers, and Mrs Acton-Payne nimbly grabbed it before Giles could reclaim his property.

"Jonty!" barked Giles's mother, "if you want what I think you want, don't shilly-shally around. Life's not a rehearsal, dear. I, at eighty-seven, know that better than anyone."

"There," she said, giving the mobile back to her son. "That has rattled his cage, as Rupert might say."

Giles and Phyllida looked at each other, speechless. "Well" said Giles, "if that's the case, I'll have that slice of cake after all."

Jonty returned to the flat, pondering. What did he want, he wondered, for whatever might be the remaining years of his life? Monica Acton-Payne, for some reason, thought she knew what he desired, but then it was difficult to imagine a more definite or decisive woman. He opened the front door, and, hearing whirring noises, punctured by the slop slop sound of water, guessed his wife was at her potter's wheel. When he and Sally had first bought the flat, he had earmarked the small room next to the main bedroom, with its old-fashioned washbasin and sideways view of the park, as a sort of minuscule study-cum-dressing room. He thought of painting it – or rather getting someone else to paint it – a dark ox-blood: a good, masculine colour, the limited wall space an excellent backdrop for his regimental photos. And he could put the campaign desk that had belonged to his grandfather under the window, and a row of brass hooks on the back of the door for his old uniforms. It would be his man-cave, his little retreat from the rest of the world. But unfortunately, just after moving to Battersea, he had gone on a course – completely unnecessary – to improve his IT skills. The Ministry of Defence had sent him to some godforsaken conference centre somewhere in the depths of rural Warwickshire, and he'd returned to find that his putative cubbyhole had been taken over by Sally and her pottery equipment. The room now resembled a children's kindergarten, with blobs of clay over the floor, and a rainbow of paint streaked up the walls. There was no curtain at the window, and the atmosphere always felt a little damp and earthy. What Geraldine would say to a mess like this was unimaginable, he thought, as he opened the door tentatively. He leant against the frame. Sally looked up briefly. "Were you thinking of making coffee?" she asked.

"I wasn't, but I could. I was just going to watch you, you know, potting something. If you don't mind."

She said nothing, and continued with her modelling. Her foot tap tapped on the electric pedal, her hands skilfully ran up and down the wet clay, caressing it as it rose up between her fingers. Quite provocative, thought Jonty. Pity she doesn't lavish the same attention on flesh. He watched for several minutes more, till the emerging vase crashed into a wobbly collapsed mound, and Sally let out an exasperated screech. "There!" she cried like a petulant schoolgirl. "Look what you've done. You put me off, standing there, watching me like that. I'll have to start all over again."

"Sorry," he said, "I was only taking an interest. That's all. I'll go and make the coffee now. Oh," he said as an afterthought, "I ran into one of my men in the park."

"You make it sound like you're Robin Hood," said Sally, humourlessly.

"You know what I mean. A chap from the Army. Nice young man with his wife and baby. Just moved to Battersea." He looked at Sally. She was pulling a face he had become familiar with – a sort of sucking in of the lips, accompanied by a sideways turn of the head. He thought for a moment.

"It's funny, you know, but every time I mention the Army, you do a special face. Like this." He mimicked her expression, then smiled, encouragingly. "It took me a while to associate the face with the sentiment, but I'm right, aren't I? I expect I'm a bit of a bore about the Army, but the thing is it's been such a big part of my life, it's difficult not to talk about it a lot."

"I realise that," she said, wiping her hands on an old rag. "Forgive me for saying this," she paused. Why is it, thought Jonty, one knows that whenever

230

a sentence starts like that, it's going to be something one doesn't want to hear? "I'm afraid I just can't bear the thought of you having been a serving officer."

That was a bit of a bombshell, thought Jonty, surprised. He was taken aback. "Well," he said, carefully, "I'm not sure what to say. This is the first time you've said anything about your, er, objections. It's not as if you've suddenly found out about me and the Army. We've been together now for – what? – two years, and you only tell me now you don't like my Service connections. What on earth is all this about?"

Sally gazed through the clay-spattered window, as she thought back to those heady days in the 1980s. She remembered the wonderful sense of companionship, the endless sitting round camp fires till late into the night, drinking cocoa and toasting crumpets. And all those other women that she had come to love, all with their different backgrounds, their different stories to tell. She'd lost touch with most of them, although she'd bumped into a few again on a couple of marches. She felt her eyes fill with tears.

Jonty sprang forward, hitting his knee on the potter's wheel, placing kindly hands on her shoulders.

"What's up, Sal? What have I done wrong? Tell me! Please! I don't want you to cry."

She shook him off and found a paper tissue to blow her nose. "I should never have married you. It was bad enough that you were still married to someone else when we got together, but even worse that you were a colonel."

"Would you have preferred it if I'd been a brigadier?" he asked, innocently enough. "Noooo," she shouted. "I hate… I hate war."

"Well, so do I. But I'm afraid as long as war exists, we will need men, and women of course, to fight it. We can't afford the luxury of lying down and letting the enemy run all over us. Think of Hitler. Appeasement didn't work with him."

"I hate the Army." She was beginning to sound like a small child.

"You know, Sal, the Army isn't just about fighting. Look at all the humanitarian efforts. At the first hint of a disaster, the armed services are there, helping."

She blew her nose loudly again, trying to regain her composure. "I'm sorry," she said, "I should have said all this, you know, when we first met. I should have been more open, more honest. But I was just so pleased to have a man, I thought, well, I'll just put up and shut up. And it didn't seem polite to tell you, especially when you went to all the trouble of leaving your wife and that sort of thing…" She trailed off.

Jonty covered his face with his hands. This was all unbelievable. She'd gone off with him because she didn't want to be impolite? And what were all these things she hadn't told him about herself?

"I just kept thinking," she said, somewhat recovered, "it was all such a shame. When we first started chatting to each other on the Tube we didn't really say much about ourselves. We used to talk about the weather, what we'd seen on the television last night, that sort of thing. I remember you saying you liked watching the nature programmes, and so did I. But you never mentioned the Army, not then. I think the first time it cropped up was when we'd gone for a drink at that café in Sloane Square, and by that stage I'd grown to like you quite a lot." She tailed off. "I'll go and put the kettle on."

Jonty let her pass, as he stood there, in that ugly little room, remembering. Of course he recalled the conversations about nature programmes. They'd always been a bit of contention in his household then, as Geraldine claimed she only had to see the opening credits of *Wildebeests in the Kalahari*, or *The Secret life of Anteaters* and she'd begin to itch, uncontrollably, all over.

"Coffee's ready in the kitchen," shouted Sally, interrupting his reminiscences. He sat opposite her at the table, stirring in milk with a large spoon. Where were all the teaspoons, he wondered, irrelevantly. He eyed her apprehensively. She opened a tin of biscuits and offered it to him. "No thanks," he said, as she took two. "I think I'd like – I need – to know more about your objections to me."

"Well, it's really not you. You're quite sweet."

"Thanks," he said, sarcastically.

"No, it's really all my fault. I should have told you more about myself, about Greenham Common, that sort of thing. It's been such a significant thing in my life."

"Greenham Common," he exploded. "You were there!" he exclaimed. He remembered the longstanding blockade at the RAF base, the women's camp outside the perimeter fence, the protests against the government's decision to allow Cruise missiles to be based there. The camp had gone on for years, but in its heyday in the eighties, the nightly news was full of those dungareed women, holding hands, united against the wickedness of men with their beastly weapons of mass destruction. He looked at her across the kitchen table in disbelief. "How much time did you spend there?" he finally asked.

"Oh all in all about five years, on and off. Mother joined me too, for a bit. She's been a lifelong supporter of CND."

Jonty thought of the frail but feisty old lady in her cottage in Hampshire, tending her chickens and her little vegetable garden. "Well, why didn't your mother say anything, if you couldn't? She must absolutely loathe me."

"I wouldn't put it quite as strongly as that. But she did say I was mad when I told her about you. I don't know, there just never seemed to be the right opportunity to tell you about my, er, misgivings."

"So what else have you done, apart from Greenham Common?" Jonty enquired, wondering why prospective wives don't come with a full curriculum vitae and several references.

"Um, well, the anti-invasion of Iraq marches, obviously. Oh, and I was a protestor on the Newbury bypass site – although it's not as if that had anything to do with war. Do you remember it? It was quite a big thing, really."

"Yes, of course I do. That was that eco-warrior guy, Swampy, wasn't it?"

"Yes, he was a lovely young man. Ever so nice. He still sends me Christmas cards. He's living in a commune in Wales now with his family."

Jonty groaned and placed his head in his hands in despair. "I'm surprised you had time to be a librarian what with all this protesting going on."

"Yes, it was difficult. But I managed to get my Chartered Institute of Library and Information Professionals qualifications despite all my other commitments."

"Well done you," said Jonty, raising his head from his hands and staring at her in disbelief.

"There's no need to be nasty. It was quite difficult you know."

"Quite difficult!" he shouted, "Quite difficult! Actually, it was quite difficult for me to leave my wife, but I thought, God only knows why, that you loved me. That you really loved me."

"Oh, I liked you... I liked you very much. With reservations, obviously."

"Obviously."

She continued, "I did think of pulling out, you know, before the ceremony at Chelsea Town Hall, but I thought it was probably all a bit late. I didn't want to upset you."

"Didn't want to upset me? It wasn't an invitation to a dance. It was a commitment to a life changing decision. A commitment which you clearly didn't want to make." He sat, baffled by her. He resumed. "And so you thought you'd leave it until now to upset me? After over a year of marriage? After all I went through, leaving my lovely, beautiful wife." There – oh Christ, he had said it.

Sally stood up. "Well of course, if you see beauty and loveliness in some sort of contrived, over-groomed, vacuous creature who must spend most of her life shopping, I feel very sorry for you," she spat out, venomously.

Jonty held up a hand. "Pax, pax," he said, "this is going too far. You're the one against war and all that. Let's say no more. I think we both know this is at an end. There's really nothing more to discuss."

She got up angrily from the table. "You're right. There isn't. Go back to that silly woman with her ridiculous dog. And don't you forget I own half of this flat. I'm going to pack up my stuff and go to mother. I wish I'd never sold my little place in Fulham. I'll ring up Wendy from the library. She's got a big estate car. She'll drive me down to Fordingbridge." She walked purposefully out of the room. It's surprising she didn't slam the door, thought Jonty, hearing her call out for Tiddlepuss.

He sat for some moments, numb. Then he picked up his phone and dialled Hugo's number. He felt nothing but relief.

Chapter Eleven

It took a complicated process of decision-making to come up with cranberry juice mixed with soda water. A Cosmopolitan for the unsophisticated, thought Geraldine, bitterly. She stood, like a sulky teenager, mulling over her fate. "Hi!" said a friendly voice. A young, fresh-faced man stood next to her. "I thought you might like me to explain the pictures to you." Geraldine looked round. Yes, the walls were covered in photographs and portraits of men, serried ranks of mug shots, yards and yards of footballers commemorated by oil or camera. What explanation could be called for? That they had ears, eyes, noses? That they all took part over many years in a pastime designed to enrage those of a sensitive and non-American disposition? I am behaving badly, she thought to herself. Come on, snap out of this. Manners maketh *moi* – that must be the watchword.

"How kind, lovely," she said, charmingly. "I've been standing here for ages hoping someone might explain things to me."

The young man's face lit up. "Let's start at the beginning, with the first known portrait of an All Saints football player."

"Super!" she said, "lead me to it."

He led. They studied every gilt-framed picture with the concentration of a microbiologist searching for clues in a Petrie glass. Each player was described, his contribution to a particular game picked over. There was something comforting, mesmerising, about the young man's voice. Awesome, he said, over and over again, and Geraldine joined in. Awesome, she replied, mechanically, hoping she would never utter the word again on her return home. They reached the very last player: Arsenio Hapgood. "What a lovely name," said Geraldine. "And a lovely guy", her young companion added. "He had just become a professional footballer after leaving All Saints, when God spoke to him. He's now a priest in Bolivia."

"Awesome" said Geraldine, peering at this paragon. She looked away. "Oh my goodness" she exclaimed, "the second half has begun. I mustn't keep you a moment longer. I have been absolutely monopolising you."

"It's been my pleasure," said the young man, sincerely, shaking her hand. Geraldine moved away and found a seat next to Hal, who was eating a hot dog.

"What d'ya think of it so far?" he asked her, through mustardy bites. "Great day, isn't it?"

"Yes, awesome," agreed Geraldine. "And inspiring, too," she added, "my mind has been wandering, here and there, and all over the place, with football-related thoughts and musings."

"You don't say," said Hal, apprehensively, chewing his sausage.

Geraldine recited:

"'The Assyrian came down like the wolf on
the fold
And his cohorts all gleaming in purple and
gold,'

"That was what first sprang to my mind. Byron of course."

"Brian?" said Hal, scratching his head, "is he here?"

"I said, 'Byron'. Lord Byron."

"You don't say," said Hal, again. He thought for a moment. "Was that the Wolves you mentioned? Are you talking about Wolverhampton College?"

"Well, yes, or no, really – I mean the Assyrian was only like a wolf. Not actually a wolf."

Hal took another bite and pondered a while. "The Syrians? Where do they come into it?"

"No," said Geraldine patiently, "Assyrian. 'The Assyrian came down like the wolf on the fold'."

"Yup, I got that one."

240

"'His cohorts all gleaming in purple and gold'."

"Purple and gold!" said Hal, relieved, clutching at something familiar. "All Saints colours!" "Exactly!" said Geraldine, beaming, "that's what made me think of it."

"Of course!" smiled Hal, edging away. "Say, can I get you something? A cookie, perhaps? I'm going to get a coffee."

"No thank you, I'm fine," replied Geraldine, as Hal hurried over to his wife.

"Gloria," he said, who was talking to Pat, "she is nuts." He pointed his finger to his head, and whirled it round, descriptively. "Who is?" enquired Gloria.

"Ellis's bit on the side, lady friend, whatever… Geraldine. I tell you she is nuts. Rambling on about Syrians and purple wolves co-habiting with God knows who. Brian came into it somewhere. She's talking like some goddammed crazy woman."

They looked over to where she was still sitting, now animatedly talking to Barb.

"It probably means something in her language, Hal, don't forget she's from England," said Pat, reassuringly.

"So you don't think I should say anything to Ellis?"

"Nah," said Gloria, "it's not going to last. It never does with him."

"Well, you know best, Gloria," he said, shaking his head. He collected a cup of coffee from the counter, then, noticing Ellis was deep in conversation with a couple he didn't recognise, glided towards them. "Hal," said Ellis, "this is the President of Wolverhampton College, and his wife, Donna."

"Pleasure to meet you both," said Hal, in a friendly manner, "it's a great game going on, isn't it? Pretty equal sides, too," he added, diplomatically. The president agreed, and his wife nodded. "Excuse me," said Ellis, "I'm just going to bring Geraldine to meet you guys. You'll love her, she's English."

Hal looked at Ellis with horror. "Are you sure that's wise?" he asked, quietly. "She's just been saying some pretty weird things to me. Seems to have a bit of an interest in Syria. I couldn't make out what she was talking about."

"Aw, that's just her accent, Hal. She's a great girl, really. You probably misunderstood her. Geraldine!" He beckoned her over. "Come and meet the President of Wolverhampton College and his wife: George and Donna Jackson."

"How do you do?" said Geraldine. "We're good," replied Mr Jackson.

"Yes, real good," replied Mrs Jackson, "and I just love listening to you English speaking. Your Royal Family is quite wonderful. Are you what they call a London cockney?"

"Um, no," said Geraldine, "I think you'd find a cockney sounds quite different from me."

"We have a friend in Utah who comes from York Shire. She sounds a little like you. Are you from York Shire?" continued Mrs. Jackson.

"Actually I was born in Roehampton. It's a suburb of London."

"So you are a cockney then," Mrs Jackson rejoined, accusingly, "if you were born in London…"

"I believe the criterion for being a Cockney is being born within the sound of Bow bells, although that must be very difficult now with modern-day traffic."

Hal gave Ellis a worried glance.

"A cockney sounds like this," pronounced Geraldine, "'allo, Missus Jackson, 'ave yer taken yer dawter up the apple and pears? She's lawst 'er dog and bone." Hal raised his eyebrows, and excused himself. Mrs Jackson expressed great interest, and claimed to be fascinated by the translation. "But what I would love," continued Geraldine, "is to know more about Utah. Where exactly is it, and do you have to be a Mormon to live there?"

The Jacksons replied with patience and courtesy, and Mrs Jackson was quite unfazed by Geraldine's query about whether she was one wife of many, and kindly explained with good humour that polygamy was relatively unusual, but tended to attract rather too much publicity.

"I'm so relieved to hear that," said Geraldine. "It must be awfully difficult deciding which wife would do what. I mean who would…"

Ellis interrupted with a loud laugh of forced heartiness. Was Hal right, he wondered? "Geraldine, my love, I think you should go and talk to Maryjo. She's been sitting there all on her own for a while."

"Perhaps she's contemplating her mortality?" suggested Geraldine, brightly, trotting off obediently.

Ellis watched her. She was gesticulating wildly. What could she be talking about now? It was true she could come out with a few strange utterances. Had he noticed that before – before this weekend away? He wasn't certain. But despite this, there was a vivaciousness about her, which, although unrelaxing most of the time, could also be most charming. Aw, he thought to himself, this isn't going anywhere, anyway. It doesn't matter. What the heck. He couldn't have come on his own to East Cork. He chuckled to himself. It was kinda expected among his friends that he would bring a date, always nice-looking, but not usually as voluble as this one. He looked at her again. He wondered, suddenly, what her husband had been like. Army officer, wasn't he? He pictured a moustached, goose-stepping, ram-rod straight disciplinarian. Perhaps that was why she was so skittish – perhaps it had all been a terrible strain being married to a militaristic martinet?

244

That was probably the explanation. She's more to be pitied than censured, he thought.

Curiously, Geraldine was thinking of her husband too. She had surreptitiously looked at her mobile phone and noticed another text message from Jonty. It must be practically the early hours of the morning back in Blighty, she said to herself, with longing, as she read: 'Hugo rang. Nice children we've got.' What a sweet thing to say, she thought, putting the phone back in her bag. Yes, they are nice. Cassie can be rather loud of course – that was her grandmother's genes, most probably – and Hugo should stick up for himself more, but on the whole they were both very satisfactory. She and Jonty had been lucky. She pictured him, sitting behind his newspaper, his paunch just lolling over his trousers, his boyish face studying the racing results, or puzzling over the crossword. It was sad that the only man she had ever loved would not grow old alongside her, but would face his dotage with a woman with whom he shared little mutual history. Did he mind that, she wondered? And did he sit there now, in his flat on the wrong side of the river, glasses falling off his nose, slumped on the sofa, murmuring 'old thing' to Sally? Geraldine had never really cared for being called 'old thing', wishing neither to be blessed with advancing age nor indeed thing-ness. Yet, after being called every conceivable endearment man could devise, she could rather fancy being an 'old thing' again.

Many hours later the game was pronounced over. One side or the other had won by a very small margin. Geraldine thought it was All Saints, but she couldn't be sure as she was so tired. Trying to make conversation with the natives had been exhausting, not to mention all the other activities of the day. She wanted very much to be tucked up in bed. Typically, there had not been enough room in the many golf buggies for all the guests to go back to the condo, and so she found herself dragging her feet yet again past the tennis courts, her blister oozing into her still-damp espadrilles – surely this would result in trench foot? – and trailing her horrid floral poncho behind her. I am a wreck, she thought. Ellis marched beside her, his energy undiminished. She wondered if she could ask him for a piggy back, but not being a ninety-pound wisp she felt she probably shouldn't. Then she remembered she didn't even know where she was sleeping.

"We'd better get our bags," she said wearily, as they were buzzed in to the hall of the condo.

"Didn't you leave your bag here, as I told you?" asked Ellis.

"You never told me to leave it here. You just told me to pack my bag. I left it by the wardrobe so it was out of the way of the bathroom."

"Looks like a bit of a misunderstanding my love." Or a foot in the mouth, thought Geraldine, remembering the earlier book signing. They seem to be big on misunderstandings round here, she muttered resentfully.

"Well I'll just go and find it, and meet you upstairs," she said.

"Yes, there'll be nightcaps and sandwiches on the top floor," replied Ellis cheerily.

She took her espadrilles off, and walked slowly down the stairs. The corridor was now back to normal, but the door ahead closed. She opened it tentatively and switched on the light. She had never been to Panama, but imagined that it, and its canal, looked very much like this room. There was a trench, about five feet deep and three feet across, dividing the bedroom in two. She was on one side, and on the other side, covered in drying cement and dust, was her suitcase.

"No," she cried out loud, "Please no…NO!" She crouched on the floor, rocking herself like a baby. "This is the worst weekend I have ever had in my life," she crooned mournfully. "I think I want to die."

Somehow – maybe it was a miraculous intervention from the long dormant Brother Herring – somehow she managed to stand up, take a very deep breath, and, as a psyched-up footballer at the beginning of a game might utter, yelled, "I will not be defeated!" She grunted and pawed at the floor like a rampaging bull. She took a running jump at the canal, flew in the air, lost her footing the other side and landed awkwardly on her ankle. The one with the blister. She was now the wrong side of the room – admittedly reunited with her suitcase – with a twisted ankle. She knew from her experience yesterday in the lift there was no point shouting. She would have to get herself, and her suitcase, back across the vast hole. She couldn't jump now, so she would just have to climb down into the trench, which had a trickle of a mud-like substance at the bottom of it, and climb up the other side. She sat gazing at the hole, contemplating her task, rubbing her swelling ankle. She decided the best thing would be to throw the suitcase across, and hope that it didn't land in the slime below, then she would somehow get herself across. She stood up painfully and threw the suitcase. It reached the other side. Then she gingerly placed her good foot on a small ledge on her side of the canal, and then tried to fling herself to the other side. Her hands caught the jagged edge of the dug-up flooring, her bad leg dangling dangerously as her good leg remained on the ledge. She was diagonally sprawled across the trench, with no hope of ever being anywhere else again.

It was in this position that Ellis found her five minutes later. His face turned from horror to amusement. "I should take a photo of this."

"Help me," Geraldine cried, "I am absolutely at the end of my tether."

With a certain amount of laughter from Ellis and screams from Geraldine, they managed between them for her to reach the other side of the room.

"I can only hop," she said, looking down at her filthy white capris.

"Oh my love," he said, "do you know what you look like. I think you have to be the most ridiculous woman I have ever met. Come on, let's get you upstairs. We're in Chick and Pat's room."

"Not with Chick and Pat?"

"No, Sweet Pea, they've had to go back to Chicago. It's all clean and ready for us."

Geraldine could hardly speak. "Has it got a window?" she croaked.

"It's got two."

"Is there a bathroom?"

"Yup, and that's got a window too."

Geraldine thought she might cry.

The bedroom was on the second floor – not big – but comfortable. She hopped into the bathroom and ran a bath, tossing off her dirty clothes. She sank into the hot fragrant water. She thought this might have been the longest day she had ever had. There was a knock on the door. "May I come in?" asked Ellis. He opened it, holding a large glass of white wine.

"There's ice in the bedroom for your ankle. I'm going up for a whisky with the boys. You take your time, Sweet Dream, and I'll see you soon."

Geraldine lay in the bath sipping her wine, occasionally topping up the hot water. You have to have the bad times to savour the good, she thought, dreamily, pulling herself out and wrapping a large, warm fluffy towel round her damp body. She hopped into the bedroom, found the ice bucket, and placed some ice on her ankle. The swelling was already subsiding. Her bites looked better – clearly the effects of Dry Martini on insect infestations deserved an article in *The Lancet*. She just managed to slip her nightgown on before subsiding into a deep, much-needed sleep.

She lay, motionless, for four hours, then woke up with a start, hearing a noise from outside. She looked at her phone. Five o'clock. There was no sign of Ellis. Delicately, she placed her foot on the bedside rug. Her ankle twinged a little, but it was definitely better. She stood up. It was still dark outside. She wondered what the noise had been – a car perhaps, or a dustbin lorry. She opened the door and walked out onto the landing. All was quiet. She remembered there was a little kitchen on this floor, so she thought she would see if she could make herself a cup of soothing herbal tea. It was the door at the end. She was quite certain of this. She turned the handle, and was just about to reach for the light switch when she realised to her horror she was in a bedroom. She could dimly see across to the double bed, two sleeping bodies spooned together, the one with his arm round the other. It was Ellis, yes, she was absolutely certain – although she was peering, contact lens-less through the gloaming. It was Ellis and – she could just make out – the young man in the chef's apron. Although presumably by now he'd discarded that.

She silently closed the door and went back to her room.

Surprisingly, she fell almost instantly asleep again, despite her dreadful trauma. When she awoke once more it was 7.30, and she was still alone. On the night stand was Ellis's watch, and underneath it a note.

'Sweet Dream. Hope you are refreshed! I have to go off early and see someone, but will be back after Mass. Chip rang to say he's had to fly Stevie to Phoenix, so won't be able to take us back to London. I've reserved flights from Chicago for this evening. We'll catch a ride to the Windy City at three! See ya! Exx'

Geraldine read and reread the note several times. Then she looked at his watch. Rolex. How could it have been any other make, she thought, wryly. But why had he left it behind? And what about last night? What was the correct etiquette in this situation?

Should she say: I accidentally opened the wrong door and saw you in bed with the hired hand. Or should she keep quiet? It was a difficult question to resolve, and one she would have to carefully consider. Meanwhile, she must get dressed. She put on her seersucker skirt and a white polo shirt, and her pink ballet pumps. She would not, she decided, be wearing any more All Saints merchandise. She climbed the stairs to the sixth floor, hoping for a cup of coffee. There was no one there except the young man in the chef's apron, and, more recently her lover's bed – although, strictly speaking, she corrected herself, it was the young man's bed. It would have been particularly unusual to have awoken in the middle of the night and found a threesome. Although anything seemed possible here. And she didn't much care, anymore. Nothing mattered except her desperate desire to go home.

"Good morning!" she said, with false brightness. The young man looked nervous. "Hi there," he said, "coffee will be ready in a moment."

"Excellent," said Geraldine. "I could literally murder for a cup of coffee after the night I've had." The young man dropped a plate. It smashed in a hundred pieces on the wooden floor. Geraldine shook a finger at him. "Butter fingers," she cried, "I do hope that wasn't Wedgwood or something." He bent down and cleared up the broken china, his face reddening.

"Hi, you early birds!" chirrupped Barb, tottering in in her ostrich mules. She was wearing an All Saints shirt, which she had belted at the waist. It was a little too short for a woman of her age.

"Oh Anthony. Is that another plate gone? What is it with you and plates?"

"I don't know, Mrs Hattencote, I'm all over the place this morning."

"Didn't you sleep well?" asked Geraldine, solicitously.

"I have to go and collect some doughnuts," he said, ignoring her question. He poured coffee into mugs and handed them to the two women without looking at them. "I'll be back shortly."

"He's useless, that one," remarked Barb, as she stirred her coffee. "But it's so darned hard getting help round here."

"He's probably good at something," said Geraldine. "After all, he's very good-looking." Barb smiled. "Yeah, but he's a butt boy, know what I mean?"

"Really?" said Geraldine, disingenuously, "Goodness, I'd never have guessed."

"Yeah, Chuck got mad at him 'cos he kept bringing his boyfriend into the condo. Chuck's very hot on security. Likes to know what's going on, who's coming in, who's going out, that sort of thing. Our place in Florida is like fucking Alcatraz. This friend

253

of Anthony's is from the liquor store downtown. Perfectly nice person, but Chuck seems to have taken against him. Chuck does that a lot. Won't have him here at night. But you know what, if I was to lose Anthony, I'd be stuffed for these game weekends. Anyway, his friend will be round later to collect the empties, so you'll see him. He may remind you of someone," she chuckled, drinking some more coffee. Then her mood darkened, her eyes narrowed. "About yesterday," she began.

What about yesterday? thought Geraldine: there were so many incidents to choose from.

"You know," continued Barb "the… er… water."

"Oh that, Barb. You know, you have been a sweet and generous hostess, taking in a guest you have never met. A guest who so far has set off two alarms, made a complete idiot of herself at a dinner party, not to mention all the ridiculous *faux pas* which just seem to come from nowhere. I've totally diminished your entire stock of white wine, and frankly, if I spent any longer here I too would be drinking copious amounts of… er… water. I quite understand. Really I do. And you shouldn't feel bad about it." She paused, "I don't suppose, um, you've tried to do anything about it?"

"Have I heck. I've been to rehab twice. Stayed off for three months, then, aw, I don't know, something happened, and I just went back on it again. I guess

I seriously started drinking vodka when I was about thirty. I found it stopped me eating, I don't know why. But it was just what I needed after three children in four years. Wow, was I a fattie then!" She looked down at her cocktail stick legs with some pleasure. "And then I found it stopped me thinking, too, which was even better. But I manage to keep it under control. No one ever sees me drunk. I'm what they call a functioning alcoholic. Chuck just ignores it. If he doesn't address a problem, then it doesn't actually exist."

"I'm sorry, Barb. It sounds awful."

"It's ok. As long as my liver functions, I'm fine. And you know what, everything looks better through vodka-tinted glasses. Even Chuck!" She cackled. "But what about YOU. What about you and Ellis? Where's that going?"

"I don't really know. He's not what you'd call the one. He's very nice, obviously, but I've found this trip quite a challenge. He seems a little different here to what he's like in London."

"Aw, tell me about it," said Barb, "they're all the same. They get here for these game weekends and they regress. Jumping around like twenty year-olds, stoopid juvenile behaviour. But Ellis has a lot going on. You know, what with his wife, and his son, of course."

"Yes, I'm not quite sure about his son. What IS actually going on there? He never mentions him – well, hardly ever. I don't even know where he lives, do you?"

"I sure know where he lives, and I reckon Ellis is there right now."

Geraldine looked genuinely surprised. "You mean he lives here? In East Cork? Why ever didn't he come to the game?"

"Because he's in prison, hun. You'd have seen it flying in. Huge great barn of a place in the middle of nowhere. One of East Cork's big attractions."

"Goodness! How absolutely awful. What on earth did he do?"

"It was a robbery that went wrong. He ended up shooting a guy in a jewellery store. Luckily the guy survived – and was able to identify Robert, Ellis's son."

"But how terrible. How could he have a son like that?"

"Aw, I don't know. Kids go wrong, don't they? Ellis was never around while he was growing up, always work, work, work came first. And Candy was a useless mother. Useless woman really. Robert got packed off to a fancy boarding school when he was ten, hated it, didn't get into All Saints, and ended up in some weird college in Montana. God knows why." Barb poured more coffee. "Then of course Candy got ill, and everything just went downhill in that family. I don't think Ellis knew if he was coming or going."

"How terrible for him," said Geraldine.

"Yeah, I agree. But I shouldn't really be telling you all this. He keeps things pretty close to his chest. Never talks about it. Do you think you'll stick with him?"

"Well," said Geraldine, pausing for time, "I'm not sure I'm quite the right person for him. I mean, it's great in London – you know, having a man to go out with. And he's been very generous to me. But there's no – what I think you'd call – chemistry. You know…"

"He doesn't float your boat?"

"Most definitely not. The boat hasn't even been launched."

Barb laughed again, "The woman he brought last year said much the same thing. Well, as far as I could understand. She was German. The one the year before was Italian, and before that Portuguese. I think there was a Pole one time, too. None of them spoke good English. We were real relieved when we heard he was bringing a Brit. At least you talk our language. Kind of," she added, as an afterthought.

"Oh!" said Geraldine, incredulous, and not a little deflated. "He must be working his way through the European Union." There was something rather demeaning about being one of so very many.

"Yeah, it's weird really," continued Barb. "It's almost like he chooses women he has no hope of ever properly communicating with. Except you of course."

But he hasn't really communicated with me very much, though Geraldine. During their expensive dinners together he'd often talked more to the waiters and the sommelier than her. Even during their Sunday lunches, seated at her Georgian card table in her little white painted kitchen, they hadn't discussed much – the ballet they'd seen the previous week, perhaps, the amusing antics of Bolly, but nothing especially personal. But then, she considered, had she ever talked about anything very significant with Jonty? When he was in the Army much of their time had been spent apart. And of course, their post-Army life had been somewhat cut short. She tried to remember when they had first met. It was so long ago. A different life, really. They had both been at university together, in the West Country. He was reading Geography, she English. They had friends in common, but it wasn't until the very last term that they had started going out. Her father blamed Jonty for her failure to shine in her Finals. "Blasted boy," her father used to remark to her mother, "she would've got a First if it wasn't for him." Geraldine's mother remained silent during these tirades.

She was quite certain that, even confined to a nun-like existence, her younger daughter would never have applied herself to scholarship. Next, Geraldine was working for a publisher in London, and Jonty was at Sandhurst. And then they'd married. She didn't even think they'd talked much on their honeymoon. They'd travelled to Venice – so romantic, Geraldine had thought – and Jonty had gone down with a bug within twelve hours of arrival, and had been confined mainly to the bathroom. It was a lifetime, thought Geraldine, of limited communication. The more she dwelt on it, the more she realised she knew very little about Ellis, and very little about her husband. Ex-husband, she corrected herself – a term that, even after two years, she had never quite got used to.

Geraldine put down her mug. There was nothing else for it, she was going to have to ask that other question running through her thoughts.

"Do you think Ellis bats for the other side, too?"

"Excuse me?" asked Barb, puzzled.

"You know…"

"What?"

"Oh nothing really." It was all too much effort. Her mind felt in turmoil, what with reminiscences about Jonty, disturbing images of male couplings and a Euro pageant of women, all once here, in this condo, struggling to make themselves understood. And she mustn't mention anything about Anthony, busy with his doughnut collecting. It might affect the delicate balance of the household arrangements. No, she would say nothing. That was the sensible thing to do.

Barb looked at her watch. "I wonder where everyone is? I think Chuck has organised transport to Mass. Will you be going?"

"Gosh yes," said Geraldine with feigned enthusiasm.

"You don't have to, hun. I'm staying put."

"No, I think I shall definitely go." I am never coming back here, thought Geraldine, so I may as well indulge in the full experience of a weekend at All Saints.

"Then it's back here for brunch – if Anthony can get himself organised – and then off everybody goes."

"I bet you breathe a sigh of relief."

"Yeah, kind of. But then it's also just me and Chuck on our own." She tailed off, "and then we return to Florida first thing tomorrow morning."

"We were going to go back with Chip, but apparently we're now going to Chicago and getting the flight from there. Ellis seems to have organised everything."

"Oh he's good at that."

Half an hour later Geraldine was standing outside the condo waiting for a lift to Mass. It would have been perfectly easy to walk, she thought, especially now the temperature had dropped, and yesterday's sudden downpour had dried to no more than a few puddles here and there. She thought about Ellis, sitting in prison, waiting to see his boy. It was a scene she was familiar with only through films and television. Would his son be behind a grille, like a wild animal in a zoo, manacled to a gun-toting guard, or would visitors and prisoners be sitting at wooden tables, their allotted time together eating into their very souls as prison officers looked on? And would he tell her about it? Probably that was as likely as a confession about last night's bedroom-hopping. At least I am no longer hopping, thought Geraldine, staring down at her now restored ankle.

A golden coloured Hummer drew up. It was an immense warlike beast, more suited to the killing fields of 'Nam than the orderly shrubberies of East Cork. Those who had elected for morning worship boarded. It was quite a climb upwards. Gloria, bursting out of too tight jeans, could barely mount the vehicle.

The journey to the Cathedral took no more than three minutes at a sedate speed. All around the campus, there was evidence of an overnight clean-up operation. Every blade of grass stood to attention, every piece of litter had been disposed of. The place was immaculate. You could eat your dinner off it.

They stopped in front of the huge doors of the Cathedral ("copied from the Baptistery doors in Florence," Hank helpfully pointed out) and spilled in. Inside, the roof soared up into the copper dome, the one Geraldine had spotted – what now seemed like years ago – as they had flown in to East Cork. It was a tremendous feat of engineering, the huge cupola, peppered with tiny glazed holes. The walls of vast stone blocks, so perfectly ordered from the outside, were scarcely visible under the elaborate decorations inside.

Saints, angels, Madonnas and Christs all chased each other round in a pantomime riot of colour. What with the garishness of it all, and the narrow shards of morning sun piercing through the dome, one almost needed sunglasses. Geraldine looked round in amazement before being ushered to a pew by Maryjo. They knelt to pray before Mass began. Gloria remained seated, but bowed her head reverently. Her jeans prevented her from bending. Geraldine closed her eyes and prayed too.

She prayed for Bolly and her family. She prayed for Ellis and his wife and his criminal son. She prayed for Mrs Mankowitz and Mrs Acton-Payne. And then she prayed for herself. She paused briefly, wondering what, in her list of prayerful desires, she would most like. She wanted to be home. She wanted that most of all. She wanted not to be bothered by things – anything, really. And she wanted, like Greta Garbo, to be left alone. Not, you understand, God, not totally alone. Not the sort of alone one reads about, where your rotting corpse is found months after your demise and no one has even realised you're not there, no, more the sort of alone where you're in a lovely little bijou residence with an apricot poodle for a quiet afternoon, and you have a hardback novel to read, and the prospect of an outing to the ballet or the theatre in the evening. That was the sort of alone she meant, God. But then, that was a problem in itself, she thought. With whom would she be going to the ballet or the theatre? Her companion of choice for the last few months had been Ellis. Did she really want to continue with that? Of course, it's nice to have a theatre buddy, and probably even better if they are gay. But Ellis was sort of manifesting himself – if that was the right word – as not gay. Really, people had to be one thing or the other so one knew where one stood.

And then there was the sex. Oh my God, thought Geraldine, suddenly. Oh my God! She had had sex with a man who had… No, she didn't even want to think about it. There are some things even unlimited numbers of antiseptic wipes cannot purge. She would have to go to one of those anonymous clinics in Harley Street. She couldn't possibly go to Dr Crean at the St John's Wood Surgery. He would merely sneer at her in a superior manner. No, she'd have to find the right sort of clinic. And give a false name. She felt hot and breathless at the thought of it. Supposing there was something dreadful wrong with her? Something permanent or even fatal? What would she tell her family? Would she suffer much? Oh, she felt wretched. Had she been standing, her legs would have collapsed, jelly-like, beneath her. She must pull herself together, she said firmly. God, please give me clarity. And strength. Now. There was nothing else for it. Ellis would have to go, the old heave-ho. She would tell him on the way home. At some point. She felt a sharp dig in her shoulder. She opened her eyes. Everyone else was standing. She quickly stood up as the procession of priests and acolytes made its way down the aisle. "It's Father Linus," whispered Gloria, "he's a heart throb."

He certainly was – tall, slim, his golden hair a little too long, he looked like a carved angel as he walked slowly past Geraldine's pew. She caught a whiff of Eau Sauvage, mingled with incense, as he trailed along, his cream silk vestment catching like a bridal train on the carpet. 'Carpet!' exclaimed Geraldine to herself, suddenly diverted from her woes. Whoever thought of having carpet in a church? It was so impractical. And unhygienic. She contemplated it as they were bidden to sit. It was a Madonna blue; the sort of covering that was closely woven and slightly scratchy. Geraldine remembered it was a type that had been very popular in the 1970s. Her own bedroom had been wall to wall in it, a sludgy shade of olive green. What was it called? It had a particular name that she simply couldn't remember. There will be increasing moments like this, she thought – trying to recall simple, everyday things which elude one's dying brain cells. She imagined Candy, her blonde curls fragrant with luxurious shampoo, sitting in her expensive home, her tiny body merely a vessel for an eviscerated mind. And then she realised they'd been though two hymns, several readings and probably many Hail Marys and a lot of bells, and she'd missed them all. She'd been too busy thinking, she said to herself, purposefully.

"Please be seated," said the Angel, as he stood in the pulpit, a single shaft of sunlight bathing his beautiful face with an ethereal glow. His voice was clear, mellifluous, almost seductive, with only the faintest trace of an American accent. His pronunciation was clearly garnered from a lifetime of travel and long sojourns in exotic locations. Had he preached amongst the poor of Haiti, laboured in the African jungle? He would probably feel more at home on the French Riviera, or the Hamptons. His hands, which he used theatrically to illustrate his point, even from a distance, looked elegantly pale and well-cared for.

But the rich need religion, thought Geraldine, just as much as the poor. Probably more, really.

"And so we turn to misunderstanding…" Geraldine's ears pricked up. For what was this weekend except a misunderstanding? She remembered the All Saints professor yesterday, in the bookshop, his history of misunderstanding not the popular choice when up against a bloody tale of Mafia crime. Perhaps he too was here today, in the congregation, still smarting at his very short queue of would-be readers. Geraldine looked round to see if she could see a bespectacled, tweed-clad, bow-tied man, looking disappointed. There were at least a dozen that met the description. She returned her attention to the sermon.

"How often have we made assumptions, only to find we have been misguided. We have allowed ourselves to be taken in by superficial appearances…"

Yes, that is true with me, thought Geraldine. I have been taken in by too many soufflés at The Ritz, too many hand-tied bouquets, and far too much fine wine. I am a foolish, soon to be elderly, muddled woman.

"Jesus was the real deal," intoned the priest. "If Jesus was with us now, he wouldn't drive up here to the Cathedral in a Jaguar or a Porsche. He wouldn't be in fancy designer clothes." That is ridiculous, thought

Geraldine, coming from a man in a silk dress. And why shouldn't Jesus have a Porsche. At least it would be quicker than going by bus.

The congregation was standing, as the priest processed out. Apparently they were all expected to go for coffee afterwards. Geraldine thought longingly of the church in St John's Wood that she occasionally attended. There, they always served a glass of Tio Pepe after morning worship. And how appropriate that would be here, she thought, later, as she stirred her weak *americano*, for a place founded by Brother Pepe Herring.

"Come and meet Heinrich Kord," said Bud, bearing down on her with a Teutonic-looking gentleman with gold rimmed glasses.

"Haircord!", exclaimed Geraldine with pleasure, "I've been trying to remember that word all morning. Thank you so much."

The man looked at her apprehensively. "Geraldine's from England," explained Bud.

The man's faced brightened. He spoke with the remnants of a German accent. "How I admire your Protestant work ethic, your Princess Anne, your London parks and your Mr Bean."

Geraldine tried to return the volley with a paean of praise for his homeland. She paused.

"And how I love your Battenberg!"

"Heinrich is a Professor in the School of Architecture."

"Super!" said Geraldine, "I'm a tremendous admirer of the Paleo-Gothic School." She beamed. "And there's such a lot of very interesting architecture round here. I love all these large stone buildings. They're very... solid. That must be a great comfort in the event of a tornado."

"Yes," agreed the Professor, "although we haven't had a tornado here since 1976, we still build to withstand excessive wind."

"I'm staying in a very curiously planned building," continued Geraldine, engaged by the conversation. "It's just opposite the tennis courts. I think it must have been designed by a madman – and I know it must be a man, because, honestly a woman would never have come up with anything as daft as this: it's on six floors, but the fourth and fifth floor is a separate apartment belonging to someone else, so all you do is go up and down, and up and down – all day long – utterly pointless flights of stairs." She warmed to her theme. "There is a lift (or elevator, I suppose one should say) but I got stuck in it for ages on my first day. And then the basement flooded with raw sewage..."

"Excuse me," said the Professor, "I have just seen a friend over there."

Geraldine smiled vaguely, and stood, holding her still-full cup and saucer, wondering whom to talk to next. She saw Chuck with Father Linus by the door, and decided to join them. Father Linus was now wearing a pair of black trousers with a very fitted black shirt. She noticed he had astonishingly green eyes and very long lashes. His hair was pushed back from his chiselled brow. Should she challenge him over Jesus's preferred mode of transport?

"I see you were talking to Professor Kord. He designed our condos," remarked Chuck. Geraldine's full cup wobbled precariously, spilling brown liquid over the priest's shoes.

"Oh goodness I'm clumsy," she said, extracting a tissue from her bag and bending down to mop the priest's feet. Italian leather loafers, she noted. Her grandmother had always told her, amongst many other recommendations of varied usefulness, to look at a man's shoes. She stood up.

"I better get this lady home before she does any more damage," joked Chuck.

"Gosh yes, I am so sorry. I hope it hasn't gone on your socks!" (a thin, fine cashmere, she observed) "And super sermon. Thank you! It's given me lots to think about!"

Chuck bustled her out of the room before she could further elaborate, and they boarded the waiting

Hummer to make their three-minute journey brunchwards. Geraldine felt the excitement mounting inside her. She was in the home stretch. Tomorrow morning she'd be in her little house, surrounded by her lovely bits and pieces and her beloved Bolly. She glowed with happiness.

Chapter Twelve

Ellis was already upstairs in the party room, half way through a Bloody Mary. Despite his perma tan he looked pale and haggard. Geraldine bounced towards him. "Do hope you had a lovely time with your friend." She noticed he was now wearing his watch, and he had a funny little ink stamp on his hand, like Cassie sometimes sported when she had been to a concert or a festival.

"Yes, well, a friend in need and all that," mumbled Ellis.

"And of course I didn't see you this morning. You'd already gone when I woke up. Did you sleep well?" She smiled at him, sweetly.

He took a large gulp of his drink. "Yes, Sweet Pea, I slept real well. And you?"

"Like the dead. For most of the night," she added. "Oh look," she said, turning her head, "there's Anthony, with a plate of chocolate eclairs."

Geraldine could barely contain her excitement. She felt like a schoolgirl at the end of term. She wanted to jump up down and sing. Barb came over to her with a huge glass of white wine. Her cup ranneth over. Surely goodness and mercy shall follow me for the rest of my days, she chortled to herself, still in religious mode from Mass.

"When do we leave for Chicago?" she asked Ellis.

"I'm just trying to sort that out, Sweetheart. We were going to hitch a ride with some old friends who are staying on campus at the Boris Inn, but unfortunately Bing's hip slipped last night after the game, and he's going to be prone on the back seat, so there's not enough room in the car."

"But we will get to Chicago, won't we?" Geraldine felt a rise of panic in her chest. "How far away is it?"

"It's about a two-hour ride by car to the airport. There's a bus which takes over three hours, if the worst comes to the worst."

"A bus?" said Geraldine, faintly.

He looked down at her and smiled kindly. "I know my princess wouldn't like a bus. I'm trying to find a limo. Trouble is, as you can imagine, they're heavily booked now. But don't worry, my love, I won't let you down."

Typical, she thought, just when one gets oneself all keyed up, something goes wrong. "If I don't get home I shall go mad," she said to him, dramatically.

He looked alarmed. "Let me get you another drink. And I'll go and make some more calls."

He came back with her refill, his phone glued to his ear. "You won't have to go mad my love. I've got the last car in town. It's coming at three."

"Yippee!" she yelled, unnecessarily loudly. Everybody looked round.

Maryjo wandered over. "You know, Geraldine, you've really dispelled all my impressions about Brits. I mean, I've always found them very reserved. And real quiet."

"Oh, but I am terribly reserved," exclaimed Geraldine, "practically totally off limits…" She truly thought she was. Perhaps this place, East Cork, changed people. Ellis certainly wasn't anything like he was in London. Even the quizzically raised eyebrow seemed to have dropped. But what was the real Ellis, she pondered? The suave pinstriped guy, smelling the wine cork, toying with a truffle, standing when she entered the room – was that him? Or was he the man in knee-length shorts and a baseball cap? The man lying in bed with another guy? Of course, we're all complex, she thought, and we're all a little bit chameleon, adapting to our surroundings. She looked round the room. Barb had her glass of 'water' in her hand. Gloria was talking to Chuck, while munching on an enormous ham roll. Maryjo was sitting next to Ellis, showing him photographs on her mobile phone. Bud was chatting to Anthony, who was whipping up a cocktail.

The comfort of friendship, thought Geraldine, is astonishing to behold. All these men, who have known each other since they were eighteen, still friends forty years on, still finding pleasure in each other's balding, broadening company. Except of course Ellis, who seemed to have retained a full head of hair and a boyish girth. What an enigma he had proved to be!

Nevertheless, she would have to think of something to say about not wishing to see him anymore. But was that what she wanted? It wasn't, strictly speaking, the problem of seeing him that bothered her. And – really – one could hardly say to someone who lived round the corner that one never wanted to clap eyes on them again. That would make walking down the street an act of peril. What if one bumped into each other, say, in the fishmonger's, would one call out 'hello', or turn one's back and walk away? It wasn't so much that she didn't want to see him, it was more that she wanted to make it quite clear that, while she was perfectly happy to be in his company – perhaps go to the occasional opera or ballet – she wanted a minimum personal space of about two feet. Yes, that was it, really. She was very happy to see him, at a small distance. But then, if they were sitting next to each other at Covent Garden that would be less than the two feet no go zone, although, of course, in these circumstances, they would be alongside, and not facing, each other. This was all quite tricky. The bottom line was, she thought… and then inwardly laughed. Really one should keep bottoms out of this, the less of bottoms the better. No, the truth was she did not want any pouncing. In fact, now she'd thought about everything so very clearly, she realised that she might just as well go back to seeing the elderly widower who'd liked opera so much. He'd rather fallen by the wayside. She'd just carry on into old age enjoying the company of elderly men who could provide pleasant conversation, and an appreciation of arias. That would be more than enough. But would it? What about a warm embrace when bad news was broken, or an arm round the shoulder after a difficult day? What about waking up and knowing someone was beside you? Someone other than an apricot poodle? She thought of Jonty, his plump number two wife busy with a shapeless clay pot.

Geraldine had never been to the mansion flat in Battersea, but had heard extensively about it from Cassie. It overlooked the park, and most of the furniture had been bought from a Scandinavian store. "Daddy had to put it all together. It's that flat-packed stuff. The dining table's terribly wobbly. I practically had to hold on to my lunch to keep it from falling off," Cassie had remarked. "Sally does her potting in the box room. She makes the most awful things – cups

275

with funny handles and jugs with irregular spouts." Geraldine had met Sally once at a funeral. She pictured her clad in thick tights and a long voluminous skirt, her fingernails caked with clay, her spectacles spattered from the potter's wheel. It just showed that men could be very unpredictable.

"We went there for lunch last Sunday," Cassie had told her that summer, "you know, when it was frightfully hot. She wasn't wearing tights. She had a pelt, Mummy, honestly. I couldn't believe it. Her legs are like an ape's." Geraldine had pondered on this often. She'd thought of Jonty and Sally, even her children, sitting at the wonky table, knocking over misshapen crockery, dribbling and spilling their food and drink like a chimpanzees' tea party. And she wondered, over her lifetime, how many days – or even months – she had spent epilating and waxing. And it turned out her husband preferred a hairy woman. And retrievers. It was all most unfair. She gazed out of the window. People were already drifting away from the condos. Improbably large cars were meandering out of the driveway. In an hour or two, all would be empty of footballing revellers.

She was wrested from her thoughts by a young man standing at her side with a bottle of white wine. "Anthony sent me over. He said you are very partial to a domestic Chardonnay." She looked up at the tall

276

young man and gasped. This was the guy from the liquor store. This was Anthony's boyfriend. And he looked like a young, red-headed Ellis.

"Yeah," said the lookalike, pouring her wine, seeing her surprise, "you've noticed. Everyone says the same. But, hey, we're not related. Just one of those things. And he's the lucky one, right, with the dark hair? All my family are red-heads. We're Irish. That's near England, right? You know, I heard that everyone of us has a double out there"

Yes, thought Geraldine, a doppelganger. Where was hers, she wondered? Somewhere lovely, she hoped. An apartment overlooking Fifth Avenue, perhaps, or a house on the Rue St Honoré. She didn't like to think of her twin slumming it, ill-dressed and down on her luck. What funny little twists and turns one's mind takes when one lets it. And this double, standing before her, was clearly the man in the bed in Anthony's room. It hadn't been Ellis! If only she'd put her contact lenses in she'd have been spared the agony of uncertainty.

However, relieved though she was, none of this solved the problem of where Ellis had actually been at five o'clock this morning. Not the staff bedroom, clearly. But nevertheless a bit of a mystery. Or maybe just another misunderstanding. Still, no batting for the other side, just one of the home team. And no trip to the discreet Harley Street clinic, she realised, with enormous relief. Oh, no, but wait, slow down, she thought, suddenly reining herself in: what about all those Euro-trash women, her predecessors? The beauty pageant of erstwhile girlfriends who had slipped through these doors? She would still need to make a trip, clinic-wards. She thought of all the advice on this very matter she had thrown at Cassie in the past. "Oh Mummy," Cassie had wailed, every time the phrase 'responsible sex' had been mentioned, "I'm a bloody nurse. Of course I'm sensible." If only I had followed my own advice, thought Geraldine. This is just further proof of my increasing senectitude.

"Are you all packed up, my love?" Ellis glided over. "The car should be here in ten minutes."

Geraldine excused herself and raced downstairs to the bedroom. She pulled off the sheets and folded them in a neat pile on the bed. She folded up the towels and put them on top of the sheets. She went round the bathroom with an antiseptic wipe. Several. She checked her bag. To her horror she realised she had never given Barb the little presents she had brought from London. She placed them on the dressing table, and, extracting a visiting card from her purse, scribbled, 'Thank you, Barb, for being a wonderful hostess. Come and see me in London.' And she genuinely hoped she would.

She returned upstairs, where the party was now breaking up. There was much hugging and slapping, and wiping of tears welling at the corner of eyes. Eventually, with many promises of everyone seeing each other again, very soon, they extracted themselves and headed for the front door.

Parked outside, attracting some attention, was a stretch limousine. It was flamingo pink, and bore the legend, in a deeper pink, 'Princess Pick Up. For your Party Princess. And Hen Nights too'.

"Goodness", exclaimed Geraldine. "I wonder whose car that is."

"Ours, my love. It was the last car available in the whole of town."

She smiled as the chauffeur opened the door for her. "Look," she squealed, "the upholstery matches my shoes."

"I guess this is definitely my Liberace moment," joked Ellis. And she laughed too, safe in the knowledge that she knew for certain Ellis didn't really mean it.

They took the route past the university to the toll road, the coppery dome a-glitter in the watery sun. Ellis put his hand on hers. "Was that something or was that something? The weekend? Wow!"

Geraldine observed that the inky stamp, presumably administered by some zealous prison officer admitting visitors for the day, had been rigorously scrubbed. The back of Ellis's hand was reddened with the ferocity of nail brush and soap. He noticed her stare, and withdrew his hand, turning to his briefcase at his feet, retrieving his diary.

"Now, what does your week look like, Sweetheart? I thought we might go to the Festival Hall. Yo-Yo Ma is in town."

"Um, I think I'm going to be a bit busy this week, what with having been away and all that."

"You're always so busy, my love," he remarked. Was there a hint of sarcasm in his tone? Geraldine looked at him. His face was impassively mild.

"What about dinner next weekend? We still haven't tried the new French place in Blenheim Avenue."

"Could I get back to you about that? There's a possibility I might be going away on Saturday to some friends who have a cottage in the Cotswolds. Bolly's coming, too," she added.

"Of course, my love. Just as soon as you know what you're doing, you let me know." He looked out of the window as the Indiana countryside passed them by.

"But thank you for this weekend. It's been such fun. I've never had a weekend quite like it," she said, truthfully.

He smiled. He knew what was happening. Yep, he could see it coming. It had happened before, it would happen again. He didn't much mind. Not at all. She was a nice woman, he thought, a bit kooky, but an amusement. Yeah, a nice, kooky woman. What the hell? It had been a bit of fun. Mind you, there was that damned apricot dog. What was all that about? That was more than kooky – that was bordering on the insane. And then some of the things she came out with. He looked at her, sitting next to him on the pink seat. She was dropping off, her eyelids sliding down over her big eyes, her mouth slightly open. Too much wine at brunch, he thought, rather cruelly. And then last night – what was going on there? Why was she coming out of that bedroom down the corridor at 5am? He hadn't been able to settle – well, who would, with the morning he'd been facing – so he'd been making himself some tea and toast in the little kitchen. He couldn't believe she was up to anything. She didn't seem interested in that kind of stuff. Frigid, or bordering on it. Maybe she was just sleepwalking? But wouldn't that be more evidence of insanity? Who was it in that play he'd seen who'd sleep walked? Lady Macbeth, that was it. She'd been insane, too. But he'd liked Geraldine, though – yes, he'd really liked her. He remembered the first time he'd spotted her in the fishmongers back in St John's Wood. There had been something so complete and definite about her, so elegant, as she had rejected several of the proffered fishes before alighting on the chosen one. Heck, she was definitely not the chosen one – how could she be? When you've had the love of your life, you don't get another. He'd go and see Candy soon. He hadn't seen her since way before last Christmas. He thought of his wife, with her mermaid golden hair and her huge pale blue eyes. They hadn't altered with her illness. She was still beautiful. He glanced again at Geraldine, now breathing deeply. She was pretty, with her little snub nose and her honey-touched hair, but not as pretty as Candy. No one was. He sighed. Then an idea came to him. He got out his phone and texted frantically.

"Oh my goodness," exclaimed Geraldine, waking up with a start, "have I missed seeing Chicago?"

"I'm afraid we're skirting round the outside of Chicago. The airport is west of the city. You've missed nothing except freeway," Ellis didn't look up from his phone. "We'll be there in ten minutes."

Geraldine removed her small leather make-up pouch from her bag and applied lipstick. "I always get excited at airports," she said, brightly.

"Do you my love? That's nice." He sounded vague, distracted. "Oh, one thing, Sweet Pea: we'll be going to different terminals."

"Sorry? What do you mean? Are we not flying back to London together? Where are you going?" She sounded distressed. He looked at her, appraisingly.

"Slight change of plan, I'm afraid. I'm going to have to fly to LA. Work problems have suddenly cropped up." He indicated his phone, "texts have been flying while you nodded off."

"I see," said Geraldine, biting her lower lip.

"I'm really sorry about this my love, but work is work. The driver will drop you at the international terminal. Go to the British Airways desk. They'll sort you out."

Geraldine looked out of the window. She felt distraught. She hated changes of plan, especially when travelling. Her face burned with rage. She pressed her cheek to the cool glass. She was more than disconcerted. Count to ten, she said to herself. Take deep breaths. Drop your shoulders. She counted. She breathed, she dropped. She turned towards him, her face composed, a smile ready.

"Poor you," she said. "I hope everything goes well." There was an air of brisk finality in her voice.

"Yes, it's a nuisance," he said "but it can't be helped." He felt a little bad at what he was doing, but hadn't he been a kind and generous companion for the last nine months? And nothing lasts forever, after all. The London office wasn't going to be as long a tenure as he'd expected. It would be Paris, then maybe, just maybe, after that he'd think about retirement. Let's see what happens, he thought.

The limousine drew up outside the international terminal, causing a small amount of amusement for the few straggling passengers standing around, their trolleys laden with suitcases.

Ellis helped Geraldine out with her bags. It was the least he could do.

"Well, thank you, Ellis," said Geraldine, pecking him briefly on the cheek, "safe travels and all that."

"You too my love," he said, returning to the car. "You too."

Chapter Thirteen

His voice rang in her ears as she walked through the automatic doors. She didn't turn to glance back. She held her head high, moving purposefully. She looked around for the right desk. She felt slightly numb as she stood in line at the check in counter. There was a couple in front of her with an enormous amount of luggage. The girl behind the desk kept weighing and re-weighing each suitcase. Eventually, Geraldine moved forward.

"What flight are you on?"

"The one to London," replied Geraldine, handing the girl her passport.

The girl tap tapped at her computer, frowning slightly as she stared at the screen. Her jauntily cut uniform and neck scarf contrasted with her pale face and smooth fair hair, swept up in a bun. She looked at Geraldine. "I have a seat for Mr Ellis Cater, but only a reservation for you. Your seat hasn't been confirmed."

"Well," said Geraldine, slowly, "I'm confirming it now. Here I am."

The girl went back to her computer and tapped further.

"Do you have an authorisation code?"

"What do you mean?" asked Geraldine, perplexed.

"These seats have been booked through Nathan Brothers's account. Mr Cater's seat has gone through automatically as he is a signatory on that account, but you, as a companion, need an authorisation code from Nathan Brothers."

Geraldine felt panic-stricken, almost faint. She gathered herself together and thought for a minute.

She spoke slowly, clearly, as if explaining to a child. "Mr Cater is now not travelling on this flight. He's had to fly suddenly, at the last moment, to Los Angeles. For work. So he's not using his seat... I, on the other hand, have an unconfirmed seat. Couldn't I just, um, have his seat?"

The girl paused, sensing the awkwardness of the situation. "I'm sorry, but it doesn't really work like that," she said, as kindly as she could. "I can't transfer tickets between passengers. And I can't issue your ticket without an authorisation code."

"But I have to get back to London." Geraldine could feel her voice rising, hysterically.

"Well," said the girl "I'm afraid to tell you that you are going to have to purchase a ticket."

"What?" screamed Geraldine, aware that people

were looking at her. She had a sudden idea. "Suppose I telephone Mr Cater and get the authorisation code from him. Would that work?"

"Of course," said the girl politely. "But if you're going to make a phone call, can I ask you to stand away from the line so I can check in the next passengers?"

"Yes," said Geraldine miserably, carrying her bags over to a small unoccupied counter. She found her phone and dialled his number. It went straight to voicemail. Hardly unexpected. She heard his confident American tones entreating her to leave a message and he'd call back as soon as he could. Yes, of course you bloody will, she thought angrily to herself.

There was nothing for it, she would have to buy a ticket. She queued up again.

"Any luck?" asked the girl.

"No, no," said Geraldine. "I think he must have taken off already."

The two women looked at each other, knowingly, the one with a certain defiance, the other with a measure of pity.

"So I'm going to have to buy myself a ticket," continued Geraldine. "Although I must say, it seems a bit of a rip-off considering Mr Cater has paid for a seat that won't get used."

"I'm afraid I don't make the rules round here," said the girl, "and I'm sorry, but I'm going to have to ask you to go over to the ticket desk. I can't sell you a ticket. I just check people in."

Geraldine picked up her bags once more, and made her way across the terminal. The ticket desk was empty. She stood, hovering over it. "Hello," she called, assuming there was someone lurking in the back. "Hello," she said, more urgently. After a few minutes of frenzied hand wringing and wondering what to do next, another navy-suited girl emerged.

"We're about to close," she said, unhelpfully, pushing her lank hair behind her ears. "The last flight boards in just over an hour."

"And I need to buy a ticket for it," said Geraldine. "It's an emergency!"

The girl, without speaking, clicked on the computer screen. "It's pretty full," she said. "There's nothing in Coach." She scrolled through slowly. "And there's nothing in Premium. There's one seat left in Club World. First is full too. It's Club World or nothing."

Now there's a surprise, thought Geraldine. And one seat paid for that's going to be unoccupied. "Right," she said, "here's my credit card."

She held her breath while the girl took her card and ran it through the system. She hadn't even bothered to ask how much the ticket was. It didn't matter. She just wanted to get on the plane.

"Ok," said the girl. "It's gone through. Here's the receipt. You need to go back to check in."

Geraldine felt depressed and dispirited. Picking up her bags yet again, she walked back across the terminal. She had quite forgotten about her inner core or her good posture. She slumped. She dragged herself over to the check-in desk. The same girl as before issued her with a boarding pass and explained where the lounge was situated. "You have a good flight," she said, as Geraldine exhaustedly turned towards Security. She was an automaton, a robot, proceeding through the airport as if in a dream. Or a nightmare, more like. She scarcely blinked, scarcely saw anything. She walked straight through Duty Free, where normally she would have lingered long, unbelievably not even noticing the colourful display of that French brand of foldable tote bags, hugely reduced for the discerning buyer.

"I am not myself," thought Geraldine, wearily. "I am an old, tired woman who has been horribly ill used." She walked heavily to the lounge, showed her boarding pass to the pleasantly smiling lady at reception, and found a seat. She put down her bags with some relief. She sat. She was so very, very tired. She found the strength to walk over to the small serve-yourself bar, and poured a very large glass of white wine. Back at her seat, glass in hand, wine trickling easily down her throat, she allowed herself a review of the situation.

Had Ellis knowingly put her in this position? She could easily have been stranded here, she thought. Supposing she had left her credit card at home, or her bank had declined the transaction? Did he care? And while it was certainly the case that she was preparing the ground for a cessation of relations with him, it was quite something else to have the rug – so to speak – pulled from under her. She had to be honest with herself (even if she was not going to be honest about this with anyone else): he had dumped her. It had been a period of dumping; first poor Phoebe, then Cassie – although she did now appear to be un-dumped. One could only hope that Hugo had decided to join the vanguard and dump the dreadful Abi, thought Geraldine. At least that would be something positive out of the weekend. And really, not that she wanted to dwell on it, but why on earth should Ellis dispense with her favours? Had she been that bad this weekend, she mulled to herself. She'd put her foot in it a few times – a foot in the mouth, as it were – and she supposed she had been a little bit embarrassing at the dinner party on Friday evening. But nothing very major. No, nothing that warranted dumping in so humiliating a manner.

She must devise a strategy. No one would be told

of the ignominious end to her friendship with Ellis. It had simply not worked out. That was it. The weekend had proven that they were just not suited to each other. And certainly no one would ever be told of the dreadful incident at the check-in desk. She hadn't even looked at her credit card receipt, nor would she until she was feeling confident enough to confront it and not scream out loud. To be fair, she acknowledged that Ellis had been extremely generous over the past few months. But perhaps that made it worse, since the final act was so unexpected. Perhaps it really was an oversight, and he intended her ticket to be paid for. The important thing, she said to herself, was not to dwell on it. Move on. Onwards and upwards. She stood up and shook off some crisp crumbs that had fallen on her lap while she had absent-mindedly nibbled.

An announcement over the tannoy indicated that her flight had been called. One step nearer home! She felt slightly cheered at the prospect.

She boarded the plane and found her seat. She was by the window, facing enginewards. The seat next to her, looking towards the tail of the airplane, was presumably the one which Ellis would have occupied, and, unsurprisingly, remained empty as the plane filled up. How very nearly pleasant she thought, a welcome glass of champagne in her hand, to finally feel relaxed, and to know that one was returning home. She looked at the inflight entertainment magazine, hoping there might be a good film or two to pass her time before sleep overtook her.

An air hostess walked up and down the aisle, offering hot towels, and checking seat belts, the pilot made various announcements, a safety video was shown, and the plane's engines throbbed into action. They were on their way. Geraldine only managed to view half of a film about a man and a woman who kept bumping into each other in unpropitious circumstances, only – one had to assume – to be reunited for life eternal in the final scene, before she drifted off to sleep. She was dimly aware of people running up and down the aisle, and perhaps even a slight commotion. Or maybe she dreamt it. When she woke up three hours later, somewhere over the Atlantic Ocean, the cabin lights were dimmed, and passengers were snuggled under blankets in various stages of somnolence. Geraldine was surprised to see that the empty seat next to her was now occupied. She was certain, she thought, though perhaps she had not been fully alert, not quite herself, that it had been empty on take-off. Someone must have moved there during the flight. He looked deep in sleep, cocooned in his duvet. She would have to climb over him to get to the lavatory, she considered, carefully raising herself up and disengaging herself from headphones and seat belt. It was quite a palaver getting out of her seat and delicately placing a leg over the feet end of the slumbering gentleman. Of course, she'd taken the precaution of removing her contact lenses earlier, and, as she said to herself afterwards, it really was very dark, but as she tried to get her other leg over, she somehow slipped and lost her balance, and fell, spreadeagling herself across the recumbent man. "Oh my goodness," she said, "I am so sorry. What a silly thing to do. I do hope I haven't woken you." There was no response. As her eyes adjusted to the dim light, she noticed he looked rather blue in the face. "Are you ok?" she asked. There was no reply. There was no doubt about it, she thought, this poor man was most unwell. She pressed a button to summon assistance, urgently, whilst simultaneously yelling, "Help, help." Soundly sleeping passengers sat up suddenly, fearing the worst. An air hostess ran towards her. "I think this man is dying!" shouted Geraldine, above the roar of the engines.

The air hostess looked relieved. "Don't worry, he's been dead for the last two hours. We did everything we could."

"Dead!" exclaimed Geraldine.

"Yes," said the air hostess. "He must have had a heart attack. There's a doctor on board. He tried CPR but it was too late. I'm afraid we had to put him somewhere. We couldn't leave him in Economy, next to a young couple with a baby. This seat by you is the only spare one on the flight. We're really busy tonight."

Geraldine eyed the corpse tentatively. He was in his seventies, grey, balding hair, in a beige tweed jacket and a now loosened striped tie. Poor, poor man, she thought. Presumably travelling on his own.

"I do think you might have told me," she said to the hovering hostess. "It was a bit of a shock, I can tell you. I fell on top of him."

"I'm very sorry. You were fast asleep when we moved him."

"Well, you could have left a note."

"It's all rather stressful when this sort of thing happens. Of course we're taught procedures to follow when we're in training school, but no amount of practice can prepare you for the real thing, can it? Let me get you some more champagne. And perhaps a herbal tea? That will calm you down."

Geraldine thanked her, and replaced her head sets. There was no possibility of further sleep. Really, she thought, what could be the odds for a passenger to be next to a dead party on both the outward and return journey? It seemed highly improbable. But at least Mr Bellingham had been in a box.

The air hostess returned with a glass and a mug of peppermint tea.

"Do you think he ought to be covered or something? I mean, I know he's got a duvet over him, but don't you think he should be fully covered? Wouldn't it be more... ah... respectful?" Geraldine suggested.

"I'll go and speak to my colleague," said the air hostess. She looked at the corpse's face. "Bless him. He'd asked for a whisky, but it was that busy back in economy, no one had got round to it. My colleague was just getting one of those little miniatures off the trolley when it happened."

Dying for a drink. How extremely sad, thought Geraldine, as she sipped her champagne. The hostess returned with a blanket, which she placed reverently over his face and torso, so that all that was revealed was his brown brogues poking out of the duvet.

"There, that's better, isn't it," she said tenderly. "I'm afraid this will delay everyone getting off the plane at Heathrow, but there's nothing we can do about that."

Geraldine had a quick word, a sort of inward prayer, with Brother Herring, should he be somewhere – available and listening – and able to assist with the poor man's soul and next of kin. Then she drained her glass. She had no faith whatsoever in the Brother's abilities, but felt this sad and solemn event had to be marked in some way. Sometime, later, breakfast was served, and Geraldine averted her eyes from her neighbour as she tucked in with relish to her croissant and fruit.

They landed at Heathrow shortly before 7am, and Geraldine could see from the plane's window the assorted vehicles of death approaching – the private ambulance, the doctor's car. She wondered whether she would be the last to exit, given her position next to the deceased. She was perfectly resigned to this. In fact, her resolve to remain calm in the face of life's strange events amazed her. She sat quietly, with her eyes closed, taking deep but measured breaths, practising her inner tranquillity.

"Are you all right?" said a voice. A young man in a crumpled suit stood in the aisle. "I'm a doctor. I thought your breathing looked strange."

"Really?" said Geraldine, "No, I am absolutely fine. I'm just looking forward to getting off this plane. I was practising my inner tranquillity, actually."

"Well there's no need to practise it for much longer. If you don't mind manoeuvring yourself around this unfortunate gentleman, I can let you out, and get on with my paperwork."

"Gosh, that would be a great relief. I'm absolutely longing to get home." She looked at the young doctor quizzically. "Haven't we met before? Aren't you a friend of my daughter, Cassie, and her boyfriend, James?"

"Of course! I thought you looked a bit familiar. I remember meeting you several times at your house in Fulham. It's great news isn't it?" he said enthusiastically.

"What is?" asked Geraldine, confused.

"Their engagement. I saw it on Facebook last night, before I went to bed."

"Their engagement?" she faltered, feeling both foolish and puzzled.

"Oh God. I'm an idiot. You haven't heard about it, have you? I'm awfully sorry, I assumed you would know, otherwise I'd never have mentioned it."

"I've been in Indiana for the weekend. News takes a while to percolate through to there. I dare say Cassie was waiting until I get home."

Really, thought Geraldine, as if she hadn't been through enough in the last few days. And to be told by a slight acquaintance next to a dead body! She felt she needed a long period of absolute quiet, preferably in a darkened room.

"Let's get you out of here," said the young man, helping her past the corpse. "You'll want to rush home now."

"I certainly will," agreed Geraldine, gathering her bags and making her way to the exit.

She emerged from immigration into the arrivals hall, a little sad at seeing all the eager faces waiting at the barrier for loved ones, and knowing there was no one there for her. She queued for a taxi, and soon settled into the back of a black cab with a sigh of relief. She looked at her mobile phone. It was awash with messages. Everything, she felt, could wait till she got home. She felt like Dorothy in *The Wizard of Oz* – clicking her red shoes and intoning, there's no place like home, there's no place like home. Although why Dorothy would want to return to Kansas was inexplicable. It was probably even worse than Indiana. They drove past Ellis's flat, without Geraldine giving it so much as a cursory glance. I am above curiosity, she thought, grandly, to herself.

"Here we are, luv," said the cab driver, "and you know what, I've been doing this job for ten years, and I never knew this was here," he said, indicating her little mews.

"Yes, everyone says that," replied Geraldine, wearily. She paid the driver and found her keys. There was silence. Her heart missed a beat with dread. Bolly always barked, even before she reached the door.

She opened the door and entered the tiny hall. Bolly limped towards her from the kitchen, a sticking plaster hanging from his ear. Archie and Jasper flanked him on either side, like burly bodyguards. "Bolly my darling," she cried, picking him up in her arms, "whatever has happened to you?" The pugs looked at each other apprehensively. Bolly managed a weak, loving lick of Geraldine's face.

"Is that you, G?" yelled Phoebe, from upstairs. "I wasn't expecting you back this early. Now, you're not to worry about a thing. It all looks worse than it is." She came down stairs, rubbing her wet spikey hair with a towel. She was still in her pyjamas.

"Have you had a great trip, G? You look well."

Geraldine very much doubted that. "What on earth has happened to Bolly? I knew about the ear. But why is he limping?"

"It was that ghastly girlfriend of Hugo's. Accidentally trod on his paw with her horrible high heels. Nothing broken. We took him to the emergency vet yesterday afternoon – bill's on the table – and he was all X-rayed and everything. Nothing serious, just a tad bruised. Bolly's making a bit of a meal of it, if you ask me. But lots to tell, G, lots to tell. While you've been swanning off, enjoying yourself, it's been all go here."

"What's this I hear about Cassie?"

"How do you know about that? Did she ring you?"

"Apparently it's on Facebook. Where IS Cassie?"

"She went back to Edinburgh late last night with James. His shift was starting early this morning. Apparently he asked her to marry him on Saturday evening. She said yes. They're going to go to Africa."

"Africa?" bleated Geraldine, "do you mean for their honeymoon?"

"No, they're going to work in some hospital outside of Cape Town. Two-year assignment. Can't remember exactly where. Actually, may have been Cape Verde. Is there somewhere called that? Honestly can't remember, G, all a bit of a whirl."

Geraldine sat down on the little gilt chair next to the door, her dog in her arms. She felt tired and a little faint.

"I think I need some coffee," she said, weakly.

"Great idea, G. I'll just dash upstairs and put some kit on. I'll be down in a min. Put the kettle on. I could do with some coffee, too."

Geraldine carried Bolly through to the kitchen and put him in his bed. The pugs followed. She stared at the pile of dirty dishes in the sink, at the saucepans soaking beside them, at the sticky granite surfaces, at the biscuit crumbs, at the greasy hob, the floor covered in nameless blobs of discarded and dropped food, and the dirty dog bowls – caked with the remains of a doggie dinner – and she screamed. She screamed loud and long, and apart from the shock on her apricot poodle's face, she really felt much better. She heard the thump of Phoebe racing down the stairs. "What's up G? Seen a ghost?"

"This kitchen is a disgrace. It is absolutely disgusting."

"Yes, well I wasn't expecting you for at least another hour. It would have been all tickety-boo if you'd come

300

at the right time. And it's only a kitchen, G, it's not life and death."

"It may be that to you, but to me it's, it's…" She was so angry she couldn't think of the right word. "It's sacrosanct."

"Hold your horses, G. Let's get some coffee down you, then you'll feel a bit more rational." Phoebe filled the kettle and slopped ground coffee into the cafetière.

"So what else has happened?" asked Geraldine, sitting down at the Georgian card table, which was smeared with jam.

"Where to begin, eh? Well, of course, you know now about Cassie. Lovely chap, James – she's a lucky girl. He was able to give Eileen some very sound advice about her fibroids."

Geraldine raised her eyebrows. "So Eileen's been round here?"

"Yes, she came over from Kilburn yesterday for Sunday lunch. I did my meatball special. Delish! Anyway, everything has gone a bit pear-shaped with the make-up woman, and, to cut a long story short, we're going to try getting back together again. I'm off to Chiswick this morning with the boys. We've decided Eileen's going to leave Pinewood, and we're going to get a bitch, and start breeding. Eileen will be a stay at home pug mum. It's worth a try."

Geraldine envisaged their little terraced house stuffed full of snuffling pugs. "You'll never be able to sell the puppies. You'll want to hang on to all of them."

"That's what Eileen said, but we're going to have to be firm. Maybe we'll keep one or two. Anyway, that's me and Eileen sorted. A new future all mapped out. Bit of a relief I can tell you. I couldn't face life without her, G, I really couldn't. Then of course we had Hugo and the ghastly Abi here. You won't be seeing her again, thank the Lord. I think Hugo has finally seen the light. It was Bolly's paw that did it. Can you believe this, G, she said it was the dog's fault. Said he'd ruined her shoes." She shook her head in disbelief.

"Did Hugo seem ok? Not too upset?" enquired Geraldine.

"Goodness me, he was as right as ninepence. I think he's realised he's better off without her. All that nasal whining and going up at the end of every sentence. Very tiring on the ears. And she's so orange! No, he's well rid of that one. He's such a lovely, kind, gentle lad. I'm sure he can do better." She rootled round in the cupboard for a packet of biscuits, and, disappointed finding there were none, opened the fridge in a quest for sustenance.

"Oh, and one more bit of news," she said, munching on the remains of a piece of Brie, "after lunch yesterday, and all the trips to the vet, and the awful

Abi ringing for a taxi and exiting in a huff, etcetera, etcetera, Hugo went over to Battersea, and Sally wasn't there. Gone to her mother's apparently."

"Well, there's nothing remarkable about that. Her mother must be nearly ninety. Probably needs her daughter's help for a while, or something."

"Ah yes, but there's more to it than that. Apparently the potter's wheel has gone, too."

"How did Jonty seem? Did Hugo mention that?"

"Yes, he said his Dad seemed quite jolly. Apparently they went to the pub and had a couple of pints and a good old chinwag. Male bonding and all that."

"I see," said Geraldine, thoughtfully.

"But what about you, G? What was your weekend like? Pretty swanky, eh, I imagine. And what about Ellis? How did it go? I thought you'd be coming back together. Love's young dream and all that." She looked at Geraldine. "Well, love's middle-aged dream," she corrected.

"Actually," said Geraldine carefully, "I don't think I'll be seeing him again. Not my cup of tea."

"I knew he wasn't your type, G. Struck me as a bit of a cold fish right from the start. And honestly, who wants an American? The accent alone would get on my nerves. You're better off without him, really you are."

"I think so too. It was one of those things that was never going to go anywhere. It wasn't very

303

serious. Waste of time really. Still, at least I've seen an American football game and been to Indiana."

"Yes, another thing to cross off the bucket list." They both laughed.

"Well, G, I must get going. Places to be, people to see. I'll get these boys out of your hair… and Bolly's! Let you get on with your unpacking and whatever it is you do with yourself all day." She slapped her empty mug cheerily in the sink and whistled a happy tune. All was well in Phoebe world, and she was going to make damned sure she enjoyed it while it lasted.

Geraldine continued to sit, ignoring the bangings from upstairs as her sister packed her bulging rucksack. She looked round the chaotic kitchen. She would tackle this first. She hadn't even looked at the rest of the tiny house. Goodness knows what that was like. But before getting up she reached for her phone. She sent messages to her children. 'Congratulations darling Cassie. Ring to tell all when you can xx,' and to Hugo, 'Sorry to hear about Abi. Hope you are ok darling xx.' She received back, 'Super exciting, Mummy! Will send pics!! Cxxxxxx,' and from Hugo, 'Better off without her, Mum. Awful cow. Hope B's paw better. Great news about C. Dad worried about you, Hx.'

She examined previous texts. Yes, there were a couple from Jonty she had missed. 'Do think v rash going off with stranger to States. Hope u ok. J', and 'R u ok? J'.

How very concise, she thought. And considerate, really. Had Ellis been a stranger? She had felt before she left London that she knew him quite well, this urbane, smooth, eyebrow-tweaking man. And yet he had seemed so very changed in East Cork. But, to be reasonable, she must have seemed altered, too. The only difference between them, really, was that he had been within his comfort zone, and she most certainly had been many, many miles away from hers. One thing was apparent: he may not have been a stranger, but he was certainly very strange. She sent a message back to Jonty. 'Now home. All well. Survived stranger danger. Gx'

And then what about Sally, and her return to Mother? Did the removal of a potter's wheel denote a final departure? Or was it just impossible to go for a week or two without the comforting whirl of wet clay circling through one's fingers? This was an unanswerable conundrum, she thought, as she assembled rubber gloves, buckets, cleaning fluids and a stout heart. She opened the back door while she waited for the tap water to heat up. Bolly skipped, all thoughts of a limp gone, into the little garden, his happiness returned.

Phoebe struggled down the stairs with her rucksack, chipping at paintwork in her wake. Much hugging and barking took place, as the pugs and Phoebe bundled themselves into an awaiting minicab. "Lovely chap," she explained to Geraldine, "he only lives round the corner from us in Chiswick. Doesn't mind the dogs and he's ever so obliging."

Geraldine watched this paragon drive off, the departure of Phoebe and the pugs instantly restoring the inner tranquillity she had been fighting for all morning.

In an hour the kitchen was gleaming and shiny and restored to proper standards. She stood for a moment admiring her accomplishment before venturing into the drawing room. Stout heart sank. The two sofas had been shoved together, to create a sort of giant padded play pen. Suspicious marks blodged the cream upholstery. There were half empty glasses and empty bottles, and a pretty Delft bowl had been filled with a smoker's detritus. The awful Abi, thought Geraldine, flinging open the window. Mrs Mankowitz walked slowly past, her blue rinse immaculate, her gnarled fingers curled round her ebony walking stick, which she always used when she ventured forth. It must 10 o' clock.

Mrs Mankowitz stopped by the open window, her silk scarf fluttering in the breeze. "Quite a party, dear," she remarked.

"Oh gosh, has it been very noisy?" Geraldine looked back in to the room. "I'll be cleaning up for ages."

"Yes, well it did seem quite busy here. Not your usual style, my dear. Never mind, I'm as deaf as a haddock as you know, so nothing much bothers me. But there did seem to be a lot of coming and going. Still, nice to see you home and everything getting back to normal. I must dash – I can't have Mr Patel selling my newspaper to someone else."

She turned and walked at a snail's pace down the mews. Geraldine tried to envisage herself at eighty-five. She strongly suspected it took Mrs Mankowitz a good two hours to get ready in the morning, and her walk to the newsagents was an agony to behold. She knew that Mr Patel had begged the old lady to allow him personally to deliver her *Daily Express*, in time for her breakfast. But she wouldn't have it. Her walk, her bi-weekly excursions to the hairdressers and outing in the Rolls-Royce to Bridge, were the punctuation marks of her life.

Geraldine scrubbed, hoovered, polished and filled a recycling bag. She felt exhausted, but knew sleep would elude her until her home was restored to its usual order. She took her suitcase upstairs, unpacked, changed sheets, and put on the first of what she knew would be many loads of washing. More hoovering and dusting, and bleaching the bathroom, and the job was complete. She returned to the kitchen, where Bolly slumbered the sleep of the content. All the usual smells of his territory had been restored, the irritating snorty creatures removed, and his own much loved person returned to him. His paw didn't hurt anymore and he'd got used to his sticking plaster. He hoped for a little bit of salmon later and maybe a walk, just to re-establish his supremacy in the neighbourhood.

Geraldine made herself more coffee. The washing machine and dishwasher whirred in the background. She turned on the radio. A noontime concert was being relayed, live, from the Usher Hall in Edinburgh, a soothing programme of Schubert symphonies. She thought of Cassie, really just a stone's throw away from the broadcast, back at the Infirmary, delivering babies. She had never observed Cassie in her chosen profession, and wondered momentarily, what it would be like being delivered of an infant by her daughter. Cassie could be so very loud and enthusiastic. Perhaps she didn't shriek quite so much in the labour ward, allowing her patients the monopoly of screaming. And Hugo? How was he, really? He didn't sound too unhappy about Abi, but did one ever know with men? She'd phone him this evening.

She took a piece of salmon out of the refrigerator (that all needs a good wipe down, too, she noted) and put it on the hob to poach for Bolly's lunch. She left it simmering while she went upstairs to shower quickly and change in the now immaculate bathroom.

She returned to the kitchen, emptied the dishwasher, hung the washing out on the wooden clothes horse she kept behind the back door, and left it to dry in the garden. I am completely and utterly knackered, she thought to herself. I can barely move one foot in front of the other. But there were still things to do before she could relax. She fed Bolly, and left him appreciatively licking his monogrammed bowl. She found, in the hall cupboard, the bag in which she had been collecting items of clothing and unwanted knick-knacks for the local hospice shop. She went in to the drawing room and removed the Limoges frog from the mantelpiece and placed it in the bag. It was the wrong shade of green, she thought.

"Come on, Bolly, walkies!" She put him on his pale blue patent leather lead, picked up the bag and her purse, and opened the door. It was a lovely afternoon, with a faint nip of autumn in the air. Leaves were already starting to fall. She walked briskly past Ellis's flat. A young man in a shiny suit, 'estate agent' stamped through his very being like 'Brighton' through a stick of rock, was shouting into his mobile phone, "Yes, his PA rang first thing. She's organising removal of his possessions. Yeah, well he had a break clause in the agreement. Nothing we can do. Corporate lets are always a bit of a nightmare. No, we'll have a new client within the week. No worries! It's a great flat."

So Ellis was moving out and moving on, thought Geraldine, just as I am. And what a relief not to encounter him again. One will be spared any embarrassment.

They had reached the High Street. They took the carrier bag to the charity shop, and then stopped at the flower stall on the corner. "Your usual?" asked the cheery geezer.

"Yes, white lilies, please. And maybe I'll take some of those," she pointed at a shallow bucket full of violets, their purplish flowers, a paler All Saints hue, contrasting with their moist, mossy leaves. She knew they wouldn't last, but she'd put them by her bed, next to the silver-framed wedding photograph. She sighed as she handed over a note. "You look tired, luv. Busy weekend?"

"You could say that," she smiled. "I went to America. Indiana."

The flower man scratched his head. "No idea where Indiana is. But I took the kids to Florida – Disneyworld – last year. Holiday of a lifetime. Never again."

She walked slowly home, Bolly padding faithfully next to her, stopping here and there. She had never, she thought, been this tired. She put the key in the lock. It now smelt like her home again. She arranged the lilies, and put them in their customary place on the half-moon inlaid table by the drawing-room door. She placed the violets, already wilting, in a little cut glass jug that had belonged to her grandmother. She took them upstairs, straightened an imaginary hump in her counterpane, and absent-mindedly sprayed herself with her favourite scent. She looked at the flowers again. No, something about the colour just wasn't right in the room. She had an idea. She would quickly pop over to Mrs Mankowitz and give them to her.

"Two ticks, Bolly," she called out, as she slammed the door behind her. She dashed across to the three-in-one house and rang the bell. Mrs Mankowitz let her in, delighted with the offering of violets. "My favourite!" she declared. "Binky used to buy me a bunch, and pin them to my lapel when we were going out. He was always such a gentleman. Speaking of which, how's yours? Gentleman that is. You must tell me all about him. But first I'll make some tea. Your usual? The tea bag briefly introduced to the hot water… and a little slice of lemon, too, dear?"

"That sounds perfect. Can I help?"

"No dear, you go and sit down with Gertie and Otto. Binky's in his usual chair. You look a bit tired."

I am tired, thought Geraldine, as she sank into the sofa, I am very, very tired. It feels like the tiredness from which one will never recover. Tomorrow I will have a quiet day at home with Bolly. Just us. No interruption from anyone.

Mrs Mankowitz entered with a tray and two tea cups. "No cake today, I'm afraid, dear. Dr Crean said I was putting on weight when I went for my check-up last week."

"What a ridiculous thing to say. I think you should eat exactly what you want. And you don't look a bit fatter. I'm really not keen on Dr Crean."

Mrs Mankowitz laughed loudly. "Oh, that could be the beginning of a song: 'I'm really not keen, On Dr Crean.' What do you think of that, Binky?"

Geraldine continued, "Last time I went to see him he said I needed counselling. Just because I started to re-arrange his desk while I was talking to him."

"Well, dear, if you need counselling, there's no hope for any of us. He should have been grateful for your tidying," replied Mrs Mankowitz, robustly. She took a sip of her tea. She'd pinned the violets to her jumper, and she closed her eyes, briefly, drawing in the scent of the flowers and the aroma of the tea. "Lovely," she murmured, "really lovely." The French porcelain clock on the chimney piece ticked softly, and the aged dachshunds breathed stertorously. It was heavenly, thought Geraldine, to be in this peaceful place. Suddenly, Gertie, not known to be quick of movement, looked up, as if someone was crossing the hearth rug. Mrs Mankowitz gazed in front of her, her old eyes softening, as if she had seen something or someone she loved very much. "Oh!" she said, then dropped her half-full cup and saucer, and slumped back in her chair.

Geraldine leapt forward. She took hold of the old lady's wrist. It was pale and knotted with blue veins. She searched for a pulse. She knew there would be none. The dachshunds sighed. "She's with Binky now," said Geraldine, soothingly, as she knelt down to stroke the two dogs. She got up, and went to the telephone in the hall.

The necessary calls made, she returned to the cosy room and sat by Mrs Mankowitz, holding her cold, old hand. That was how Gordon, Mrs Mankowitz's son, found her, tears pouring down her face, when he arrived twenty minutes later.

"It was terribly, terribly sudden," explained Geraldine. "We were just chatting, and suddenly she said, 'Oh!' It wasn't as if she was in pain or anything. And I am sure she saw your father. It was like he had got up from his chair and had gone over to her, arms outstretched, to fetch her."

Gordon eyed her cautiously, then wiped away his own tears. "I never thought she'd go. I know that sounds silly, when she was so old. But you're right, she does look very peaceful."

There was a ring of the bell. The dachshunds in their grief managed some hearty woofing.

"I'll answer that," said Geraldine.

Dr Crean stood on the threshold. "I am Dr Crean," he announced.

"Yes, I know," said Geraldine, "I am one of your patients."

"Really?" he said, peering at her carefully. "Oh yes, I remember you. You have OCD, if my memory serves me well."

"Your memory does not serve you well," said Geraldine, severely, "I merely have very high standards. Now, perhaps you would like to come in and deal with the matter in hand – poor, dear Mrs Mankowitz's death," she continued haughtily, ushering him in.

"Well, *you* would grant me a very great favour, and considerably relieve me of my professional burden, if you could do something with those dratted dogs," he replied, pompously.

Gordon emerged, blowing his nose like a trumpet. "I'm her son, doctor." He offered his hand.

"I never shake hands," said Dr Crean. "It's medical suicide. Is she in there?" He brushed past officiously.

Gordon remained standing wanly by the staircase. "Geraldine," he said, "I hate to ask you this, but could you do something for me? Could you take the dogs to your house? Just for a while till I sort something out for them?"

Geraldine swallowed. What would she tell Bolly? "Of course, Gordon, let me find their leads, and I'll take them back with me now. I'll leave you to it, but you know where I am. Don't hesitate to come over if you need me." She squeezed his arm.

Bolly was reclining on one of the cream sofas when she arrived back with the dachshunds. He looked in horror as the two sausage dogs waddled over to the fireplace. He glared at Geraldine enquiringly. "Yes, I know, it's terribly unfortunate," she said, " but we must do our best to make them welcome. They have had a dreadful upset." She knew perfectly well this would not be a temporary measure. Gordon lived in a small flat on the fourth floor – with no lift – just off the Marylebone Road. She was quite certain there would be no possibility of a berth there for elderly dogs; no, she and Bolly would just have to be very brave and give Gertie and Otto the best possible home for their old age. She went into the kitchen to find more dog bowls. She looked at the timer on the cooker. 6 o'clock. What a very long day! And what a horribly sad ending to it all. Although, she supposed, when one has to go, to go quickly in a comfy chair, and to be reunited with the man one loves, is the best possible exit.

She found an unopened bottle of Chablis in the refrigerator. One that the name that will never be spoken of again had given her. She opened it and poured herself a large glass. She took a packet of salted almonds from the cupboard and decanted them into a little bowl.

She went back to the drawing room, placing the glass and nuts on the découpage tray on the needle-point stool. She lit a scented candle. She sat down and raised the glass to her lips. The tiny mews seemed to be awash with cars coming and going, attending to the passing of Mrs Mankowitz, awkwardly manoeuvring in the narrow space. The doorbell rang. It was Gordon. "Come in," said Geraldine, "you must be absolutely shattered."

"I do feel a bit all over the place, but I won't linger. I'm going back to my flat. They've just taken her away, and there's so much to do. I've locked everything up. I'll let you know what all the arrangements are, you know, the funeral, that sort of thing. It will definitely be Golders Green. That's where Dad was despatched."

Geraldine smiled sympathetically. "Let me know if you need anything. I'm going to miss your mother dreadfully. She was such a wonderful character. I really would like to help," she said.

"Well, you're already being an absolute saint having the dogs. I'm not a dog person. Never have been.

Funny, that, isn't it?" Geraldine agreed. "Oh, there's one other thing. I thought I ought just to mention that I know mum has left you the Rolls. She was ever so fond of you, and of course, I'm more of a bike man. Just thought you might need a bit of warning. Size of it and all that."

"Goodness," said Geraldine, taken aback, "how very, very kind of your mother to remember me… I am quite lost for words."

"Well, yes, as I said, I thought you could do with a warning. I'm off now, but thanks for everything. I've ordered a cab to take me home. It's waiting for me at the end of the mews, so I'll be going. Thanks again, Geraldine, you were a good friend to my Mum."

Geraldine went back to the drawing room. "Well," she said to the assembled canine company, "that's a bit of a shock." Yet another one, she thought to herself. She wondered quite what she would do with the yellow Rolls Royce. She imagined herself, with Bolly and Gertie and Otto, all motoring off together. Bolly and Otto would be in bandanas, and Gertie could wear a silk ribbon round her neck. She sat down again and reached for her glass. From outside she could hear the sound of a diesel engine. A taxi drew to a halt right by her window. She put the glass back down. Surely that couldn't be Gordon returning. Really, it was becoming just like Piccadilly Circus here. A moment later the door bell rang. The four occupants of the room looked at each other, before three of them decided to bark.

Geraldine opened the door, hesitantly. In front of her stood Jonty, red cords a little crumpled, the expression on his face shyly sheepish, his old army duffel bag on the ground beside him. She opened her mouth to speak, but found nothing would come out. Jonty smiled, uncertainly.

"Hello, old thing," he said.